The Accidental Gangster

Part 2

D J Keogh

The Accidental Gangster: Part 2

David J. Keogh

Paperback Edition First Published in the United Kingdon
in 2016 by aSys Publishing

eBook Edition First Published in the United Kingdon
in 2016 by aSys Publishing

Disclaimer

This is a work of fiction. All characters and incidents are
products of the author's imagination and any resemblance to
actual people or events is coincidental or fictionalised.

ISBN: 978-1-910757-47-5

aSys Publishing
http://www.asys-publishing.co.uk

This book is dedicated to the memory of the twenty one victims that were murdered on the 21st of November 1974 by the IRA. I also wish to dedicate it to the families and friends of those that lost their lives on that terrible night and also to the other six victims caused by the bombing that served sixteen years in prison for a crime they didn't commit.

In loving memory of Hazel, Chrissy, Don and Frankie Fewtrell.

This story, although inspired by actual events, is purely for entertainment.

The actions and personalities of the characters featured in this work, in no way reflect the real life characters of the same name.

Note from the author

Broaching the subject of the Birmingham pub bombings was always going to be a difficult task for me. The memories of those times are still raw in the minds of those who lived through that awful night and in a small way when compared to the victims and their relatives and loved ones, the events of that night affected me deeply, and still do till this day. Only now, forty odd years later can we look back on those awful times and perhaps, question the facts that were given to us by the authorities without racial stereotypes clouding our minds like they did back in the 70s. There have been many conspiracy theories that have floated around over the years, but one thing is for sure, there were MI6 and ex British Army connections within the Birmingham IRA during the times of the bombings that never came to light at the time. Also the police knew of information provided by a reliable source within the IRA, that the men who became known as *the Birmingham six*, were never members of the IRA and had nothing to do with the bombings of the *Tavern in the Town* and the *Mulberry Bush* on November 21st 1974. The police also had information about those who actually *did* plant the bombs as early as November/ December 1975. This is stated in Chris Mullen's excellent and courageous investigation during the 1970s in his brilliant book, *Error of Judgment*. Chris Mullen states that the information was withheld from the public to cover the mistakes made by the Serious Crime Squad. I think the reasons they had to hide the facts may have been a little more sinister than that, perhaps, a little too close to the establishment for comfort.

I have used language and terms in this work to bring to life the times and atmosphere of the early 1970s. The book features language that we now, quite rightly, would never use. Racism and prejudice were rife during the times in which this story is set and although I have used certain racist terms, I have used them sparingly and only when a character within the book is stating their personal opinions. I personally have suffered from much anti-Irish racial discrimination throughout my life, so would like to point out that I have included some remarks made by the characters only because I feel it adds to the realism of the book.

On behalf of Abi and myself, I would like to thank all of the Fewtrell family, friends and especially those people who bought the first book and have left such amazing reviews or sent us kind messages and also for their help and encouragement in writing parts 1 & 2 of these books. I would also like to thank surviving brothers, Johnny, Gordon, Roger (Bomber) and of course, Eddie Fewtrell, for these amazing stories.

D J Keogh

Foreward

My father Eddie Fewtrell always says,
    "Every cloud's got a silver lining." I think he is right. The reason why my family's night clubs did so well during the depression of the early 70s was, I'm sure, because people need an escape when times are bad. My mother and father provided that escape for thousands of people during a time when Birmingham needed it most. That decade was an incredibly important time for my mother and father as well as the rest of the Fewtrell brothers. The building of their night club empire during late 1950s and early 60s was the learning curve that finally paid off, fifteen years later in the mid 1970s. Of course along with the success of their businesses came the temptations of fame and wealth. I would be lying if I said my mother and father were saints, of course they weren't. They were young, wealthy and powerful and the world was theirs for the taking, but amidst all that, they never forgot the poverty ridden streets of Aston of the 1950s or the people they shared those streets with. Perhaps that's the reason why they went to such lengths to keep hold of what they had literally, fought for. Some of the content of this story was painful for me to see in print at times, especially some of the things about my beloved mother Hazel, but we felt it was important that *her* story be told as well. We also felt that it was important that everyone sees things as they really were, instead of portraying a perfect fairytale family like so many other books. My husband has constructed this book from his many private conversations with my family in particular my mother and other friends of my family about how things really were back then. There are so many amazing, daring, bizarre and

deadly things that happened to my family over the fifty years they ran their night club empire and this story just sets out a few of them, we hope you enjoy it!

Abi Fewtrell

The Accidental Gangster

Part 2

Opening Night

Chapter 1

He had to admit it, it was one of the best punches he'd ever seen. In boxing terms it was known as a *bolo* punch, *bolo* being the filipino word for machete, the name of the punch derived from the action of cutting elephant grass with the long bladed weapon. Left fist held high to distract the victim, the right follows through in a low sweeping arc, bringing the fist in underneath the jaw, to catch the victim by surprise. In this case it certainly did, as a matter of fact the punch could have only been more devastating if it had *actually* been a machete that had been used. The big gypsy's fist, as broad as a shovel, connected with the doorman's jaw, knocking his head back and lifting the fifteen stone bouncer a good twelve inches off the floor. The doorman fell backwards across a table, spilling drinks and smashing glasses as he fell, unconscious before he'd even hit the floor. He lay in the doorway to the bar, his body making little quivering movements as if he were connected to the main's electric. Somewhere deep inside the bouncer's mind he may have been struggling to regain consciousness, but all he managed to do was make a gurgling noise from his shattered jaw; teeth, blood and spittle dribbling down the side of his mouth. The gypsy looked around the crowded bar, his four friends continued pummelling anyone that got in their way.

He looked across the bar, his eyes scanned the room looking for his next victim, stopping at the white faced, bar manager. The gypsy snarled, showing a set of yellowing teeth, mostly missing, each gap telling a story of a previous fight. He kept his gaze on his prey. He came on, throwing anyone that crossed his path to his side as if they were nothing but a bag of rags. The gypsy raised his arm and pointed at the manager.

"Ye ... I'm gonna fecking kill ye ...!" His thick Irish accent and speed of tongue made the words hard to understand, but it was obvious to Brendan Hodgson, the owner and manager of the *Grapes Bar*, that there would be no reasoning with this one. He stood frozen like a rabbit in headlights, unable to run or even raise his fists, his arms felt like lead, his legs gave a tremble. He knew what was coming, closed his eyes and waited ... WHAM ...! Stars, thousands of stars exploded in his head, set against the blackness of the infinity of his mind, they danced around like a cheap fireworks' display, popping and bursting behind his eyes until they slowly faded to nothing.

* * *

Brendan Hodgson was a Manchester lad through and through, he loved his home city and hated to leave it, but his beautiful, black country girlfriend, Wendy, had persuaded him to head the eighty miles south, to the boom town of Birmingham so that they could be closer. The fact he hardly knew her didn't stop him. His friends called him *Hodgy*, but he didn't have any friends in the city as yet, just people he'd met through the re-opening of the *Grapes bar*.

He had been to Birmingham plenty of times, mainly playing soccer against the local teams of Aston Villa and Birmingham City. Playing soccer isn't really the right term, sitting on a bench every match day and training with the stars of the team mid week, is the right way of saying it. Oh, Hodgy liked to tell people he had played for Manchester United for the past three years, but all he really did was take the two hundred and fifty pounds a week and go through the motions. He knew he'd stay on the bench but the money was enough to smother his pride and he sat, watched, and kept his mouth shut whilst the going was good. His father wanted him to go into the family business, and after leaving school he considered it for all of ten seconds before running off to his Manchester United soccer coach to sign a contract with the team. After three years of sitting on the bench the club finally let him go. He'd had the foresight to see the situation wouldn't last forever, and after the initial euphoria of spending his first few wage packets on flash clothes, presents for his mum and a brand new Ford Capri, he had saved the rest of his money religiously for the rainy day he knew would eventually come.

Birmingham's boom era was well and truly over. The inevitability of decay had started to creep along the hairline cracks in the ever-expanding concrete planted in the early sixties, allowing the weeds of disrepair to take hold in the once fashionable city. The 1960s tidal wave of industrial expansion flooded the outlying villages and towns creating new, tree lined suburbs for the middle classes. The working class were simply piled on top of one another in ghettos rising to the sky in the form of huge, grey, high rise blocks that towered above the factories, shops and motorways, like so many sentinels staring down from the smoggy sky above the heartlands of Great Britain. The 1970s had rolled into town like a juggernaut, squashing the dream of a Brummie utopia. If the hedonistic days of the 1960s were the celebration, the 1970s were the come down. Crippled by the opposing, immobile objects of trade unions and management, the city had been plagued by a three day working week, which in turn led to daily power cuts across the city. If that wasn't bad enough, the freezing, grey drizzle of the winter that year highlighted an edge of danger for the citizens of Birmingham, brought about by the ever present, terrorist threat from the IRA.

Hodgy didn't see any of this, he only saw Wendy, the cute, mousey haired girl that had appeared out of nowhere with her long legs and wide smile. She talked about Birmingham as if it were Las Vegas and Hodgy was intrigued to say the least. He had looked around Manchester for a business to invest his cash in, but with the ever increasing pressure from his father to go in to undertaking, he had jumped at Wendy's idea and come to Birmingham, ready to invest and finally stand on his own two feet. He'd always thought Birmingham was a bit of a backwater compared to Manchester and he had taken great pleasure making fun of Wendy and her family's funny accents, which all seemed slow compared to that of the Manc lads he hung around with up North. On his first night out in the city Wendy had taken him to a swanky bar called *Rebecca's Brasserie*, where he'd been introduced by Wendy to the owner; a fellow called Eddie Fewtrell. Eddie had been told by the huge doorman that went by the unlikely name of Nobby, that the lad played for Man United and, just like that, he was in. Eddie treated Wendy and Hodgy to champagne by the bucketful, introducing the young lad around as if he'd known him for years. Hodgy mentioned to Eddie about a possible investment in a business in Birmingham and asked whether he had any suggestions. Eddie's mood had changed instantly, rising from his barstool at the end of the long bar, he wrapped his arm around Hodgy's shoulders.

"Follow me our kid! I got *exactly* what you're looking for," and intrigued, Hodgy smiled and gestured to Wendy to follow them, she smiled but just stayed where she was, enjoying the free bubbly. Hodgy followed Eddie through the crowded bar to the front door of the club and Nobby swung the glass door open, smiling.

"Cheers Nobs," Eddie said passing. Hodgy smiled at the huge man, Nobby gave the lad a slow wink which seemed somehow inappropriate. Hodgy's smile shrank and he followed Eddie, feeling unsure about the look in the doorman's eye.

Eddie stood in the middle of the road, *John Bright Street,* the evening traffic of mainly taxis stopped and he just stood there pointing at an old pub diagonally opposite to *Rebecca's Brasserie.*

"*The Grapes,*" he said, without turning to look at Hodgy, "it needs a few quid spending on it but it'll make some cash if it's fixed up, and this part of town is the place to be right now, our kid." The pair stood in the middle of a small crossroads, gazing at *the Grapes* pub, a dirty grey concrete building that had been built in the mid sixties. The taxis waited quietly for them to move. Hodgy couldn't understand why the traffic had just stopped. None of the taxi drivers were blowing their horns or becoming agitated at the two men stood in the middle of the road, holding up the traffic. If this had been Manchester the taxi drivers would've been out of their cabs by now and kicking off. Eddie noticed the look of confusion on Hodgy's face.

"Never mind them!" Eddie pointed at the waiting cabs beginning to stack up along the road. "Let em fucking wait! They'll keep their traps shut if they know what's good for em." Rather than reassure Hodgy however, Eddie's words added to his confusion. He grabbed Hodgy's arm and led him across the road.

"I can get the lease on this our kid, it looks like a dump now, but if you spent . . . I mean *invested* about ten grand in to the place you could do very well here." Eddie smiled, gesturing towards the building with open hands, as if he were a magician about to turn the grey slab of wall into a Disney castle. "Don't take any notice of what it looks like now, think about the location, a few grand and it'll be a gold mine."

To Hodgy the pub looked like a shit hole from the outside, somewhere he wouldn't have been seen dead in. Eddie led him through the doorway into the dimly lit bar. Hodgy's first impressions had been correct. The place *was* a shit hole, inside *and* out. A filthy dump that hadn't seen a clean since the day it had opened. Long, dark brown velour benches ran along the walls, their seat coverings ripped or slashed by years of *Stanley* knife vandalism. All the promise and optimism of the 1960s that had gone into the original design of the pub, had been bludgeoned to death by the time the 1970s had trundled into town.

There was a distinct, soft smell of urine that seeped from the toilets, giving the customers a promise of what lay within the white tiled latrines and the glow of the yellow light shades on the nicotine stained ceiling increased the sensation of filth. The smell had settled on the expressions of the bar staff, who all had a look of bitterness about their faces. On the other hand, the scowls of the staff might have been brought on by the fact that they had spent their lives serving watered down ale to the dregs of Birmingham, in this city centre, concrete bunker.

The staff looked shocked when the two walked in. What customers there were, moved away from the door as if a wild dog had wandered in from the street. A chubby man appeared behind the bar, pushing the middle aged barmaids out of the way.

"Evening, Mr Fewtrell," nodding a head full of tight, curly, freshly permed hair, that gave him the look of a cherub, his youthful, plump, tired face smiled without any real commitment. He gestured to the men to take the freshly vacated barstools at the bar. "What can I get for you Mr Fewtrell?" His yellow t-shirt was too small for him and his little breasts gave a wobble, as he forced himself to smile. Hodgy could see the man was terrified and trying his best to hide it. If Eddie Fewtrell noticed the fear in the barman's eyes he didn't show it. Eddie ignored the barman's question.

"See what I mean? It's all here, just needs bringing up to date." Hodgy nodded, seeing the pub as it could be, rather than what it was.

"Yeah, I see what you're saying," he said, his smile trying to hide his true feelings. "I could do something good here."

"That's right son, and you've got a good sized kitchen on the first floor and a top bar on the third floor for private functions, weddings, christenings and the like. I make a lot of money from private parties." The barman looked bemused.

"Yes we are just waiting for the funds to fix the place up. Mr Fewtrell sorted out the lease for us and ..." Eddie looked at the chubby man sternly, who in turn stopped talking instantly. There was a silence in the bar broken only by the sound of buses trundling along the road outside. Hodgy nodded and smiling he turned to Eddie and shook his hand.

"I'll have it!"

"Can I get you anything Mr Fewtrell?" The barman said, his voice faltering.

"Yeah," Eddie replied, "you can get the fuck out of my pub, Charlie!" The barman's usually flushed face, turned instantly white.

"But I thought we had a deal?" he began to say but Eddie butted in.

"You can take that up with Nobby, I'll send him over and you can tell him all about it." The barman turned to the women behind the bar. He struggled for the right words.

"Eh . . . alright girls we're gonna shut up for the night. Just get your stuff and go." One of the women confronted him.

"*What?*" she was looking at the barman, but talking about Eddie. "Who the fuck does he think he is, coming in here telling us to clear out?" The woman was obviously a friend or relative of the cherub and was trying to defend him, but the barman wasn't having any of it.

"Shut the fuck up Rachel . . . that's Eddie Fewtrell!" He smiled at Eddie as if Eddie hadn't heard the exchange, Eddie just gave an expressionless stare back.

"Twenty four hours Charlie . . . understand? Twenty four hours and Nobby will be here to pick up the keys and you don't want to mess our Nobby around do you?" Eddie said with a false smile. "Get all your gear and fuck off, anything left here after that is mine, understand?" The barman gave a desperate plea.

"But we had a deal?"

"Yeah but you broke the terms Charlie, you said you were gonna fix the place up but you've done fuck all. You're taking the piss son, " Eddie slammed his hand on to the counter, "you broke terms son."

"How?" The chubby man said, a bead of sweat breaking his brow.

"*How?*" Eddie replied.

"How?" Charlie said again.

"You sound like a fucking red Indian, Charlie!" Eddie laughed at his own joke. Hodgy stood back, not wanting to get involved in the little drama playing out before him.

"How did I break the deal Mr Fewtrell? "

"However I say it's fucking broken that's how, besides as I said, *you* were meant to fix the place up." He replied so that everyone in the room could hear. "I gave you six months rent free so you could put some cash into the place and you've just pissed it up the wall at the Chinese casino, you're into them for five grand Charlie, *five grand.*" He held his hand up, his fingers spread out to emphasise the figure, he let the words sink in. Charlie seemed shocked that Eddie Fewtrell knew about his gambling debts. "Don't think I don't know Charlie, I know everything that goes on in this town." Eddie had raised his voice so that everyone in the pub could hear him now.

"Twenty-four hours Charlie, I don't need a run in with the chinks. If you owe them money you don't get to run a business with me, simple as that mate." The barman seemed to shrink in stature. His chubby face now flushed red like a scolded school boy.

"If I were you Charlie I'd get out of town cos those lads don't fuck around, Kung Fu and all that, you'll be visiting *Earlswood Lakes* if you're not careful." Everyone in the pub knew what that meant and everyone knew it wasn't said lightly. Charlie the cherub nodded.

"Yes Mr Fewtrell . . . thanks for being so understanding." A touch of sarcasm in his voice, Eddie picked up on it.

"You cheeky little twat," he was starting to lose his temper now, "I'm saving your fucking life here son, you ungrateful little toe rag. You just ain't cut out for this type of life." He reached across the bar and grabbed the man by his t-shirt, tearing it around the grubby collar. He pulled the man across the bar until they were face to face. "You had your chance and you fucked it. Now get your stuff and fuck off!" He held the man for a second and looked behind him at the bottles of alcohol hanging from the wall on their optics. "Leave the stock too, if anything's missing I'll come looking for you Charlie." Eddie let go of the man's t-shirt. Charlie instantly collapsed behind the bar, all but disappearing except for his curly perm which stuck up behind the bar like some sort of blonde poodle. Eddie patted it and laughed. He turned to Hodgy. "The poodle comes with the pub Hodgy old son." He gave a short laugh. "I think he wants a scooby snack," both men burst into laughter. "Come on," he continued, gesturing that they should leave, "we'll sort you out a deal, Hodgy." Once outside he stopped Eddie.

"That was a bit harsh wasn't it?" He gestured to the pub doorway. "That bloke nearly shit himself." Eddie shook his head.

"Nah you got me all wrong our kid." He put his arm around Hodgy and they continued to walk back to the *Brasserie*. "I back *winners* not losers Hodgy, that kid was taking the piss and if I don't show a bit of strength then they'll *all* take the piss son, *understand?*" Hodgy nodded, unconvinced.

Eddie and Hodgy crossed the road back to *Rebecca's Brasserie*. They sat back on their barstools joining the, by now very drunk, Wendy and struck a deal over a hand shake. Hodgy could see Eddie was a powerful and feared man, but somewhere inside he felt excited by that power, *scared* but excited nonetheless.

Eddie Fewtrell was a good looking man in his early forties. Blonde, powerfully built and six feet tall. He had come through the London:Birmingham gang warfare of the 1960s, unscathed and unstoppable. The Fewtrell family clubs had grown from humble beginnings at their illegal speakeasy at the *Bermuda club* in the late 1950s, to a small empire of night clubs and pubs throughout Birmingham by the early 1970s. Business was good and getting better. Now the Birmingham gangs of yesteryear had been broken, the city was wide open and now belonged to the Fewtrells alone or so they liked to think. Their gang, the Whizz mob was more or less just a group of friends and family now. No reason to keep a gang together unless there was an enemy to battle against, and no one who knew anything in Birmingham, would dare going up against Eddie Fewtrell and his six brothers. It *had* been seven but Frankie Fewtrell had died suddenly in 1967. They still made a formidable force that you either stood behind or ran from. The family were supported by a back handed but well organised system that existed between themselves and elements within the Birmingham police and council. This kept things running smoothly in the city on both sides of the law. Things had certainly changed since the early days, when, *at which time,* the council and police had used everything legal and illegal to prevent the Fewtrells' steep climb out of poverty, from the dirty streets of *Aston* to where they had now come. Birmingham owed the family for keeping the cream of the London underworld out of the city and Eddie and his brothers weren't ever gonna let them forget it.

* * *

Hodgy regained consciousness three hours after being knocked out by the gypsy. The travellers had left the pub virtually straight after. Why they had come there was a mystery to all. It was the opening night of the *Grapes Bar* and invites had been sent to all and sundry so maybe they had got one by mistake? People had just started to arrive when the didikoys had stepped through the doors, throwing punches as they entered. Hodgy sat at the bar, trying to remember what little he could of the incident. Bruised but nothing broken, he had asked Eddie to supply a few doormen for the *Grapes*, but only one had shown and *he* wouldn't be showing up anywhere again too soon; his jaw had been shattered completely by the devastating punch Hodgy had witnessed.

Most of the guests that had arrived before the fight started were beginning to calm down and chat about the fight to others who had missed it, not the best impression for an opening night. Hodgy told the bar staff to pour some champagne on the house for the guests who hadn't already left. He chose a good looking girl to wander around the room, serving the drinks from a silver tray. He crossed the room and put on a selection of songs from the juke box. When the mood began to lighten, he told the bar staff to bring out the buffet.

Around seven thirty, two men showed up. Their open collar shirts, loose ties and black and brown leather safari jackets attempting to disguise the fact that they were plain clothed police officers, however it was obvious to all exactly who they were. They began asking about the fight and this confused Hodgy as he hadn't even reported it. The two scruffy officers sat at the bar, already smelling of booze.

"I'm Dixon and this is Jimmy," the policeman said with a Gloucester accent. "Serious Crime squad," he continued, expecting the words to impress the young bar owner, a serious look on his face. Hodgy looked at the two men, shook his head at their arrogance but remembered his manners.

"I'm Brendan Hodgson . . . but everyone calls me Hodgy," he held his hand out but the men ignored his hand and just nodded. "Can I get you some drinks lads?" He offered, the police men nodded simultaneously. He gestured to the bar girl for some champagne but the Gloucester man rose from his seat and put his hand across the tall champagne flute before the girl could pour.

"We'll have a couple of whiskeys Hodgy, I ain't drinking that shit." Hodgy nodded and pulled up a bar stool.

"So you've had a bit of trouble?" The other detective spoke for the first time. He was a short, ugly man with a thick, Belfast accent. His hair had disappeared on top and lay in a dark shaven shadow around his ears. He looked like he hadn't washed or shaved for days. Hodgy nodded.

"Yeah but it's hardly a *serious* crime gentlemen." The Belfast man shook his head.

"It's all serious to us Mr Hodgson," he stared at Hodgy without expression. "That an Irish name? Brendan?" he continued. He just gave a confused shrug, he took the whisky from the barmaid and slid them across the bar to the policemen.

"Yeah . . . somewhere along the line, think my grandfather was Irish, but *everyone's* got a bit of Irish in them somewhere, haven't they?"

"*I* fucking haven't!" The Belfast man rose from his stool, obviously offended. Now it was Hodgy's turn to be confused.

"But you're Irish . . ." he began to say, the other police man butted in.

"Jimmy, cut this proddie shit out! We're here to ask him a few questions and show him he's got a bit of back up, not to launch into one of your fucking anti catholic speeches, for fuck's sake!" The Belfast man sat down and took the whisky. Dixie gave him a sharp glare.

"Sorry Mr Hodgson," the Belfast man said hesitantly.

"Eddie told us to drop in and say hello. Eddie's a friend of mine from the old days." The Gloucester man took over the conversation.

"Can you tell us what happened here?" Hodgy shook his head.

"Well, one minute they were punching everyone in sight and the next, apparently they knocked me out and just left, or so I've been told . . . I was unconscious."

"They were *Irish* you say?" The Belfast man spoke again, Hodgy looked at him quizzically.

"I didn't say they were *anything* . . . but yeah, they were, gypsies too, big fuckers, the big one that punched me nearly took the head off my doorman."

"Dirty Fenian bastards!" Jimmy began to rise from his chair again. Dixie placed his hand across the Belfast man's chest and pushed him back down into his seat.

"For fuck's sake Jimmy give it a rest! Irish this, Irish that, they ain't *all* fucking Fenians you know."

"Oh ain't they? Well let me tell ye . . ." Dixie butted in.

"*Enough!*" He said, shutting the other man down mid flow, showing his authority.

"Look, Eddie Fewtrell asked me to drop in and introduce myself, that's why we're here, *not* the fight." He left the sentence hanging. "Maybe I'm not making myself clear. We are protection for you Mr Hodgson, *legal* protection . . . you won't get any shit from anyone if you take us on board." The words started to make sense to the young man. "This type of thing won't happen again Hodgy . . . we'll make sure of it."

"How do you know? . . . I mean these blokes just turned up and started . . ." Dixie interrupted,

"We know who they are. We'll head down the Irish centre in Digbeth and start knocking some heads together. They won't do it again and once the word goes around you're on our books, trust me, no one will bother you again."

"What's this Irish thing?" Hodgy asked, confused.

"Well Birmingham's an Irish city . . . didn't you know son? The Irish run this city." Dixie couldn't believe the Manchester lad didn't know about the Birmingham Irish, he continued, deciding to scare the kid, "especially the IRA."

"*Fenian bastards!*" Jimmy muttered, Dixie gave him a sideways glance.

Anyway they'll be up here collecting for the *cause* every night and once they get in here you won't get rid of em . . . unless they know you're one of *our* pubs of course."

"The *cause?*" Hodgy asked. Jimmy spoke up.

"The cause . . . you know . . . buying guns for the IRA so they can have a united Ireland." Hodgy shook his head.

The detective was right. The Birmingham Irish had embedded themselves in the city like so many ticks on a dog's belly, the longer they stayed, the deeper they dug in and the larger they got. The potato famine of 1845 had sent the human tsunami of poverty stricken, half staved immigrants across the Irish sea to the middle of England, to the very heartland of their old enemy. Initially there had been trouble between the newcomers and local gangs but after twenty years or so, a thin mist of peace lay over the city. Local gangs began to work with the Irish and soon Birmingham had an endless supply of hard working, cheap labour and in return they had a new place to establish themselves and grow, and grow they certainly did. By the late 1950s it was said that the city was home to quarter of a million, first generation Irish immigrants. Integration was, at that time, an unheard of concept. Many of the shops and pubs still displayed signs that read *No Irish, No Blacks, No Dogs* right up to the early 1970s. Many of the indigenous population of Birmingham only ever saw the Celtic tribe when it displayed its numbers and power on the St Patrick's day parade traditionally held on the Sunday before St Patrick's day. Thousands would gather outside the Irish centre in the Irish quarter of the city, Digbeth, to march under the banners and flags of their Irish counties, led by marching pipe bands of fife and drums. It was a celebration of their success in the city and a way to show solidarity to each other in hard, racist times. But the Celts were also proud of the city that had been named after the Irish–Norman Lord of Athenry De-Bermingham.

The St Patrick's celebrations were viewed very differently by those taking part to the non-Irish residents of Birmingham, to *them* the march was a show of power, corruption, even a fund raising event for the Irish Republican Army. The feeling with some in the city was one of having an enemy amongst them; a Fenian enemy plotting to creep in to the house in the middle of the night to kill everyone.

"Sorry I've never heard of anything about all this," Hodgy lied, everyone had heard of the troubles in Northern Ireland and how these troubles were about to spill over on to the mainland any day now. The violent scenes of street fighting in Belfast were shown on the news every night, but it wasn't something he wished to get into right now. "Anyway I've got guests arriving and more that needs attending to, so . . . how much is this "protection" gonna cost me?" he asked finding it hard to disguise his irritation.

"Shhhh . . . !" Dixie held his finger up to his mouth, looking around the room to see if anyone had over heard him. "Two hundred a month Hodgy." He let Hodgy think about it for a while.

"That's a lot of money," he replied, alarmed at the sum.

"Yes it is, you're right," Dixie continued, "but for that you won't get any trouble from anyone . . . including the law . . . you can stay open all hours, no raids, no license times, no shutting at fucking ten thirty at night like all the other mugs. You just pay us and stay open as long as you want. You'll triple your normal takings and do it without having to look over your shoulder" The deal was starting to sound more attractive.

"Two hundred and that's it." Hodgy held his hands out flat, Dixie nodded, Jimmy spoke up.

"And a few drinks on the house every now and then sonny . . . just for good will's sake." Jimmy smiled an unconvincing, thin lipped smile. Hodgy held his hand out and this time the policemen were eager to take it.

"Ok two hundred a month . . . but not tonight." Dixie and Jimmy nodded. The two men stood and threw the whisky down their throats before accepting another.

"You've made the right decision son. We'll drop in next week and sort all the details out." And with that they turned back to each other and began talking in hushed tones.

Hodgy realised he was no longer welcome in the conversation and returned to rest of his guests.

"Has he gone?" Dixie asked the Belfast man.

"Ai . . . he's gone." Jimmy replied looking over the other man's shoulder. Dixie seemed relieved.

"I told ya it would be easy didn't I?" The detective raised his glass and smiled at the other man. "I've got twenty three pubs doing this Jimmy . . . It all adds up to a pretty penny at the end of the month, I mean you can't live on the police wages can ya?" Jimmy just shrugged and smiled, unconvinced. "Well this is the deal Jimmy, I'll cut you in on this one and every pub after this, but the twenty two I did on my own are mine. I like to keep that little list secret, that's fair enough ain't it?" Again Jimmy seemed uninterested. Dixie saw the bald man's lack of interest and took it for greed, he continued. "That's the deal Jimmy, I know you've only just arrived in Brum, but that's the way things operates in this town . . . in Belfast you might do it differently, I don't know, take it or leave it mate." Jimmy nodded weakly.

"Ai I'm not too bothered about a bit of cash here and there Dixie. To be honest, I can't see myself being here too long so . . . yeah, that deal's cool with me." Dixie smiled and held his hand out, the bald man shook it without any conviction and drained his whisky glass.

"Come on, I'll introduce you to Eddie Fewtrell, he virtually runs the night life in this town." Jimmy shook his head.

"Oh sorry Dix, I should've said, I have business down in Digbeth at the Irish centre." Dixie gave him a puzzled look.

"What the hell's a Fenian hating proddie going down the Irish centre for?" Dixie said with a laugh. Belfast Jimmy looked embarrassed realising he'd said too much. He raised his index finger to his nose and tapped it, then gave a sarcastic smile saying.

"You've got your secrets Dixie . . . and I've got mine." With that he turned and left the pub. Dixie watched him leave before turning to Hodgy, who had been watching the two men's conversation from the corner of his eye, and gave the young man a smile and small salute before following the other policeman out of the front doors to the pub, each man going their separate ways.

Hodgy stood and watched him as he left through the glass doors on to Hill Street. His attention was drawn away by the ten or so smartly dressed guests that were climbing the small steps to the bar. He stepped forward and greeted them, ushering the group towards the bar area which had now taken on more of a party atmosphere. The juke box had lifted the mood and people were already beginning to dance on the little wooden patch that acted as a dance floor in the middle of the room. The high energy sound of *Slade* boomed out from the flashing box and the dancers followed the beat.

"Come on feel the noise!"

The gravelly-voiced singer screamed the lyrics.

"Girls grab the boys!"

Hodgy smiled and grabbed a glass from the circling bar girl holding the tray of champagne and then joined the dancers. He was lucky, he tried to convince to himself, after all this whole thing had just fallen into his lap and the more he thought about the police protection, the late opening hours and the revenue that that would bring in, the more he believed it. Eddie Fewtrell had kept his word and had sorted the lease out very quickly and Hodgy had sunk almost twenty grand of his hard earned into the place to bring it kicking and screaming out of its 1960s nightmare and into the 1970s. Eddie had offered a deal with M&B brewery with everything on a tab through his company, something to do with tax, but Hodgy didn't really understand any of what he was talking about, so he'd just given Eddie the go ahead to sorted it all. He hadn't even had to go to the solicitors to sign the lease. The beer, spirits, carpets, furniture, the staff, even the juke box was all sorted by Eddie Fewtrell. Hodgy hadn't been too keen on the idea of a juke box, preferring DJs, until Eddie had pointed out that dealing with DJs could be a pain in the arse.

"They'll drink ya beer and shag ya missus, that's all they're good for, stick with a juke box our kid, it'll cost ya fuck all and *they* have to pay to listen and dance, not you." He could see the big box with its flashing lights and booming speakers was a money spinner, Eddie had been right.

Hodgy was starting to relax now. The night was going well, even the *Birmingham Evening Mail* had turned up to review the place. He danced and chatted with the locals and began what he hoped would be some new long lasting friendships. The only person missing was Wendy. She had been a bit non-committal since he'd made the deal with Eddie. Before that she'd been doing all the chasing but now it was *he* who was doing all the leg work. She answered his calls yes, but he was sure he was starting to hear a begrudging tone in her voice whenever he asked her out on a date. The last few calls had been answered by her parents who insisted she was out of the house. He was sure she would show her face at his opening night though or at least call, so he kept his ear open for the phone, even though the music was blaring. Around nine thirty Eddie Fewtrell walked through the door with the huge doorman Nobby stood slightly behind his shoulder. He waited in the doorway to be noticed before entering further into the pub. As he strutted into the room towards Hodgy he shook hands and gave kisses to almost everyone he crossed paths with. He seemed to know everyone there, or at least everyone knew him. He came to Hodgy with a broad grin spreading across his face.

"I told ya didn't I our kid? It's a blinder." Eddie was looking around the bar at the new decor. "It looks fucking great. We're gonna make a few quid here mate." Hodgy didn't know whether he was talking to Nobby, who was still standing at his shoulder smiling or himself.

"What you drinking Eddie?" Hodgy asked smiling. Eddie seemed more interested in the growing crowd than anything else.

"Eh . . . nah it's alright Hodgy . . . I gotta get back to *Rebecca's* . . . I'm expecting a big crowd tonight." He turned to leave. "See ya later our kid." With that he left, without looking back. The big doorman held the front door to the pub open, as Eddie passed him and stepped outside on to the street. Nobby turned and gave a smile, then followed Eddie outside.

Hodgy grabbed another glass of champagne from the girl with the tray. For the first time he had an uneasy feeling about Eddie but he pushed it to the back of his mind as he lifted the bar hatch and went through to his little office behind the bar. He sat with a huff in the swivel chair and looked at the phone, deciding if he should call Wendy or not. This feeling of unease made him feel very alone all of a sudden. He realised that he knew no one in the bar, they were all friends of Eddie's, he'd sunk almost all of his cash into the venture and it was beginning to dawn on him that he might not be the one in control of this business. Yes, it had his name on the alcohol licence over the door, but he was starting to think maybe he had been a little too eager to let Eddie pull the strings and Eddie was all too happy to pull them.

"Briiiinngg, briiing . . ." The phone came to life and Hodgy jumped in his chair. The phone's trill seemed loud in the little office. He gave a sigh and smiled, grabbing the ivory coloured hand piece, he sat back in his chair stretching the curly cable that joined the hand piece to the phone.

"*The Grapes* bar." He said, importantly.

"Beep, beep, beep . . ." Whoever was on the other end of the line was busy pushing their coins into the call box . . . "Beep, beep . . ." the line went through.

"Wendy, where are you?" Hodgy expected to hear the young girl's thick, black country accent on the other end of the line but the phone line gave a soft crackle. He could hear traffic in the background and wondered if it was coming from the other end of the phone line or if it were the buses rumbling along their routes outside. "Wendy . . . ?" he said again.

"This ain't Wendy, sonny, this is the IRA . . ." A voice with a thick Irish accent without emotion spoke on the other end, the man left the words hanging.

"Stop fucking around!" Hodgy said and gave a nervous laugh, wondering who it was on the line.

"Like I said son . . . this ain't Wendy. This is the *feckin I.R.A* . . . there's a bomb in your pub," he said the words slowly, deliberately. "Tell the police . . . code word . . . *double XX*" The

Irishman waited for a second to see if Hodgy would say anything, then he hung up. Hodgy held the phone to his ear listening to the soft brrrrrrrr on the dead line, expecting someone to admit it was all just a joke. He couldn't believe all the drama on his opening night, and now this. He pulled himself together and placed his fingers on the phone's little black buttons where the handset usually sat and cleared the line. He dialled 999 and a crackly voice came on the other end almost immediately.

"Police, Ambulance or Fire?" The lady's voice answered. He felt foolish suddenly.

"Police, Ambulance or Fire?" The woman repeated in the same expressionless tone.

"Police, please luv." The line went dead for a second and then a man's voice came on the line.

"Police, how can I help?" The man's voice sounded far away.

"I'm the owner of the *Grapes Bar* on Hill Street in Birmingham." Hodgy searched for the right words for a moment, then decided to say it as simply as possible. "I've just had a phone call from someone who said he's in the IRA, telling me there's a bomb in my pub." The line went quiet. "It's probably a wind up," he continued.

"Did the man say anything else sir?" the phone operator asked. Hodgy searched his memory.

"Yes, yes he said to say . . . code word, double XX?"

The operator went quiet, then another man came on the line.

"Hello, sir you need to get everyone out of the pub straight away . . . straight away . . . this is not a hoax!" Hodgy took a while to take in the words. The dramas of the day making him confused.

"What do you mean, not a hoax?"

"Sir, you need to exit the building right now. The code word is accurate." The man's voice seemed concerned. "We have officers and bomb squad on their way to you right now."

"Bomb squad?" Hodgy repeated, half questioning.

"*Get out now sir!*" The man almost shouted his command.

Hodgy placed the receiver down on the phone and stepped out of his office. He strode across the dance floor, pushing his way through the dancers, ignoring the offers to dance. He reached the juke box and pulled it away from the wall, making the record jump inside, the needle skidded across the vinyl record sending a loud scratching noise through the speakers of the machine. Hodgy bent and yanked the plug from the wall and the sound stopped instantly. Everyone in the room stood in silence waiting for an explanation.

"BOMB SCARE . . . !" Hodgy shouted. No one moved, some even shrugged. "We have to clear the pub, there's been a bomb scare!" Hodgy expected a panic to break out, but the Brummies were used to bomb scares. They had been happening on an ever increasing basis over the past twelve months, so this wasn't anything new for them. Reluctantly the large group of men and women started to grab their jackets and coats and carrying their drinks, they began to saunter out on to the street. Hodgy went to the front door of the building and ushered the people past him down the little steps. He felt like the captain of a ship, his duty was to get everyone out and he would be the last to leave his sinking ship. As the crowd gathered on the street in the soft rain, a black police van pulled up to the curb and uniformed officers jumped from the rear doors and began pushing the group along the street towards Eddie's bar. Hodgy watched as the large group of people began to spread out along the road wondering what to do, then, above the noise of the traffic, music began to play. Hodgy looked across at *Rebecca's Brasserie*. The huge doorman had swung the door open and the music had been cranked up so loud it was filling the street. Nobby held the door open without even looking onto the street and let the music encourage the group to make their way across the road and in to Eddie Fewtrell's bar. Hodgy stood there holding the door to his pub open, his mouth dropped and a gormless expression took over his face.

"Cheeky fucker," he managed. One of the policemen saw his expression and gave a snigger. That was too much for Hodgy. He let the door slam and stormed across the road to *Rebecca's Brasserie*. Now that the crowd were inside, Nobby had let the door shut. Hodgy pulled the glass doors open and stormed inside. Nobby stepped in front of him.

"Everything ok son?" he said in a deep, gravelly voice.

"Where's Eddie?" he replied, his anger rising, Nobby gave a grin and pointed to the stairs.

"He's upstairs in the VIP room." He made a brushing gesture with his hand. "Go on up son, he's waiting for you," he said laughing. Hodgy turned and crossed the room, as he did so, he was sure the small groups of people in *Rebecca's Brasserie* were staring at him, hidden giggles and conversations began as he walked towards the stairs. He could feel their eyes in the back of his head, the paranoia brought on a cold sweat and he began to panic little. What had he got himself into? He crossed the packed bar as fast as he could and ran up the stairs covering two steps at a time.

"I'll fucking tell him!" he said to himself, "steal my customers will he!" He reached the top of the stairs and turned along a narrow corridor until he reached a small bar on the first floor. The place was dimly lit and very plush. He could see Eddie sitting at the end of the bar surrounded by a group, only Eddie was facing the stairs, everyone else had gathered around him and he held court, talking in his usual exuberant manner. Hodgy stormed into the room and walked around the group until he stood right in front of Eddie.

"Alright Hodgy?" Eddie said, smiling.

"Just what the fuck's going on Eddie? You're stealing all my customers!" Eddie looked the lad up and down and just laughed. The others joined in and for the first time Hodgy looked at the other people in the group. His eyes locked on Wendy who was stood next to Eddie, her back to him, leaning her elbow on the bar.

"What are you doing *here*?" he asked her. "I'm having my fucking opening night across the road, *remember?* I bought a pub ... Wendy ... Wendy, I'm talking to you!" The girl looked embarrassed but continued to ignore him, she shrugged and looked at Eddie for support. The crowd sniggered again. Hodgy looked at Eddie, a feeling of jealousy creeping over him when a man to his right butted in,

"Wendy works here Hodgy ... she's working tonight," he slapped a friendly hand on Hodgy's shoulder. Hodgy shrugged it off and turned to look at the man.

"What do you mean she works...?" Hodgy stopped mid sentence. The realisation that the man on his right was one of the detectives he'd met earlier that night hit him like a punch. "You're...you're..." he stumbled on his words.

"Dixie...I'm Dixie." The man held his hand out. "We met earlier, ya silly bastard," he said laughing. "Have you got a bad memory Hodgy? That could be very useful!" The whole group burst out laughing and Hodgy looked around the faces of the rest of the group.

He turned back to Eddie, eyes wide and began to say something but the words just weren't there. All he could do was stand there in his grey silk shirt and flared, high waisted trousers feeling like a clown, trying to work out what was going on. Eddie smiled.

"Sit down son, relax, have a drink." A huge hand rested on his shoulder.

"You heard Eddie," a deep Irish accent said softly in his ear, "sit down and have a drink pal!" Hodgy turned to the voice and came face to face with the big gypsy that had knocked him out at the beginning of the night. He nearly jumped out of his skin.

"Th...that's...him, that's the bastard that punched me!" Sniggers broke out again. The gypsy laughed a booming laugh. Hodgy looked from face to face.

"So *you* did the bomb scare then?" He addressed the gypsy, confusion washing over him. "Why?" He turned to the detective, his mind swimming. "You said I was under your protection." Hodgy pointed his finger at Dixie's face and Dixie stepped forward into *his*.

"You said *not now* Hodgy, if you want our protection, you have to pay up son, until then you're easy prey." Hodgy backed away. He turned to Eddie for some kind of explanation. Wendy left Eddie's side and sat in the corner next to another, dark haired woman that Hodgy hadn't noticed before.

Eddie stood up. He gestured with a nod of his head for everyone to leave and without question everyone stood, and taking their drinks with them, they filed down the stairwell until only Eddie, Hodgy and the dark haired woman were left in the VIP room. Hodgy held his arms wide.

"What the fuck's going on Eddie? I trusted you." Eddie's usual smile dropped.

"Look son, this is how it works. You run the pub . . ." Eddie left the words hanging. He continued, "I'll pay you a hundred quid a week just to run the *Grapes bar*, everything else . . ." Hodgy interrupted him.

"What do you mean pay me a hundred quid a week . . . it's *my* fucking pub!" Eddie stood in silence for a few seconds, not breaking Hodgy's stare. Hodgy looked away.

"Like I said," Eddie continued patiently, "it *is* your pub son yes, but even though you paid for it to be fixed up, that's only the price of running an operation on my patch, *understand?*" My brothers and I paid for this little bit of Birmingham with our blood son and let me tell ya, it didn't come cheap." Eddie gave Hodgy a huge grin, as if the smile on his face would explain everything, it didn't. Eddie saw his confusion. "Look the tinker and the bomb scare have got fuck all to do with me, let me make that clear." Eddie took a sip from his whisky. "All the receipts and the lease are in both our names not just yours, it may be your name above the door, but the beer contacts are mine, the furnishings were all bought in my name, so in fact . . . it's *our* pub son, you can run it and get your tonne a week and no hassles. Dixie wants paying too though, so that'll come on top, but you got the function room so anything you earn there will be yours, I can't say fairer than that Hodgy." Hodgy was dumbfounded.

"A backwater full of thickos," Eddie continued. "That's what you said to Wendy ain't it?" Hodgy was shocked that his girlfriend had been so unfaithful. "Well you'll find out just how untrue that really is son. There are some right hard bastards in this town Hodgy, we may talk funny but we can run rings around people like you son. Wendy said you had plenty of cash, she was right . . . good girl our Wendy." Hodgy lost his temper

"Well fuck you, I'll fucking . . ." he didn't get any further than that. Eddie's hand came up in a lightning fast strike, his open hand slapped him hard around the face nearly knocking him off his feet. Hodgy's jaw was still sore from the gypsy's punch and he backed away unsteadily.

"You ought to be very careful how you talk to people in Birmingham son. There's some very nasty people in this town, me being one of them." Eddie drained the glass, his temperament changed. "Look son, I like you and that's why we put on this little show on for you. If I just let you get on with running things on your own," Eddie stopped and searched for the right words, "well they'd fucking eat you alive son, protection rackets, Irish, blacks, gypsies, there's still a few of the old gangs knocking around who would try and move in. Without me you'd be like a lamb to the slaughter. You'll get your tonne every week," Eddie stopped and laughed, "look Hodgy, I'll tell ya what I'll do . . . cos I do want you to get on . . . as I said, I like winners . . . you run the place I'll pay you *two* hundred quid a week . . . *two* hundred a week, and you'll get the party room . . . that's all yours." Eddie opened his hands to emphasise his true intentions. Hodgy gave a small smile, Eddie picked up on it immediately. "That's the spirit son. Now, no hard feelings it's just business. You'll get used to it kid, and remember any hassle, you just come straight to me and I'll get one of my lads to sort it." Eddie nodded to himself with approval. "That's a lot of money Hodgy, more than fair," with that he smiled, turned and walked downstairs to the crowd below.

Hodgy sat on the edge of a table and let out a deep sigh, his anger subsided. He'd been stitched up, but not as badly as he first thought. He tried to find the good in the situation. He was surprised by how he felt, the thing that upset him most wasn't the cash, the protection or even the punch from the giant gypsy, it was Wendy, he liked the girl. He couldn't work out if she just worked for Eddie or was his girlfriend. He heard a shuffle in the corner and realised the dark haired woman was still there and staring at him.

"Cheer up bab . . . it ain't all doom and gloom." She rose from her chair, crossed the room unsteadily and stood in front of him. She was handsome, older than Hodgy maybe in her mid thirties and very beautiful. Her dark Italian looks and style didn't suit her thin Birmingham accent. Her eyes wandered over the lad, drinking in his youthful good looks. He reminded her of the actor Robert Redford; his blonde hair swept to the side in a parting that displayed his deep brown eyes. She scanned his face, his olive skin made him seem even younger than he actually was and by the way he stared at her she could tell the attraction between them was mutual.

"Did you think Wendy was your girlfriend?" she said slowly, savouring her words ending the sentence with a sexy, drunken giggle. Hodgy nodded, embarrassed. "She's an escort, she ain't your girlfriend, she's anyone's as long as you got the cash." She waited for him to acknowledge her words. He shook his head. "She's a pro . . . prostitute, a fucking whore!" She barked the words, growing more angry as she spoke, obviously upset by Wendy's presence in the bar but unable to do anything about it. Hodgy just looked blankly at her. "Come on handsome have a drink and relax!" She said, calming herself down, she walked behind the empty bar and grabbed a bottle of vodka from the counter.

"Are *you* a . . . a . . . ?" He searched for the words.

"*NO!* You cheeky bastard . . . I'm Hazel . . . Hazel Fewtrell . . . Eddie's wife."

Hodgy gave a little laugh.

"I'm not sure but I think your husband just ripped me off." Hazel looked shocked.

"Do you know how many people would want the deal Eddie just offered you? Some people would kill to be where you are right now." Hazel held out a glass to the young man and smiled, Hodgy took the glass and said,

"Oh and just where is that then?" Hazel just shrugged and gave another giggle.

"I'll tell you where that is handsome . . . you're under the Fewtrell's wing that's where, the *safest* place in Birmingham." He thought he heard a touch of sarcasm in her voice. Hodgy raised his glass to Hazel.

"Well it would've been nice to have had a choice wouldn't it?"

"*Choice?*" she replied drunkenly, "*choice* has got nothing to do with it bab." She walked around the bar and came closer to the blonde man who stood a head higher than herself. The effects of the alcohol making it increasingly difficult to hide the attraction she was unexpectedly starting to feel towards to him. She came closer and he pulled her into him, his actions confirming the feeling was mutual. She chinked his glass, smiling. Slowly, she raised her head meeting his dark eyes with a look of sexy mischief.

"Welcome to Birmingham bab, welcome to Birmingham."

A Grave Amongst the Trees.

Chapter 2

Zafa Khan stood amongst the tree line, watching the beginnings of another week climb across the horizon in a thin line of smoky purple and orange light. The sunrise reminded him of his home land in the Peshawar region of Pakistan. Each second the light grew, bringing different shades of reds, oranges and yellows, pushing out the last remnants of darkness that held on to the edges of the sky. The few stars still hung in the frosty, morning light were put to flight as the edge of the golden orb finally broke the curvature of the earth, the new day had begun. Zafa was lost in his day dreams. Sunrises in the mountains of Peshawar were far more beautiful than here in Birmingham. The red dust kicked up by a million feet in Islamabad two hundred or so miles to the east, made for glorious sunrises. The deep, red sun silhouetting the minarets and mountains, as the ancient call to prayer brought the humble people on to the streets as it had done for centuries. Happy memories, well at least some of them were. He shivered, his long, herringbone tweed coat was no protection from the icy breeze that danced around the trees and the sudden gust brought him back to his surroundings.

He looked down from his vantage point on the Lickey Hills that overlooked the city of Birmingham. There were no minarets, no calls to prayer, only red brick houses, car factories and trees, lots and lots of trees. That's why he was here. He could tell from the soft rumblings in the distance that the city was awakening and the Monday morning rush hour had begun down in the suburban streets far below. He turned and walked back into the forest, the tall pines were still green even after such harsh weather. Most of the trees still had their needles, which hung onto their branches, stubborn against the stiff, cold wind. He crossed the brown forest floor silently, the fallen fir needles that had succumbed to the winter winds cushioning his steps until he came to the place where his men were digging. He looked at their faces, stern but obedient, he was their leader, their chief, he worked and thought on their behalf, his decisions affected all of them and their families.

They had followed him to England from the mountains of Peshawar and now he must provide for them the best way he could. He didn't really understand the Christians, or their nailed god who seemed to forgive them for anything, without punishment and only love. These people seemed to celebrate decadence and debauchery as if it were at the very heart of the civilisation they had built since their God's crucifixion, two thousand years before. Perversion seemed to be in their souls. A pious man, Zafa didn't agree with it but that didn't mean he couldn't profit from it.

Zafa Khan's strength lay not in his fist but in his ability to out think his opponents. Make no mistake, Zafa was a killer, he had proved that several times, but now he was chieftain too and only showed his violent side when his men or his opponents *needed* to see it.

He had many opponents back in Pakistan, the last of whom was his benefactor Kahalid, the local warlord, a brave but ignorant man. He had made the mistake, like many others, of being blind to Zafa's ambitions. Kahalid had asked Zafa's father if he could have Zafa as his driver, a well respected position within the small community of hill farmers and in reply his father, almost bent in two with pride, bowed his subservient head to the warlord. Zafa, however, was disgusted at the decision made on his behalf and at his father's behaviour, but hid his feelings until the time to strike arrived. Zafa bowed and kissed the arse of Kahalid for three, long years. Always smiling, standing in the background, avoiding eyes and never questioning, only adding a soft word of doubt here and there in the ears of Kahalid's enemies. Slow and subtle, like a pit viper, he would let his prey wander by their own free will into the ambush. Kahalid would be alienated from his men by Zafa's sly words, softly spoken until the time was right to strike. Zafa saw the mercy in Kahalid as weakness.

A reporter from a German newspaper had come to visit the area in the mid 1960s, she was tall and blonde, the local children had taken to her smile and golden hair and gifts of sweet chocolate. She was well liked by the older women too, even though she was often seen with her head uncovered. The Imam had personally given her the traditional head scarves the women of the region must wear, insisting she should wear one whenever she was in public. But the reporter, being young and western, hadn't taken the Imam seriously, which in turn led to the men of the villages craving her attention. Kahalid had told his men to leave her to get on with her business in the region, that she would soon leave. He told them that they must be more open to westerners, who would bring opportunities for the young ones to the region. Zafa agreed, at least to Kahalid's face. However, in the shadows, Zafa had made plans to take the blonde woman and move her on. His contacts in Islamabad had assured him they had someone from Saudi Arabia that wanted such a woman and would pay well. To Zafa it wasn't just business, this was his chance. Taking the woman was easy. Men who had become loyal to him had been only too happy to help with the kidnap. The promise of gold had helped sway their weak minds, but the offer of the naked woman tied up in the back of the flatbed lorry had sealed the deal. The deal with the Islamabad gang was made and the woman was sold to a Saudi prince through several third parties, and never heard of again.

Kahalid came to Zafa's home at dawn the next day. He was with his men, all armed, ready for revenge against the man who had sold his guest into slavery and undermined his authority. The confrontation hadn't lasted long. Zafa was waiting for him with his own warriors. They caught the ageing warlord by surprise. The barrel of an AK47 placed against Kahalid's head as the swing of power took place in this coup amongst the mountains.

Zafa had already thought out the punishment for the insult of being made Kahalid's driver. His men were given the choice to either swear their oaths to him or to die. To Zafaf's surprise many of Kahalid's men chose the latter, all were bound, their throats slit and then left to bleed out in the red dust.

The warlord was marched outside to the car he'd arrived in only minutes before. His hands bound, he was made to kneel beside the ancient dusty jeep. Zafa took the heavy, steel, wheel brace from the old, olive green ammunition box, that acted as a tool box for the car. Zafa pushed the man's head onto the rim of the jeep's tailgate, and there, in that beautiful, deep red, morning sunrise, as the call to prayer echoed through the valleys, he smashed Kahalid's skull to a pulp with the wheel brace. The other men who had chosen to live dared not to step forward and stop him. Zafa had created his own group within the village, bought and paid for with the gold from the sale of the woman and now the swing of power was complete. He was chieftain. He would lead his people and he *had* lead them west, to England, to this wet, fat country, full of weakness and perversions. That's how he found himself on the Lickey hills that cold morning, standing over a shallow grave, awaiting the girl stolen from the streets of the city for the deadly enjoyment of another, rich, white man.

* * *

The Lickey Hills stand on the edge of Birmingham's massive sprawling suburbs. The five hundred acres of woodlands have sat to the south west of the city since the days when the Norman overlords had used the forests as hunting grounds. The Victorians also enjoyed the hills for an afternoon stroll through the pines, oaks and fir trees, riding donkeys from the little tea rooms that sat at the centre of the national park, trotting up the hills as if on safari. Every Sunday the working class would swap the industrial bleakness of the city for the nature the woods had to offer. The little businesses catering for the weekenders boomed, reaching a peak in the years before World War One, when during the summer a mop, fair or circus could be found at the cross road village at the edge of the national park. These events were attended by thousands in their day, but times and fortunes had changed. The downward spiral had begun in the late sixties, when groups of hippies and bikers could be found tripping on the psychedelic, liberty cap mushrooms found in the fields that surrounded the forest. Every now and then, gangs of three or four hundred scooter boys and skinheads would roll into the wilderness on their customised Lambrettas and Vespas, pap, pap, papping, their machines at break neck speed up and down the roads, in clouds of sweet smelling, two stroke oil. Gang fights between the greebo bikers from the black country and the skinheads had become par for the course over the weekends and gradually the families that had enjoyed the forests for a moment of solitude just faded away. Only horny couples looking for a quick knee trembler amongst the trees would brave the gauntlet of opposing yobs by racing in their father's Ford Cortina for their ten minutes of ecstasy in the forest.

There were some forest rangers that worked for the forestry commission and policed the area but they were too few and too stretched to cover the whole forest, and anyway, what were a few forest rangers going to do against a gang of twenty bikers from Wolverhampton, high on psychedelics?

* * *

Zafa knew about the rangers and he knew they would be in the area in the next few hours, so he was eager to get on with the business in hand. He went to the van that held the dark haired girl. His men had finished digging the frozen earth and joined him as he crossed the forest to were the van was parked. Haroom was already waiting at the rear doors to the van. Zafa could hear the girl kicking the van's doors, more in a protest than an effort to escape. If she had known what was coming she may have tried a bit harder.

Haroom was Zafa's second in command. At six foot six he was a huge man. Unquestioning and totally loyal in the face of death, he had been tested many times in Pakistan and always stood his ground. Zafa trusted Haroom with both his and his family's life. The big man had no family of his own, he was here to serve his chieftain and nothing more. He liked it that way. He wasn't the fastest thinker but his warlord did the thinking for him. Haroom liked to think with his fists, knives, guns and had a medieval imagination for torture.

Zafa went around to the cab of the light blue, Ford transit van. He slid the cab door back. The man inside was sitting in the cab wrestling with a bottle of champagne, his fingers pushed under the cork but the cork refused to budge. The man had his eyes closed to protect him against the champagne's expected pop. His hands were just too weak to free the cork from the *Don Perignon* bottle. He opened his big puppy eyes in shock at Zafa's intrusion. Zafa stood at the door, shook his head and smiled.

"We're nearly ready Mr Raven." The man sat looking as if he were about to cry.

"I can't open the fucking bottle . . . the fucking cork's stuck or something!" His eyes pleading, he held out the bottle to Zafa, who took the bottle and squeezed his thumbs around the neck and the cork instantly shot out with a loud pop, arcing its way into the trees. "A-haa . . . I must've loosened it for ya." He pulled a champagne flute from the map shelf on the dash board and offered it to Zafa. The Pakistani shook his head.

"I don't drink, thank you." The man in the cab looked confused and shook the glass in his hand, gesturing to Zafa to pour the champagne. Zafa understood his meaning.

"Cheeky bastard." he thought. He poured the golden liquid into the flute and looked the man over.

Mr Raven, *Gary Raven* as he was known on stage or *Budgie* as he was known to his sycophantic friends, was in his late twenties. He was a frontman for one of the glam rock bands that had stormed the pop music charts and he was living his moment of fame like a young Caligula. His tour of the major music venues had slowly become more and more debauched back stage. It had started off with the one or two teenage girls that had been hanging about outside his dressing room, invitations were given to an after show party, all innocent fun. Things changed after his single *Wanna Rock and Roll* had jumped into the top thirty, bigger venues and more dates were added and the tour rolled on, the TV music show *Top of the Pops* wanted him to appear. After the TV show, B.B.C. D.J., Jimmie Saville had explained to him that this wasn't going to last forever and he'd better enjoy it while he could and told him that he was one of the chosen few that could do anything they wanted, as long as he kept his mouth shut. The more celebrities, MPs, judges and members of the aristocracy that were involved in these orgies the safer they were, because if one fell, they all fell. He introduced Budgie to other celebrities who had similar interests and these TV and music stars could be found waiting for him when his live shows finished, with them they brought cocaine, lots and lots of cocaine which shifted everything up a gear. The activities in his dressing room had changed from boyish pranks with teenage girls to well planned orgies, almost romanesque in their debauchery. Now instead of one or two girls he could pretty much have his pick of the litter. The longer the tour went on, the further the boundaries were pushed. Eighteen year olds soon turned to sixteen, then fourteen, girls or boys (of any age) were herded into his dressing room backstage by his roadies, celebrities or unsuspecting parents. Children and teenagers abused as their parents stood smiling on the other side of the dressing room door, humiliated and raped for his perverted entertainment.

Budgie had bored Zafa on his way to the *Lickey Hills* with his talk of the *ultra-violence* he had enjoyed in the, now banned movie *A Clockwork Orange.* He had been so taken by the film that he'd even had his clothes designer make a glam rock version of the costume worn in the film, and here he was, sat in the front of a Transit van in a forest, wearing his silver bowler hat covered with tiny mirrors, black eye make up over one eye, just like the hero in the movie. Silver shirt, trousers and braces and knee high silver boots with six inch platform souls finished off the outfit. If the business at hand hadn't been so serious, Zafa would have happily slapped the lad around the forest. He could see the displeasure in

Haroom's eyes that they had to deal with this buffoon, but money was money and this lad had plenty of it. Two thousand pounds for tonight's little perversion, six months wages to most people. Budgie had assured Zafa at their first meeting that he had already enjoyed *ultimate sex*, as he described it, before. However, Zafa could see by the lad's eyes that he was lying, but the ridiculous, blonde haired man with the cigar had assured Zafa that Gary was ok to deal with, so plans were put into action.

The red haired girl skipped out of work looking forward to Friday night out with her friends. She had caught her bus on the New street city terminus, as she had done every day since leaving school a year before. The double decker bus took its normal route, trundling through the wet streets of Birmingham but had broken down just on the edges of the red light district of *Balsall Heath*. The passengers exited the bus as commanded by the conductor and waited for another in the cold drizzle. The girl had become impatient though, and crossed the road towards *Canon Hill* park and started a short cut through the floral gardens to her home. That's where she had met Haroom. He hadn't said anything to her, there was no talking or grooming. He had just stepped out from the shadows and punched her. She saw him approaching and smiled her sweet smile, she could've run but she was too young, too sweet to think that something like this could happen on the streets of Britain's second city. Haroom had brought his fist up so fast she hadn't had time to react and now here she was, two days later, hands tied behind her back, being frog marched barefoot across the freezing forest by the large Asian man. Haroom took her to the edge of the freshly dug grave. The hole in the ground was only three feet deep and its sight brought a fresh struggle from the gagged girl. She was screaming something, but the gag muffled her protests and Haroom just pushed her in, face first. She fell hard on the frozen earth. The fall winded her, and she stopped her struggling. Haroom looked down at the girl, her white skin pale in the dawn light contrasted against the dark, cold soil. Her little mini skirt had worked its way up her thighs, her little, white, flowery knickers made her look even more innocent. Haroom wondered if the silver man would appreciate that. Zafa looked across to Haroom who nodded.

"It's time Mr Raven, she's ready for you." Budgie looked like he'd forgotten why he was there. "The *girl* Mr Raven, she's waiting for you." Budgie plonked the big black champagne bottle on the dash board and began struggling out of the van. His platform boots making the process difficult. He tumbled out of the van and Zafa caught him, helping him to his feet. Raven stood there swaying in the morning light. Zafa pointed to the grave. Budgie nodded and began across the forest towards Haroom. Zafa signalled him with his fingers that Haroom should leave. Haroom turned and walked back to the group of three men waiting on the tree line who were watching the frosty sunrise, backs to the woods. Zafa had told Mr Raven that he had over a hundred whores and he could have his pick of them, but the silver man had wanted to do everything his way. He had the cash, so the pop star had got his wish.

Budgie stumbled through the trees, his silver boots slipping every now and then on the dead fir leaves under foot until he stood at the foot of the grave. He saw the girl for the first time. She had turned herself over and she now lay on her back looking up into the evergreen trees above. Her eyes widened with surprise at first sight of Gary Raven, then her look turned to recognition. Budgie realised the girl knew him, she began to struggle once more. Gesturing for him to help her, Raven began to snigger, the girl thought he was there to rescue her. When she saw him laugh the girl froze, the realisation that the man on the poster in her bedroom she had idolised, wasn't a hero coming to her rescue, he was the *reason* she was here.

Zafa watched the silver man amongst the trees, how ridiculous he looked, he felt ashamed to be involved with such an dishonourable business, but he couldn't tear his eyes away from the arrogant pop star. He had seen some things . . . he had *done* some things, killed, tortured, his mind ran back to the CIA man who had come to the mountains from Islamabad, and how he had screamed when he had been skinned alive. But none of the horrors that he had been involved with in Pakistan had presented such a bizarre sight as the scene before him now.

Budgie climbed down into the grave. The girl lay still, eyes wide in disbelief. He ran his hand over her bare legs and up to her knickers but pulled his hand away when he felt her cold skin. He stood back up shaking his head.

"She's fucking cold!" he shouted towards Zafa. Zafa raised his arms and shrugged.

"She's going to get colder the longer you leave her there." He waved his hands gesturing Raven to get on with whatever he had in mind.

"Two grand . . . two fucking grand . . . !" Budgie shouted, turning back to the girl. He unfastened his sliver studded belt and let his sparkly trousers drop to the floor. His white arse almost glowing in the semi darkness of the trees. Zafa watched the man as he fumbled with his cock, "I can't do it while you're watching," he said without turning.

Zafa turned away, embarrassed. Budgie knelt down astride the girl and started to masturbate. The girl began to struggle once more, she brought her knees up under Raven's groin and kicked. He saw it coming and shifted his weight the kick missed his groin but went on and caught him in the jaw. Budgie stopped what he was doing, a look of horror growing in his eyes. "NOT THE FACE!" he screamed at the girl. He slapped her hard around the head. "Just stay still and let me do this, then we can both get out of here." The girl began to calm, believing the pop idol, she stopped kicking and lay still, and there on the Lickey Hills on that frosty October morning, Gary Raven, glam rock star, raped that innocent, nameless girl in her own grave, as part of his sick ultimate sexual perversion.

Zafa, Haroom and the other men had wandered off towards the tree line and were stood smoking and sniggering about Mr Raven's ridiculous costume. The men questioned how Zafa had come across such a weird young man. By the time Zafa had explained that he'd been introduced to Gary Raven after his show the previous night and as far as he knew the singer was still drunk from the night before, the pop star had returned from the grave, zipping his trousers up as he hobbled across the forest back to the van.

"I'm done now mate!" he shouted over to the group, "come on . . . I'm fucking freezing." He stood at the van's window flicking his hair. "Get me back to me hotel I need to get me head down." Budgie climbed into the van and began drinking from the champagne bottle again.

"Was that it?" Zafa called, "are you finished already?" Zafa half ran through the trees, his eyes flicking towards the grave. "Mr Raven . . . are you finished?"

Gary just slammed the transit door. Zafa turned back to Haroom and gestured towards the grave. Haroom nodded. Zafa climbed back into cab.

"Was that *it*?" The young man nodded, a look of embarrassment growing on his face. "We went to all this trouble so you could have a three minute fuck?" Gary turned to the man.

"You got paid didn't ya . . . what you moaning about?" Zafa lost his temper.

"That girl is going to die in that cold grave because you wanted a three minute fuck . . . you're lucky I don't throw you in with her you little piece of shit!" Gary looked shocked.

"I thought you were cool . . . be cool." he said swigging from the bottle. "Tell em to hurry up I need to get me head down." Zafa's head swam with rage. He wanted to rip the boy's head off but he controlled himself. After all, the lad was right he had taken the money and now he had to complete the deal by burying the girl. He opened the van door and stepped back out into the cold air. Haroom and his men had started to fill in the grave, he couldn't see the girl but he could hear her muffled cries as the cold soil began to be heaped on to her body. Zafa slammed the door.

"Haroom!" he shouted. " Haroom!" The big man turned to his master's voice. "Kill the girl. Don't bury her alive, she's suffered enough." He began to walk across the space between them. As he came close Zafa became aware of someone standing amongst the trees about twenty yards away. Zafa froze. Haroom, who was still looking at his boss saw Zafa stop and stare into the trees. Haroom followed the stare until he found the figure. Unlike Zafa who had frozen, Haroom didn't hesitate and weighed up the situation in the blink of an eye, he grabbed one of the shovels and began to sprint towards the man. The forest ranger reacted too slowly. He held his hands up towards the sprinting man, trying to reason with the giant as he ran toward him. But as Haroom drew near, the ranger realised that he was witnessing a murder and they weren't going to let him live, so now *he* was their new prey. He turned too late and began running away, panic had grabbed him and he kept looking behind to see the progress of his attacker. If he had kept his wits, if he had used the trees to his advantage and run like the wind he might have escaped. But he didn't, he only half ran and stumbled amongst the tree roots, until Haroom was upon him. Zafa and the others held their breath, willing their man to bring his prey down as he sprinted like a cheater across the space between the trees. Haroom swung the shovel and brought it down with a dull *BONG* of steel clashing on the skull of the ranger's head. The khaki clad man fell in a hump, the dead weight sending up a plume of fir needles flying into the air. The man lay shivering on the forest floor his skull smashed by the blow, nerve endings creating the dance of death that Haroom had seen many times before. Without hesitation, Haroom grabbed the collar of the fallen man and dragged him back to the graveside. He made it look effortless. Zafa knew that Haroom had avoided a disaster. If the man had gotten away, it wouldn't have taken long before the police found the grave and then Zafa himself. The man was still quivering when Haroom threw the ranger on to the half buried girl. Zafa retuned to the van, swinging the door open he grabbed Budgie's arm and dragged him from the cab. The pop star protested.

"What the fuck are you . . . ?" Zafa slapped the back of his hand around his face. Budgie was more shocked than hurt. "Just who the fuck do you . . . ?" SLAP! Zafa hit him again. He dragged the stumbling pop star back across to the graveside, he pointed down at the dead ranger and the now blood-soaked squealing girl.

"One body, two thousand pounds . . . two bodies four thousand pounds!" Gary Raven looked shocked.

"Who the fuck is he?" Budgie turned to the man holding his arm in a tightening pinch.

"Two thousand pounds more, Mr Raven." He held his hand out, the pop star looked amazed.

"I ain't got that kind of money on me now mate have I? I ain't even got pockets in these fucking trousers . . . I just came off stage for fuck's sake." Zafa nodded at Haroom who suddenly grabbed Budgie by his black, tousled hair. Haroom almost picked the man off the ground with his huge arm, Budgie was left dancing, only his toes touching the ground.

"Now listen well my little silver friend. If you don't want to end up in the ground with these pair of unfortunates then I would put a civil tongue in your mouth when you talk to me and start thinking where you can get the money from!" He gestured to Haroom to release Budgie, who fell down to his knees instantly grabbing the back of his hair to make sure Haroom hadn't pulled any out. He looked up at the big man and began to say something, but before he could, Haroom raised his foot and gave the man a stiff kick. Raven gave a girlish shriek and fell face first into the grave, landing on top of the dead ranger. The girl at the bottom of the pile let out a gasp as all the wind was knocked out of her again. Budgie could see the girl beneath him, her eyes wide with confusion and fear.

"No . . . no.!" Budgie shouted, he spun around in the grave so he was lying on his back looking up at the two Pakistanis. "No . . . I'll pay . . . I'll pay . . . just get me out of here . . . Jesus get me out!" He began to panic. Zafa nodded once more, Haroom bent and grabbed Budgie's out stretched hand pulling him upwards without any effort. The pop star landed on his knees, the mud from the grave staining his silver trousers, he began to cry. "What did you do that for?" His voice sounded more like that of a child's now. "I wanna go now, I'm fucking freezing and this ain't fun anymore." Zafa grabbed his collar.

"My money . . . I want my money Mr Raven." Zafa bent spitting the words into Budgie's ear.

"Get me to a phone box, I'll . . . I'll call Eddie Fewtrell." Gary stuttered. "He'll get the money for ya."

"Eddie Fewtrell?" Zafa bristled.

"Mr Fewtrell . . . Eddie Fewtrell . . . he runs *Barbarella's club* where I played last night. He still owes me the cash from the show, I'm meant to pick it up today." Budgie could see the look on Zafa's face. Zafa shook his head and held his hands up to stop Budgie's babbling.

"I *know* who Eddie Fewtrell is . . . but do you *know* Eddie Fewtrell?"

"Well I know he ain't someone you mess about with," Budgie grew more confident. "Mr Fewtrell ain't gonna be too happy about the way you've treated me either." Budgie was bluffing, he hardly knew Eddie Fewtrell, but what he *did* know was that Eddie would have buried him alive himself had he known about the perverted things Budgie was getting up to. "So I suggest you get me to a phone and then back to my hotel and then, if you treat me nice and Mr Fewtrell says so, you can get your fucking money." They stood in silence in the growing frosty wind, the branches shuffling above their heads. Budgie looked at the two Pakistani men and he could see Zafa was running things over in his mind.

"Mr Fewtrell is your manager? . . . and does he manage lots of people like you?" Budgie shook his head.

"NO ! He ain't my manager. He owns all the clubs in town, that's how I know him. I played his club last night, *Barbarella's*." Zafa stood quietly for a second.

"You may be of some service to me Mr Raven." Budgie looked between the two men realising he was still in deep trouble and there was a real chance that he could end up in the grave alongside the dead ranger and the girl.

"Oh yeah . . . and how might I be of service then?" trying to sound cocky. An agonising silence fell between the three men. Budgie was expecting Haroom to throw him in the grave at any point so he began to run through various escape scenarios; scenes from old movies played through his mind, *The Heroes of Telemark, James Bond,* but all he could do was silently curse his silly, silver platform boots which made any chance of escape impossible. There was a muffled scream from the grave that broke the silence and all three turned towards the hole in the ground.

"Fill it in!" Zafa straightened up and patted Haroom on the shoulder. "Come on Mr Raven, let's get you into the warmth of the van," he said smiling. Budgie couldn't help a nervous snigger.

"Yeah, now you're talking. There's no point us all falling out is there?" Zafa gave Gary a thin smile.

"Let my men fill in the grave and you can drink your champagne in the van. I want to talk to you about this Eddie Fewtrell."

"Don't worry he's got the cash." Budgie said nervously.

"No . . . no, we don't need to worry about the cash anymore, it's just a . . . a misunderstanding." Raven nodded, unsure what Zafa meant but went along with him anyway.

"Yeah, misunderstanding, that's right." He gave a nervous smile.

"Instead of paying me that cash I'd like you to help me at some point in the future where Mr Fewtrell is concerned, Gary, can you do that?" Zafa said charmingly. Gary Raven shook his shoulder length, black hair in the stiffening breeze, mustering as much dignity as he could.

"I think I can do that Mr Iqbal . . . no problem." Zafa pulled Budgie up by the scruff of his silver collared shirt. He stood up unsteadily on his six inch platforms, and smiled at Zafa. The pair began to turn towards the van. The other men came around the graveside, shovels in hand began to fill in the hole. The girl in the grave began to shuffle and scream, her screams stifled by the choking gag and the ranger's dead body lying on top of her, its weight pushing the air out of her lungs. Budgie stopped and turned back towards the grave, a look of sorrow on his face. He walked back to the graveside and could see the terrified girl's eyes begging him for rescue.

"I want to watch!" Gary said a wry smile on his face. Zafa shrugged.

"It's your money Mr Raven . . . you must do as you please." Zafa had lost interest in the scene, "Eddie Fewtrell." Zafa said to himself, he mulled over the name, "Eddie Fewtrell." He said the words again slowly. That name kept coming up every time he tried to put some business on to the streets of the city and it irritated him. None of the Birmingham dealers who did a small trade in uppers and downers would even *talk* about selling anything stronger in his clubs than pep pills. The problem was, the business Zafa had in mind was heroin, pure white heroin from the poppy plains of Afghanistan, he could get a never ending supply from his friends and family still in Peshawar. Yes, the whorehouses made money, but if he could get a foothold in Birmingham with heroin, *then* he could make his fortune and be a gold giver to his men, a warlord, even a Pakistani king to his people. Eddie Fewtrell was going to have to be paid a visit, and shown a bit of Pakistani muscle, or even better, get someone else to bring this western dog into line. Zafa pondered over the name as he watched the young man in silver against the green of the forest. What type of world had he brought his people to? He sat back breaking his view of the perversion amongst the trees and drew deeply on the cigarette, a plan forming.

Chapter 3

Davey Keogh was 10 years old, a bright, academically unremarkable and somewhat confused little lad, nevertheless he had a couple of things going for him. His first communion was over and done with and he could say his prayers on his own from start to finish. No small achievement for a young Catholic boy, and now he would spend his whole life making decisions influenced by that infamous Catholic guilt. On a brighter note though he could play the guitar and had a fine voice. He even performed the songs, his mother had forced him to learn, in front of a small audience of auntys and uncles, cousins and friends. He didn't like these songs though; they all spoke of loving Ireland, leaving Ireland or fighting for Ireland, long, heart-wrenching songs about the girl that was left behind or great battles against the English. They bored him. He preferred the rock bands he saw on Thursday on *Top of the Pops*, like *Slade*, *Ziggy Stardust* or *Gary Raven,* songs that his older brother listened to on the old Dansette they shared in their bedroom. Davey couldn't understand why, if his mother and father loved Ireland so much, they had left the place six months ago and moved to dreaded *England* in the first place.

He hadn't had too many friends in Ireland, not like here. Here in England he was suddenly top dog amongst ten of so boys of around the same age that met two or three times a week at the

Birmingham Irish centre in Digbeth. The boys were from all over the city and never saw each other except when they formed their little gang at the Irish Centre, whenever their parents brought them down to the social club. To the parents this wasn't just a social event but also a place to pick up next week's work and perhaps some gossip from back home in Ireland. To Davey and the other boys it was a place to show off your sliding skills; sliding at break neck speed across the packed, polished dance floor on their knees, without hitting any of the jivers, was regarded as one of the cool things to do, as was climbing on stage with one of the big show bands that came to town on tour from Ireland. Once up there, the boys would score 'cool' points from their friends by annoying the frustrated musicians; pick up a spare guitar, detune the bass, kick the lead singer. These were all big scorers for the gang, but Davey had topped them all during a performance by one of Ireland's top show bands *The Indians*, by climbing inside the bass drum unnoticed whilst the band were playing their first song, and staying there for the whole three hour show. As the gaggle of screaming children grew around the front of the stage, the band had no idea about the stowaway until he emerged from the bass drum during the encore, a huge smile on his face and almost deaf in both ears.

Thursday nights at the Irish centre were never the liveliest of nights, not because of the lack of people, the club was always packed, whichever day of the week it was. Tuesday nights were lesson nights: Irish dancing in the main ballroom and piano accordion, penny whistle or guitar in the small, back room. The lessons didn't put off the would be drinkers though, far from it. The groups of mainly men, freshly arrived from Eire and looking for the start, could be found skulling back pints and smoking in small groups. These groups of men usually consisted of brothers, cousins, friends or just people from the same county back home. Everyone needed a start on the job and the best place to find it if you were Irish, was at the centre. The blacks had their clubs over in *Handsworth* or *Lozelles* where they did the same, but this was the *Irish* club. That's not to say there were no black folk to be found in the club, plenty of black people drank there, and the

Irish, who were generally living in the same areas as the Caribbean immigrants, thought nothing of it and welcomed them as friends. Even a young Pakistani fellow called Mo would skirt around the tables in the club on busy nights selling alcohol that had fallen off the back of the proverbial, amongst the various Irish and Catholic clubs, pubs and bars throughout the city and he was a popular chap. Mo's sideline on dodgy toys made him even more popular with the kids.

* * *

Davey was adding to the cacophony of different musical instruments being practiced in in the back room by strumming his guitar to a rhythm being tapped out by his music teacher, Mr O'Sullivan. The teacher was very proud of his star pupil. After the lesson had finished, Mr O'Sullivan would rap his pen against a pint glass, signalling the other tutors and students to quieten down and listen. Then he would encourage Davey to give an impromptu performance to the other pupils and drinkers alike, as he did every week. Davey would sing songs with titles and melodies that either made you sad or proud to be an Irish patriot. The men at the bar, hard working class men, would stop and listen in silence to the young lad. Every week Davey would see one of the big men secretly wipe a tear from his eye as the song's words struck a chord with its listener. After Davey had finished, a pint jug would be passed around the room and filled with change, tips for the lament or rebel song, and Mr O'Sullivan would take his share and leave a pound or two for the boy. On this particular night Davey was instructed to sing a particular Irish rebel song. Mr O'Sullivan had insisted that Davey play it and looked nervous when Davey had grumbled about the song. The guitar teacher had pointed to a blonde haired man at the bar that had just returned from Ireland who had requested it.

"Davey, he's a very important man and he might give you a big tip if you play the song." Mr O'Sullivan could see Danny wasn't convinced. "It's his favourite song Davey . . . and he *is* very important," he continued, in a patronising tone, "so play the song for the man, good lad!" He patted Davey's head and sat on one of the little stools to the side of the boy. Davey looked over at the bar.

"Who is he, is he famous?" The man had his back to Davey and was chatting to a group of other men in subdued tones. He pulled the small guitar against him and began the song.

"He will be soon, Davey, now play the song there's a good lad."

The room was an L shaped affair, 1960s style, brown, wooden tables and matching chairs ran along the length of both walls, the deep blue, beer soaked carpet matched the cushions on the seats and the long, blue curtains were pulled back on ties across the windows on the outside wall. A dim light came from the country style, moulded glass light fitting that hung from brass brackets from the artex ceiling. Outside the street lights shone through the frosted glass, bathing the room in a yellow light that seemed to make the place even dimmer than it already was. The yellow light rested on the ever present, cigarette smoke that floated in an eye-watering ghost like mist that sat on the air, about three feet off the ground. Davey drew in a deep breath of the smoky air and began the song.

"*When apples still grow in November.*" The man continued to talk within the tight circle.

"*When blossom still blooms from each tree.*" Davey continued, but the man still talked. Davey raised the volume of his voice.

"*When leaves are still green in December.*" The man stopped talking. He turned to watch the boy. Davey could see the man clearly now. He was tall with short blonde hair, bright blue eyes and a scar that ran down his left cheek. He looked dangerous, Davey thought, but also, he had something else about him, an air of nobility, a stubborn proudness that fascinated Davey.

"*It's then that this land will be free.*" The room fell silent as if by turning to listen, the man had given everyone in there an unspoken command to be silent.

"*Where are you now when we need you?*" A barmaid fumbled with a glass behind the bar and the man with blonde hair gave her a sharp look. She put the glass down softly, resting her hands on the counter, joining the other listeners.

"What glows where the flame used to be," Davey's voice cut through the smoky air, a maturity in it that disguised his youthfulness.

"Are ye gone like the snows of last winter." Davey stared at the blonde man now, singing the song just for him. The man began to mouth the words without any sound his eyes closed.

"And only our rivers run free . . . and only our rivers run free." The boy deliberately strummed the final chord slowly, to emphasise the sadness of the song and as he did so, he could see the blonde man's blue eyes sparkle with tears.

The room stood in silence for a breath, then the man clapped his hands together and the whole room erupted into applause. Davey watched his reaction, but unlike all the others in the room who stepped forward with loose change tips for the pint jug being passed around, he just turned his back and carried on his conversation with the huddle of men at the bar.

Davey's father Paddy stood just inside the door to the back bar smiling, still in his work clothes, his big, black, donkey jacket damp from the drizzle he'd been scaffolding in all day. He just caught the tail end of the song and his smile made obvious the pride he felt for the boy. Paddy Keogh was a scaffolder by trade. A lover of family, Irish music and his Catholic faith, he didn't show much emotion except for when his children gave him need to, and this was one of those occasions. Davey met his smile with one of his own and as his father crossed the smoky room he could see he was hiding something behind his back. Paddy had decided to surprise Davey with one of Mo's knock off toys, he had bought it from the little asian when he had bumped into him as he entered the club. Paddy rested his hand on the boy's shoulders and then brought his hidden hand from behind his back, placing a long box on its end on the table next to Davey. The boy almost screamed with pleasure, grabbing at the box greedily, his eyes ran over the doll inside its transparent, plastic fronted container with big letters running reading *Action Man*. The little camouflaged uniformed soldier figure inside stared out at him, a scar ran down the figure's cheek, his head was covered with a small green plastic beret with a gold brooch on its up turned front rim and a little black plastic

L1A1 rifle held in his gripping hands by two tiny brown elastic bands. Davey's father patted the boys' shoulders, gesturing that it was time to leave, now that his guitar lesson was over. The boy rose from the table, guitar in one hand, action figure in the other and followed his father blindly, staring at the toy and grinning from ear to ear. Davey began to show the brightly coloured box to his friends who were also having lessons on various instruments around the room. A small hubbub of children began to gather around Davey and his new toy. Davey turned to the men at the bar, still huddled in a small group.

"Excuse me." Davey said to the group of men. "Excuse me!" Davey repeated and this time the men turned to the boy. The blonde man smiled at the child. "Did you like the song . . . you knew all the words?" He addressed the blonde man directly, Davey's father looked embarrassed.

"I'm sorry lads." Paddy apologised. "Come on Davey let's go son!" He tugged his son's arm but Davey dug his heels into the old carpet.

"Do you like my *Action man*?" Davey held the doll up to the men. The smile dropped from the blonde man's face as he caught sight of the *Action man*. His father turned to pick him up.

"Come on son." Paddy said with a nervous laugh.

"Stop!" The man ordered but Davey's father carried on. "Hey!" The man shouted this time and his father froze and, turning slowly to the man at the bar he smiled nervously.

"Eh, Davey has to get home . . . it's a school night." He faltered. The man took no notice of Paddy and addressed the boy.

"That was a nice bit o playing there son, did ya daddy teach ye that song?" as he said the words he moved his eyes from son to father.

"No, me Mam made me learn it." The man came away from the bar and squatted down beside the boy. He ran his fingers through the boy's hair and looked up at Davey's father.

"You're missing out on some of your fatherly duties, wouldn't ya say?" Davey's father looked puzzled. "This wee lad's got a real talent for singing the old song so he has, maybe you should make a bit more of an effort to teach him his Irish history." Davey's father's face flushed with embarrassment.

"He knows all he needs to know." He replied nervously. The man, still squatting by the boy, held his hand out. Davey understanding the meaning placed the *Action man* into his open hands. He took the box and rose to his feet, he stood six inches taller than Paddy but slouched in his shoulders so he could look straight into the other man's face. He held the box with the doll inside beside his face.

"And is this *all he needs to know?*" He gave the box a little shake, Davey's father looked confused.

"It's a toy." He said looking from the box to the man.

"It's a British soldier," he said sternly, "or more to the point, it's an anti Irish, British propaganda toy." Davey's father shook his head confused.

"It's a what?" He said, unable to grasp the concept of a propaganda toy. The man turned to the boy and squatted back down beside him, he spoke softly.

"Tell me sonny, what kind of soldier is this?" Davey began to feel uncomfortable. He looked around the room for encouragement from one of his friends, but the room remained silent. The young boys and girls had stopped their playing and lessons, and, along with the older people and music tutors, sat in silence watching the scene unfold.

"Tell me son, have ye ever heard of the IRA?" Davey turned back to the blonde man. Davey nodded. "And what do ye know about the IRA sonny?" Davey looked towards his father for an answer. "Don't look to your da son, it's me that's asking the questions."

"Come on Davey!" Paddy pulled his son's hand, the blonde man stood and blocked the way.

"Let the boy answer the fecking question!" He said under his breath. He let go of his son's hand and clenching his fists he turned to the man.

"We all know who you are . . . we all know what you stand for." Davey felt the aggression between the two men and finally spoke up.

"They're bad men!" He tried to remember the term the man on the BBC news had used, "Terrorists!" he eventually blurted. The man looked triumphant. He stared into Davey's father's face, his bright blue eyes sparkling.

"Fecking terrorists?" He said without breaking his manic glare. "Is this the type of *Irish* history you're teaching your son?" Davey's father had had enough. He dropped his voice.

"You may be something big in Ireland, you may be something big to these sheep that follow you, but you mean fuck all to me. Now get out of my way or I'll . . ." The blonde man laughed.

"Or you'll what . . . oh you're a hard man are ye? Well tell me tough guy . . . are ye bullet proof are ye?" Davey's father snarled into the IRA man's face.

"You coward, hiding behind your guns. You're the reason we left Ireland in the first place, to get away from the troubles, and yet, here ye are stirring up more shite here in Birmingham. There seems to be men like you all over the world." On hearing that the man grabbed Davey's father collar, but Paddy managed to bring his hands up and blocked the man's arms. There was a short scuffle until the man stepped back to throw a punch, as his arm drew back it was grabbed by the small, bald man with a strong Belfast accent.

"Not here big man! Not in front of the wee ones anyway!" The Belfast man spoke softly. "Come on big man . . . we've got business to talk over. McDade will be here in a minute." The blonde turned to the Belfast man and nodded, the name seemed to bring him to his senses.

"Ai, you're right Jimmy." He turned back to Davey's father. "This isn't over though, not by a long shot, and you boy!" He pointed at Davey, "If I see that fecking British soldier in here again I'll take it off ye and burn it." He almost spat the words at Davey, then turning his back on father and son he rejoined his friends at the bar and carried on talking as if nothing had happened.

Mr O'Sullivan joined Davey and his father.

"I'd leave now if I were you." He addressed the pair, ushering them both through the door to the main room of the club. They stepped into the big room until they were out of sight of the IRA men, Davey's father turned to the music teacher.

"Who the hell was that?" he asked, his lip quivering with rage. The music teacher looked shocked. He came in close to Davey's father and half whispered.

"Jesus Paddy, that's Jan McGowen, you can't go messing with him!" Davey's father shook his head.

"Never heard of him. Who's the bald Belfast fella then?" Mr O'Sullivan's eyes widened. He ushered them further into the big hall until their voices were almost drowned out by the Irish dancers cracking their tap shoes against the sprung dance floor.

"They're very dangerous men Paddy, the new breed of IRA . . ." He left the words hanging.

"New breed?" Paddy replied.

"New breed . . . that's right." He nodded, his thin eyes blinked behind his thick glasses. "Do ye not watch the news Paddy? The situation in Northern Ireland is spiralling out of control. It's only a matter of time before it spills over here, then God help all of us!" Paddy pulled his son to his side protectively, the music teacher continued. "These new lads play by different rules: men, women, even children, everyone's a target. The catholics are as bad as the proddies, and these lads don't give a shite about the men of 1916." He shook his head as if he'd just said something sacrelegious. Davey looked up at the two men, bemused.

"Who are the men of 1916 Dad?" Paddy blushed and smiled weakly at Mr O'Sullivan.

"You *know* Davey boy . . . your grandpa and his brother, they fought at the GPO in Dublin in the 1916 uprising against the British." He paused as if the boy could work out the rest for himself but he couldn't, so Paddy continued. "Your Mam and I took you to see the bullet holes in the walls . . . remember?" Davey nodded and smiled even though he couldn't really remember anything about their recent visit to Dublin, except that his Uncle Christy had been pick-pocketed on one of the bridges that ran over the River Liffey.

"Jesus Paddy . . . he should know his heritage." Paddy glanced down at his muddy boots and nodded like a scolded child. "Anyway you'd better steer clear of that fella. He's trouble, always has been, I don't know who the Belfast fella is though, he's just shown up on the scene and seems to know everyone, they call him Belfast Jimmy but I must say there's something about him I don't trust. I've heard things being said . . ." The music teacher stopped himself as if he'd already said too much and changed tack." McGowen's people settled here from Cork years ago, but he's been living in Belfast for about five years and just returned back to Birmingham. I don't know what he saw over there, but he's been radicalised to the point that he's become a bloody fanatic in my opinion. All he seems to do is spout on about blood on the streets of Belfast and how the Brits are gonna get a taste of their own medicine, that's all he rambles on about from dawn till dusk. He sees himself as some kind of freedom fighter . . . as I suppose they all do, Paddy. Someone must like him though, because they've made him head of the Birmingham IRA." The music teacher stopped talking. His eyes ran over the children dancing in lines across the huge room. RAT-TAT-TAT. Their feet stomped and flicked the floor in perfect timing. "Look at that Paddy, it's a grand sight to see the little ones keeping it all alive." RAT-TAT-TAT, the sound was deafening loud, like a hundred drummers snapping their sticks across a hundred snare drums. Paddy and Davey watched the dancers gliding across the wooden floor as if they were floating, legs kicking head high, arms tightly held by their sides. The dance teacher screamed something about shoddiness to individuals amongst the group, but to Paddy, Davey, Mr O'Sullivan and the watching parents, they seemed to move as if they were one. After a while the dancers' unity fell apart. The dance teacher began to scream at her students again and Mr O'Sullivan turned back to father and son.

"Anyway . . . remember," he said quietly, "give Jan McGowen a wide birth." He gave Paddy a serious look. "If you mess with him, you're messing with the IRA."

Back in the rear bar to the club the group of IRA men were planning a summer of operations that they hoped would bring the British government around the table, hoping to force the extradition of British troops from Northern Ireland and free the six counties in the north, thus creating a new united Ireland and ultimately bringing seven hundred years of British occupation to an end. Every man within the group believed that their actions would bring about the end of the war and victory for the Irish nation. All except one, Belfast Jimmy. As he listened to the plans he searched the faces of the dreamers and schemers around him. They were made up of two types, either bitter men that had seen their families and homes destroyed by the war, whose hearts were filled with poison and hatred towards the British and were incapable of a clear diplomatic thought. Or dreamers who saw themselves as Celtic warrior poets, whose eyes were filled with the images of the gallant men who had fought for freedom in 1916 and the days of the *Black & Tans*, when the wind shook the barley. He was no different. He hated the men around him, not just the IRA men but every single one of these catholic bastards that surrounded him. He didn't really know why he hated them with such venom, it was just the way things were, always had been and probably always would be. The hatred ran through his protestant blood with so much power that he had no choice but to accept the job offer from the Midland Serious Crime squad, to go deep under cover within the Birmingham IRA, and here he was. They had pulled him out of the Royal Ulster constabulary in Belfast to do this job and he intended to do it well. Superintendent Ronnie Fletcher, whom he hadn't actually met yet, but had been warned was a colourful character, had instructed him to infiltrate the terrorist cell and to encourage the IRA to commit a terrorist act so bloody awful it would destroy the grass roots support they enjoyed within the Irish community in the United Kingdom, and ultimately turn the British government and its people against anything Irish for years to come.

Belfast Jimmy was only too happy to help.

The City Foxes

Chapter 4

Hazel Fewtrell sat in her metallic green, Mercedes sports car watching the endless traffic in the rush hour dance that happened every week day around four thirty in the afternoon. The cars, buses, taxis, scooters and bikes hissed past her on the dark wet road, sending plumes of spray behind their rear wheels. The traffic lights reflected off the wet, black tarmac illuminating the spray, creating tiny rainbows in the blue light of dusk. The Mercedes engine idled, heating the car, stopping the windows from steaming. Hazel was in two minds whether to stay or leave now whilst she had the chance. She glanced this way and that, her eyes darting at the passers by. Eddie had eyes everywhere and she knew that her car would be spotted at some point, then the endless questions would start.

Eddie had changed, *she* could see that, even if everyone else was too busy trying to win his approval. Hazel had been there since the beginning, when they had nothing, when the things they had worked so hard to achieve looked like they would all just fall apart and everyone and everything seemed against them. She shivered when she thought about the gangs they had battled with over the past ten years.

"Bad times," she thought, scenes played over in her mind, but somehow things had seemed more satisfying in the early days. She

56

felt more involved back then, Eddie had needed her more: her advice, ideas, approval and her love. However, those days were gone and in her mind they were never coming back and now an ever growing void grew between them, filled with suspicion, accusation and possessiveness on both sides. In Hazel's eyes Eddie had become a caricature of himself with a hundred sycophantic side kicks to back him up and do his bidding, whilst she, the brains behind the operation had been written off as simply a housewife and mother to their three children. After all, it was she who had come up with the idea of a live music venue in Birmingham, booking the top acts around the country and cornering the market in the second city for the best live music venue around. She had even found the warehouse the *Cedar club* now stood in and had had to argue with Eddie to get him to even *consider* the idea. Ultimately it was she who had helped Eddie Fewtrell become the man he was. She listened to his never ending gripes about the other brothers or people around him, and watched as he undermined them so he could remain top dog. She had initially encouraged him and his confidence had grown and grown until he finally declared himself the 'King of Birmingham Clubland' in the late sixties. Conversely it was also her that had listened patiently to his desperate confessions in the early hours of the dawn, sitting on the edge of the big old four poster and almost sobbing, he spilled out events he'd been involved in the past. Hazel still couldn't truly read him after all this time. Eddie always justified his deeds by saying he'd done them for his family, but as the years had rolled on she could see his motivation had changed and now she was starting to think he might be doing it all for himself.

"It's easy to do something bad Haze," he would say "it's living with it after, that's the hard thing." The bad things, as he called them, usually meant a beating. Someone somewhere was about to, or had just gotten a good hiding. Usually, if the beating went well there was no mention of it again, but they didn't all go well and that's when the dawn confessions would start. Eddie had so many people around him on all sides of the law that most of the time he wasn't even directly involved. Well she was fed up of playing Eddie's game which was one of the reasons she was sat on the heated, cream, leather seats watching Birmingham trundle home through the cold drizzle in the late November twilight. She was waiting for her lover, well, soon-to-be-lover, if she had her way. To be truthful the man had been reluctant to begin with and he wasn't really in the bag as of yet. He obviously fancied her but Eddie Fewtrell cast a long shadow across the city and hiding anything from him, even something trivial, was becoming harder and harder for anyone close to him.

Hazel wound the window down and threw the *Rothman's* cigarette end out in to the deserted car park. The glowing, orange, ember quickly vanished in the soft rain, she watched, transfixed at its final struggle against the rain. Ridiculous comparisons between the embers and her life ran through her mind, until she felt the cold air on her skin refreshing her senses, dragging her out of her day dream.

"Ten more minutes," she said, shaking her head, looking for any excuse to leave but too stubborn to follow her gut instinct. She wound the window up, the drizzle had began to ruin her make up as it blew through the gap in tiny droplets. The cold shocked her into a moment of clarity.

"What am I doing?" she asked herself. Images of her children ran through her mind, the look on Eddie's face when Abigail had been born, against all the odds, and here she was, about to throw it all away, and for what?

She felt angry though, angry that Eddie had pushed her away and now she had been forced to find the attention a woman needs from someone else. Eddie wasn't the greatest of lovers, but he was *her* lover. She just wished Eddie realised that, instead of screwing half the club's bar staff. Hazel gave a little laugh, she had no proof of his indiscretions, but she just believed it *was* happening. She was so fed up with all the bullshit Eddie came out with to cover the tracks of his affairs. Don Fewtrell was at it too, or at least that's what she had been told. How he managed to pull anyone was beyond Hazel. He had virtually lost all the hair from the top of his head and had taken to wearing a bizarre, peroxide blonde wig in a

1950s style quiff, that made him the centre of many a cruel joke. Gordon, Johnny, Bomber and Chrissie had a different approach, they seemed to still have their feet on the ground. Maybe it was the women they had married that grounded them, who could tell. One thing was for sure, they didn't seem as caught up in their own self importance as Eddie and Don had become.

That's how Hazel saw things anyway, and it was certainly true of Don Fewtrell. His bombastic ways had begun to annoy all five of his brothers until it had reached the point where, according to Eddie, not one of them wanted to work with him at the *Cedar club* anymore. Eddie had told her how he had had to break up a huge row, in front of the customers, between Chrissy and Don about Don's unhygienic habit of washing his wig in the glass cleaning machine behind the bar. Eddie was at a loss as to what to do with his flamboyant brother, until out of the blue Don approached Eddie with the idea of opening his *own* club. He had found a restaurant on Newhall Street that had come up for sale but he needed Eddie to front the deal, which happily he did as it prevented a full on fall out amongst the brothers.

Eddie was on a roll, he had jumped from the *Bermuda club* in the late fifties, to the *Cedar club* in the early sixties, and with the cash the club had generated he had opened another live music venue called *Barbarella's*, and on it went, *Rebecca's* (named after his eldest daughter) made four clubs and another cabaret style club named *Abigail's* (after his second child) was just about to open.

Hazel pondered over the businesses and family as she sat watching the passing traffic, waiting for her elusive lover. She lit another cigarette and gave a little chuckle, the image of Don's wig floating amongst the glasses, lightening her mood. During the last few years it had become more of a struggle keeping the family together, in fighting had started, brother against brother, wife against girlfriend, the coppers against everyone, but when trouble came, as it always did, the brothers always stood together.

"Cut one and they all bleed." That was the quote repeated by anyone that had been unlucky enough to have had a run in with the Fewtrell brothers. In the early sixties the Krays and the

Richardsons, two of London's toughest criminal gangs had found out to their cost just how true that quote was. Things had moved on since the dark old days and now Eddie Fewtrell *was* the Godfather he had always pretended to be, but however tough, ruthless and menacing he was and make no mistake he could be very menacing, he was still one of the funniest and most charismatic men to ever walk the streets of Birmingham. People liked him. They *wanted* him to succeed. The dodgier the deal, the more extreme the story of gangsterism, the more the club goers loved him, as long as it wasn't *their* collar he was feeling. That was something Hazel could never understand because she knew the man, warts and all, his beginnings, successes, strengths, flaws and weaknesses. To everyone else, the average Brummie, the Saturday football hooligan, the petty villain, skinhead, rocker, soul boy or disco dolly, he was already a legend, a celebrity in his own right. He'd seen off the Krays as well as all the other gangs who had tried their chances in Britain's second city and now he *ran* Birmingham. Nothing sells better or is more attractive than rumours of dodgy dealings from the underworld going about its business and Eddie was more than happy to let the rumours run. Eddie Fewtrell gave the average Brummie a chance to shake hands and have a drink with a so called gangster and walk away to tell the tale.

A loud BEEP from a car horn brought Hazel out of her thoughts and back to her surroundings. She watched the traffic creep along the road in front of her.

"I've waited for him long enough," she thought and, taking a last drag on the cigarette, she wound the window down and flicked the white stick out into the rain to join the other butt end. She blew the smoke into the cold drizzle and pulled the automatic gear stick into drive, the sports car gave a little lurch forward as the gears engaged, she pulled forward, and began edging slowly on to the pavement ready to join the oncoming traffic heading into the city and on to the Hagley Road. Just as the green Mercedes was about to pull out on to the road, a short burst from a car horn caught her attention. A beige Ford Capri was approaching her on the same side of the road flashing its head lights. Hazel recognised the car and pushed on the brake pedal, stopping her car just before it had joined the traffic. The Capri pulled into the deserted car park, its driver waving as he passed Hazel. She froze for a second, not knowing what to do, her eyes darted around her to check she wasn't being watched. There was still time for her to drive away and save herself from the shit storm that was coming her way should Eddie find out about this little, clandestine meeting. She put the car into reverse, an excited tingling feeling running through her loins. Hazel pulled her Mercedes up next to the Capri so that the two drivers were face to face and wound her window down.

"So you finally plucked up the courage to turn up then?" She said to the man.

The man leaned out the window and stroked her face with his soft hand.

"How could I resist?" he said charmingly. Hazel could see a look in his eyes, a look she recognised, he had the same look in his eyes that she had in hers. He seemed distracted, scared. The two sat making uncomfortable small talk for a short while, all the time their eyes darted this way and that, checking the passing cars and buses for faces they recognised, anticipating that at any moment they would be spotted by one of Eddie's men and their secret feelings exposed.

* * *

Stanley Kay, stood in the bay window of the *Wheel Club* casino, sipping the cup of tea the owner of the club had made for him. Eddie Fewtrell had asked him to call in to the *Wheel Club* to talk to the Italian head waiter, Gianni Paladini. The club owner wasn't too happy about the meeting but he wasn't going to argue with Stanley. Eddie wanted to poach the Italian to head his new venture, *Abigail's Cabaret Club*. As a matter of fact, Eddie wanted *all* the staff at *Abigail's* to be Italian. He wanted a cosmopolitan feel to the place and Gianni knew all the Italians in town, thus Stanley Kay, licensee to *Barbarellas* had been dispatched to the exclusive *Wheel club* to coax him into jumping ship, but for now, Stanley's attention was elsewhere. His eyes scanned the deserted car park of the now derelict, victorian hotel that lay across the road. The bay window of the *Wheel Club* was covered in condensation but he left the moisture on the glass to hide his position. He was watching the green Mercedes and the beige Ford Capri parked alongside one another in the deserted car park. He knew the green car, or at least he knew the driver. He watched as the man in the Capri climbed out of the driver's seat and opened the Mercedes door. The woman stepped out in her long sheepskin coat, its collar pulled up high, partially hiding her face, but he could clearly see it was Hazel Fewtrell. The man, on the other hand looked unfamiliar to him. The pair stood close to each other, he saw their hands meet tentatively, secretly, fingertips climbing into each other's clasp. They constantly watched their surroundings, checking the passing cars, desperate not to be seen, like two city foxes. Stanley remained hidden behind the steamy glass, only his silhouette could be seen in the early evening's blue light. The couple climbed into the back of the Capri. A shiver ran down Stanley's spine.

"This would have to be handled delicately," he thought. He liked Hazel, but he was Eddie's man. He sipped the tea watching the little cameo play out across the road. A violent scenario running through his mind as he played out the end game to Hazel's little affair.

"Hello . . . you wanted to see me?" An Italian voice broke his gaze. Stanley turned to the sound of the young Italian man, his handsome face questioning why Eddie Fewtrell's man had asked for him.

"Gianni Paladini?" Stanley smiled.

"Yes." The Italian said puzzled.

"Get your coat mate, you don't work here anymore, Eddie Fewtrell wants you." Gianni shook his head, none the wiser.

"Sorry . . . I ehh don't understand."

"Christmas has come early for you Gianni," he let the words sink in. "You are now the manager of *Abigail's* Cabaret club, so get your coat, I ain't got all day."

Gianni was confused he'd seen Mr Fewtrell at the *Wheel club* several times, often served him drinks and he seemed a decent sort of guy, but Gianni had heard the scary rumours that surrounded Eddie Fewtrell and for the life of him couldn't put the rumours with the man. Either way, with Eddie Fewtrell's help, the worm had definitely turned for Gianni Paladini even if he didn't know it at the time. Gianni's interest in football and his native Italian language would soon put him in the perfect position to exploit the brilliant football talent about to emerge from Italy, and Eddie would be there to help him.

Chapter 5

Dixie looked exasperated, Eddie had never seen him so animated in the fifteen years he'd known him. They sat at the long bar in *Rebecca's* club, sipping mugs of tea made for them by the cleaners who skittered around in the background of the dark club, the middle aged women disappearing and reemerging from the shadows, sweeping and polishing away the evidence from the night before. A dank odour of old beer and fags mixed with the smell of bleach and spray polish, the cleaners carried on oblivious to the toxic stink.

"Look Eddie, I'll get one of the uniforms down here to sort it, I don't deal with this shit anymore, you know that." Dixie said impatiently. Eddie had called Dixie about a minor disturbance the night before. He knew really that Dixie wouldn't be in a position to help, but Eddie had called him anyway, mainly as an excuse to catch up with his old friend, it had been around three or four months, and Eddie knew a lot can happen in that time, this was a chance to catch up on the city cop gossip. Dixie's Gloucester accent hadn't diminished in all the years he'd lived in Birmingham and for some reason the accent reminded Eddie of the old days, when he was just getting started in the early sixties. Dixie had been a beat copper back then but with a little help from Eddie he'd now risen to become a top detective in the newly formed Serious

Crime squad. They had a 'you scratch my back I'll scratch yours' relationship that concealed a deeper friendship.

"Look I know you're busy Dix, but I ain't seen ya since ya got involved in the new squad down Steelhouse lane cop shop. How long's it been now, three months?" He smiled but couldn't help having a little dig. "You too good for us now are ya?" Dixie laughed.

"Fuck off Ed." He turned to his fellow detective who had arrived with him that Eddie had never set eyes on before. "If only he knew ay Jimmy?" The Belfast man sat on one of the high bar stools further down the bar, holding a mug of tea just been made for him. He just shook his head. "Don't fecking involve me Dix, I'm just here for the tea." He took a sip to emphasise the point, he wished he hadn't. The tea was bitter and scalded his lips. The Belfast man grimaced. "Jesus I thought the British were meant to be the masters at making tea?" He plonked the cup down on the wooden bar top in disgust, the tea spilled on the counter, Eddie bristled.

"Well the cleaners made it and they ain't British." He retorted. "They're duck eggs ain't they?" He took a sip from his own tea as if to prove the tea was drinkable. He tried to hide his reaction to the vile, brick red liquid. "Tastes alright to me." He smirked at the Belfast man.

"Duck eggs?" Jimmy questioned. Dixie rolled his eyes.

"Duck eggs . . . Irish," he explained. Jimmy just shook his head, unable to make the connection.

"Duck eggs." He repeated.

"Duck eggs are green ain't they, so that's why we call Irish people duck eggs." Dixie turned back to Eddie and shook his head in disbelief.

"Where I'm from we just call em *Fenian bastards*." He said the words venomently and laughed to himself.

Eddie gave Dixie a dark stare. He leant around his friend in order to talk directly to this stroppy little Belfast man.

"My mother was a duck egg!" He said the words as if they were a challenge. "From Dublin . . . does that make me a Fenian Bastard then?" The Belfast man looked embarrassed.

"Ehh no I . . ." he stumbled on his words. Eddie cut him short.

"Who the fuck is this Dixie?" Eddie spoke directly to Dixie as if the other man wasn't there. Dixie gave Eddie a weak smile.

"Jimmy, go have a look around the club!" Jimmy gave Dixie a confused look. He continued. "Just fuck off somewhere . . . anywhere . . . I'll meet you back at the car in an hour." The Belfast man didn't move, insulted by the way he'd been spoken to. "Go on DCI Feeny . . . fuck off and that's an order, I'm talking to an old friend here." The bald man didn't move. Eddie stood up, unable to hide his frustration. He walked behind the bar and took a bottle of cheap scotch from behind the glass counter. He slammed the bottle in front of the Belfast man.

"There you go son, on the house . . . now no hard feelings but . . . fuck off!" The bald detective sat for a second, staring at Eddie, a growing hatred filling his eyes. Eddie pushed the bottle towards the man, the two men stared at each other for an uncomfortable few seconds before Eddie gave a false smile, gesturing with his head that the man should leave. The small Belfast man grabbed the bottle and without saying a word, dropped off the high stool and stormed out of the bar into the corridor that led to the busy high street outside. Eddie turned to Dixie.

"Who's that horrible little bastard?" Dixie shrugged.

"I don't know Ed . . . he's just come down the line from Belfast . . . no one knows anything about him down the station as far as I can tell." Eddie's brow furrowed, puzzled.

"He's one of Ronnie Fletcher's lot, that's all I know." Eddie turned to watch the man leave. As the Belfast man walked down the dark corridor he could see the silhouette of another man coming inside the front door of the club. The man smiled as he passed the shorter, bald man.

"Alright mate?" Chrissy Fewtrell said as he reached the Belfast man. Jimmy Feeny ignored him, his mind elsewhere, lost in rage. Chrissy stopped and watched him walk on.

"I said . . . alright mate?" He shouted after the man, shocked at the other man's rudeness. Chrissy saw Eddie and Dixie sitting at the bar ahead of him.

"Hey Eddie!" he called through to his brother. "What's up with Kojak?" He gestured with his thumb towards the man, about to step outside. Chrissy raised his voice so the man would hear him. "He's got a face like a well bummed arse."

Dixie and Eddie burst into laughter. Chrissy joined the two men in the bar, he stepped behind the counter and pulled himself a beer, still giggling at his own description of the Belfast man. He took a sip and smiled.

"Dix!" he nodded and raised his glass, with a cheeky grin.

"Chrissy," Dixie raised his glass and chinked the two together, "been a long time mate."

"It has mate, too long." Dixie looked Chrissy over, nothing had changed since he'd last seen him; still lean, full of muscle, a shock of pitch black curly hair that hung in a shaggy mop over his bright, blue eyes. Of all the brothers Chrissy was the fighter, as hard as they come and didn't mind showing it whenever the opportunity arose, which it did, quite often. Incredibly loyal to his family, Chrissy was the one you wanted with you when your back was against the wall, no doubt about it.

"Who was that miserable twat?" Chrissy nodded towards where Jimmy Feeney had left a minute before. Without wanting to repeat everything over again Dixie just said.

"He's one of Ronnie Fletcher's DCIs . . . Belfast Jimmy Feeny"

"Well that's *all* you need to know. Ronnie Fletcher's a first class cunt!" Eddie gave Chrissy a nod. "You've got some charm you have our kid," he started to laugh, "a face like a well bummed arse . . . where do you get em from Chrissy?" All the men burst into laughter again. "Come on, let's go through to the office, it stinks in here." Dixie was relieved, the smell of the cleaning products had been irritating his eyes but he hadn't wanted to say anything. He followed Eddie and Chrissy into a dark corner of the club and through an almost invisible black door which opened on to a short, brightly lit corridor. Chrissy held the door open for Dixie but didn't follow.

"Are you not coming Chris?" Dixie asked, the other man shrugged and shook his head.

"Nah got a show to organise for next weekend. I've got a band auditioning."

"I thought Hazel did that sort of thing."

"Nah she's got the kids now ain't she, don't see a great deal of her anymore, I think Eddie keeps her locked away in his castle." Chrissy patted Dixie on the shoulder "Anyway I get the chance to see if there's any good looking birds in the show . . . first dibs if you know what I mean." Dixie gave a short laugh,

"You've never changed you, Chrissy boy, you were always one for the ladies mate." Turning, Dixie followed Eddie. The two of them continued into a small back room with two small desks and walls covered in old posters advertising bands that had played in the clubs in the past, that acted as Eddie's office. Eddie reached into a green filing cabinet and produced a bottle of Irish whisky.

"It's not too early is it?" He questioned Dixie, Dixie shook his head.

"Never too early Ed." Eddie wasn't too keen on whisky, but he had heard Dixie had started to drink a fair bit since joining the Serious Crime squad and knew from the old days that Dixie was partial to a touch of smooth Irish blend. Eddie poured the golden liquid into the two small glasses and pushed one of the glasses over towards the detective.

"There you go pal." He placed the bottle back in the filling cabinet and slumped into the old, leather arm chair behind the desk. "So Ronnie Fletcher's back in town then. I'd better watch me back." Dixie looked puzzled.

"You know him I take it?"

"Oh I know that fucker alright . . . fucking ponce." Eddie almost spat the words. "He fixed my old man up for a drink driving charge, cost him three months of his liberty."

Dixie looked shocked.

"Three months for a d and d . . . bit harsh?" Eddie took a sip of his whisky and began to calm down.

"Nah . . . Fletcher stitched him up good and proper, said my old man had attacked him and spat in his face." Dixie raised his eyebrows.

"Well did he?"

"Yeah ... of course he did, but he was still stitched up." Eddie replied with a small laugh. "My old man had left his keys behind the bar and Fletcher had gone and made the landlord give him the keys and he'd planted em on my old man, of course Fletcher knew old George wasn't going to take that shit, so my old man had a go didn't he? ... three fucking months ... did him the world of good." Both men sniggered. "He'd been drinking too much anyway and he hadn't had a decent meal since 1965." Dixie a laughed and slapped the table.

"Go on." Eddie continued.

"So when they banged him up he was made up, three meals a day. Anyway most of his pals were serving time in Winson Green prison at the time so it was like going on a holiday for old George ... but that's not the point. Fletcher stitched him up." Eddie's mood turned darker. "If that fucker's back in town then we've all gotta watch our backs. It looks like Ronnie's looking for trouble, he really hates us Fewtrells, any chance he gets he'll cause me a load of shit I don't need. Let me know about any raids Dix, will you?" Dixie nodded.

"Of course Eddie, you know I will."

"You say that Belfast bloke's one of Ronnie Fletcher's lads?" Eddie continued, Dixie shrugged,

"No seriously, he just turned up out of nowhere." Dixie crossed the room and stared through the dirty glass that overlooked a set of narrow, red brick alleyways that ran behind the club. "I tried to talk to Fletcher about it but he's keeping schtum about what Belfast Jimmy's doing here in Brum."

"Belfast Jimmy ... what's his real name again?" Dixie laughed.

"His name's Feeny ... Jimmy Feeny, but the lads down the station nicknamed him Belfast Jimmy."

"Very original." Eddie laughed. "Well he don't like the Paddys does he?" Dixie turned.

"Well that's the *understatement* of the year ... he fucking hates em, fucking Fenian this, Fenian that, he's probably one of them orangemen you see on the telly." Eddie gave a little grimace, picturing the black and white images he'd seen on the continual BBC news coverage of smartly dressed men in bowler hats and orange sashes, as they marched through the catholic areas of Belfast, fifes and drums blaring, the immaculately dressed men flanked by camouflaged, British soldiers protecting them from their catholic Irish enemies that lined the Falls road area of Belfast.

"You mean like that ... priest?" Eddie searched for the name.

"Ian Paisley," Dixie said sternly, "and I wouldn't let him hear you say he was a priest, he's a *reverend*." Dixie said the words in a grand voice and gave a mock bow.

"Reverend? Priest? What's the fucking difference, they're all as mad as each other." A short silence fell over the two men.

Dixie turned back to the window. He stared down into the alleyway that ran parallel to the club. The alleyways behind the club had once been a useful thoroughfare for deliveries to the once busy area in the Victorian days of horse and cart, but had since fallen into disrepair and were now full of rubbish scrap and long grass, that grew between the black cobbles. He scanned the area from his first floor vantage point. Something caught his eye, a movement, only small, he focused on the shadows, change in light, more than a movement. He thought his eyes were playing tricks on him, then there it was again. As he watched one of the shadows he saw another further down the alleyway, his eyes began to detect other movements all around. He hadn't seen them before but now the little grey and black shadows were everywhere. There were rats, lots and lots of rats. The little dark shapes openly scurrying around the old beer crates and bits of scrap in broad daylight behind the club. The fact the rats were out in daylight meant the whole area was infested and there was either no room back at their nests or they had found a good food source. He watched the little grey creatures as they went about their business.

"Northern Ireland." He said whimsically to no one in particular. Eddie perked up.

"Ya what?" he enquired. Dixie turned back to him.

"Northern Ireland . . . that's why Belfast Jimmy is here, he's either on the run from someone naughty in Belfast or . . ." Eddie took over.

"He's here undercover trying to infiltrate . . ." Dixie joined Eddie in finishing the sentence. "The Birmingham IRA!" both men fell silent, trying to work out the reasons why Ronnie Fletcher had insisted that Jimmy Feeny be transferred from Belfast to Birmingham. Eddie poured another whisky for Dixie.

"Are you not joining me?" Dixie asked, sounding disappointed.

"Nah I got to sort out a party for the ITV lot that are coming to town and I got staff problems; you know, bar staff not showing up for work blah blah blah, the usual." Dixie smiled.

"I wish I had your problems Ed." Eddie smirked.

"Fuck off Dix, all you do is swan around collecting your protection money and nicking unfortunate dick heads that are stupid enough to cross *my* path." Eddie laughed, smiling at Dixie to let him know he was only winding him up.

"Nah Ed . . . we've got something serious on our hands, something we've never seen before, well, not in Birmingham anyway." Eddie leant forward, elbows on his desk resting his pointed fingers on his chin.

"Sounds interesting!" Eddie had seen Dixie wasn't himself earlier but had thought it was to do with the Belfast detective getting under his skin.

"We think we have a serial killer in the city." Dixie left the words hanging.

"Cereal killer . . . what type of cereal, cornflakes?" Eddie repeated. Dixie looked at his friend and saw the look of confusion on his face.

"Not fucking cereal . . . fucking *serial.*" He shook his head in disbelief. "As in series." He could see his explanation had made no difference to Eddie's expression.

"A serial killer is someone who kills people in series rather than random. All the victims or the way they've been killed or taken have something in common." Eddie shook his head.

"I thought you meant he was hitting them over the head with a cornflakes box for fuck sake, *evil bastard*." Eddie burst into laughter. Dixie didn't see the funny side of Eddie's joke. "So it's got nothing to do with cornflakes then." Eddie said feigning ignorance.

"This is bad Ed, stop fucking around, we've had this type of thing before, in London, you know, *Jack the Ripper,*" he said the words dramatically. "America has had this phenomenon more than we have, New York, Los Angeles, you know Charles Manson type of thing, weird stuff. I read about it somewhere. Anyway America, yeah I can see it ... but not here in Brum."

"Are you saying there's someone killing people here in Birmingham?" Dixie smiled.

"Ah, that's my point. Yes we've got a killer in our midst, or at least I think he's killing them, what we have is a group of girls that have all gone missing since November 1970." Eddie shrugged.

"Well people disappear all the time. I feel like doing it myself every now and then. get away from bloody Hazel!" he laughed at his own joke. When he saw Dixie wasn't laughing he became serious once more. "They've probably just had enough of the shit and fucked off elsewhere. You know the type, foster home girls or even Borstal. They've been skipping for years Dix. Who could blame them?" Dixie drained his glass and slid it across the surface of the desk towards the bottle of *Jameson's*. Eddie took the glass and poured more of the whisky and slid it back.

"Well that's just the point Eddie, these girls all had something in common. They're all around the same age, sixteen to twenty, all from *good* homes, jobs, boyfriends, young, pretty and innocent. Someone's either collecting them, killing them or both. Sixteen girls in three years Ed. That's a lot of women. *All* taken off the street by the way," he emphasised. Eddie sat expressionless, he could see his old friend had really taken this case to heart. Usually Dixie was pretty easy going but Eddie could see this case had really gotten under his skin.

"Any bodies?" Dixie nodded.

"Three so far."

"Where?" Eddie enquired.

"*Spark Hill, Small Heath, Aston* . . . there was no effort to hide the bodies they were just dumped in the flower beds. That's where the pattern falls apart." Eddie shook his head, shocked that he hadn't heard about the grim discoveries.

"They were all sexually abused with veins full of smack." Eddie began to pay more attention.

"Drug addicts . . . maybe prozzies?"

"No, like I said they were all," Dixie checked himself "*are* all family girls." Eddie could see why he'd started to drink more now, the pressure of police work was getting to him but he kept this observation to himself.

"You say *he* . . . it could be them?" Eddie let the words sink in. "How do you know it's not a gang or something? Blokes have been enticing birds into whorehouses for hundreds of years Dix, sounds like as good an explanation as anything else, to me."

Dixie shook his head.

"We've raided all the whorehouses we know of, but it turned up nothing. We didn't find any of the girls and no one knew anything about it, even our reliable grasses have heard nothing. It's just weird." Eddie agreed.

"Well that's the first thing that went through my mind, why haven't I heard anything about it? I mean everyone talks to me. Anyway why ain't the papers picked up on it yet?" Dixie smiled weakly.

"That was my idea." He sipped his whisky and grimaced at the drink's sharpness. "I learned that the Americans don't leak things to the papers as it gives the killer the attention that he craves." Eddie huffed.

"Well it's been three years Dixie and they're still disappearing off the streets ain't they? Maybe you should be warning people about the killer, or killers?" Dixie drained what was left of the drink and placing his glass down on the desk reached across and shook Eddie's hand.

"I'm out of here . . . keep your ears open will you? We need all the help we can get mate." He turned to leave, crossed the room and drew the door back, Eddie smiled.

"Will do Dix, and remember give me a shout if that wanker Ronnie Fletcher decides to pay me a visit, won't you?" Dixie stopped before leaving.

"Oh by the way . . . you got a rat problem." Eddie squirmed.

"R.A.T.s . . . where?" Eddie couldn't never bring himself to say the word as he'd always believed it to be bad luck and so always spelled it out instead.

"Out in the alleyway behind the club. It's over run with them." Dixie watched Eddie's body tighten up. Dixie had seen Eddie enter fights and situations that would make bigger men terrified, Eddie hadn't ever once backed down, not in all the years Dixie had known him, but mentions *rats* and he was like a child. "Won't be long before they're inside the club if they ain't here already Ed." Dixie continued.

"I fucking hate r.a.t.s . . . I'll get someone in to sort it out Dix." Dixie let the door shut behind him, leaving Eddie alone in his office. Eddie rose and stepped from behind the desk and went to the window. He looked down at the messy alleyway behind the club. At first he couldn't see anything and began to doubt Dixie had seen anything at all. Then he caught sight of the first rodent, the little black rat ran inside a rolled up piece of carpet that had been dumped there years before, the sight of which sent a shiver through his spine. He stood at the window in the cold, empty office, watching the creatures below him with a mixture of disgust and fascination, unable to tear himself away.

"R.a.t.s . . . that's a sure sign of bad luck," he thought to himself.

Chapter 6

Jimmy Feeny stormed down the dark corridor of *Rebecca's* nightclub, bottle of whisky in hand and a spiteful scowl on his face. He hadn't even noticed Chrissie's greeting as he had passed him in the corridor. He stepped out into the grey daylight. The endless Birmingham winter drizzle hadn't stopped for days and the soft rain forced him to shelter under the huge red and white sign of the night club. He stood there trying to work out what to do with himself. The way Dixie and Eddie Fewtrell had humiliated him swam around his mind, making him dizzy with rage. If this had been Belfast he would've just made a few phone calls and these two bastards would have been looking down the barrel of a gun. *Then* they'd have shown him the respect he felt he deserved. He mulled over revenge for the insults as he stomped through the rain.

Jimmy scanned the road looking for a taxi, but the road was quiet, grabbing the collar of his short, leather jacket around him as if it would protect him from the rain, he began half running down the street, towards the main road where he could see the buses and traffic heading in and out of town along Hill Street. His flared jeans flapped around his legs, almost tripping him. As he reached the street corner he saw a red phone box about two hundred yards away, standing on the opposite corner of the road.

Choosing his moment, he sprinted through the heavy traffic until he reached the other side of the street and stepped inside the phone box. He was already soaked through from the drizzle but the relief from the shelter of the red phone box was instantly replaced by the stink of urine. He placed the whisky bottle on the small, metal shelf and gingerly picked up the receiver. Jimmy looked over the handset and saw that whoever had used the red box as a latrine had also spat all over the mouth and ear piece to the handset. He shook his head in disgust.

"Filthy bastards," he said to himself. He took a handkerchief from his jacket and wiped the handset down, then stuffed the filthy hanky behind the metal case of the phone until it couldn't be seen. He dialled the number to his headquarters and waited for the beep beep beep to stop, showing that the call had been answered. Jimmy pushed the door of the phone box until it opened an inch or so. The small gap letting in some fresh air to the confined space, diluting the overwhelming smell of urine. *Click,* the sound indicated that the receiver on the other end of the line had been picked up, Jimmy slid the ten pence piece into the machine. The coin clunked into the cash box at the bottom of the grey metal machine and the call went through.

"Who's calling the Golden Shot?" said the crackly voice on the other end of the line. Jimmy stood in silence for a second or two, he could hear distant laughing on the other end.

"Hello . . . who is this?" he enquired, worried that he'd called the wrong number.

"Who is *that?*" Jimmy pulled the receiver from his face and looked at the hand piece, puzzled.

"This is Jimmy Feeny . . . is this the Serious Crime squad HQ?" Laughter on the other end again, then a voice shouting to someone in the background.

"Belfast Jimmy's on the line boss." Jimmy Feeny was finding it hard to contained his rage at being ordered to fuck off by Eddie Fewtrell, finally burst into a string of profanities at the person on the other end of the phone.

"You fecking wee bastard, wait till I get hold of ye, I'll fecking ring your scrawny neck so I will. What kind of a cowboy fecking outfit are ye running here answering the phone like that ye wee bollox ye?"

"D.C.I Feeny? This is Ronnie Fletcher, your commanding officer." Jimmy's outburst stopped immediately at the sound of his master's voice.

"Eh . . . sorry sir eh . . . I eh." He was lost for words, in the background he could hear the giggling and sniggering continuing.

"You need to get your little Irish arse into the office Sonny. You're not meant to be over here on a jolly, you know." Jimmy bristled at the words.

"I'm not on a *jolly* sir, I've been dumped in the middle of town by that fucker Dixie you teamed me up with. I do NOT want to be working with him and I don't know my way around as of yet. I need a ride back to the station."

"Get a fucking taxi you stingy, little Irish bastard." The voice on the other end said.

"I can't see any sir, that's why I'm calling you," he said, hiding his outrage at being called Irish. The voice became serious now.

"Well, where's Dixie, why can't he give you a lift?" he snapped.

"He's with Eddie Fewtrell . . . they wanted to talk privately so they kicked," Jimmy stopped mid sentence and rephrased his words, "they asked me to leave them to it, they had private business to talk over." He knew the words would drop Dixie in the shit with his new boss. There was a silence on the other end. Jimmy pushed the door wide open now so he could breathe real air instead of the piss stinking, foul odour that was making his eyes water, then beep, beep, beep . . . his money had run out.

"Where are you?" The voice hurriedly said.

"Hill street," he replied and the line went dead. He slammed the receiver down and searched his pockets for another coin but found none, only a five pound note. Holding the door open with his foot, he sheltered from the freezing rain which had started to become heavier and was now showing the first signs of sleet. The voice hadn't said if they were coming to pick him up or not. Jimmy stood in the open doorway of the phone box for a minute, cursing Birmingham and everyone in it.

He looked up the street and saw a steamy windowed cafe. Outside the cafe's front window was a line of stripped down scooters parked along the pavement, indicating the place was open and probably full of scooter boys or skin heads. Jimmy left the red box and strode through the sleet towards the welcoming looking cafe. As he passed the scooters he looked over the machines, none of the scooters bore any resemblance to the Lambretta, his father had once owned. These scooters had been stripped of all their panels and leg shields, exposing their engines and wiring which made the machines look more like weird, two wheeled insects than a form of transport.

He stepped inside, the humid air hung thick with the smell of grease and cigarette smoke. The skinheads and suedeheads who owned the scooters were gathered in small groups around two pinball machines at the rear of the cafe. One couple were swaying to the slow, deep beat of a Caribbean Ska tune played on a crackly 45, that thumped from the old, chrome juke box that stood in the corner. Its chrome shine lay hidden beneath a glaze of grime that had built up over the years. The group of seven teenagers looked dishevelled, as if they hadn't slept for a couple of days and were obviously working off the amphetamines they had consumed over the weekend at the Northern Soul all nighter. Jimmy turned to the man behind the counter.

"Frothy coffee please pal." Jimmy lay the fiver on the faux marble counter next to the huge, steaming coffee machine. The thin Mediterranean with the greying, greasy quiff behind the counter snatched the note up.

"A'vent you gotta any-ting smaller mate?" He snapped, holding the note between his hands, looking at the watermarks on the blue and white five pound note.

"No, I need the change anyway." Jimmy said still frowning. The man finished scanning the note and just shrugged and turning to the till drawer he said over his shoulder.

"I'll bring it-a over mate, tak-a seat." Jimmy stood impatiently, drumming his fingers on the counter.

"What's the craic with this lot then?" He gestured through to the back of the cafe towards the teenagers with a nod of his head. The man behind the counter rolled his eyes as he slammed the change on the counter. The group were partially hidden by the frosted glass surrounding the service area. He stared through the glass and could make out the teenagers.

"They-ve been-a here since we opened at six o'clock in-a morning." Jimmy took a napkin from the counter and wiped the rainwater from his bald head.

"They're up early eh?" He said sarcastically "Must've shit the bed?"

"NO-a they beena bladdy dancing . . . *all night* for God's sake . . . to their bladdy black man's music!" Jimmy sniggered at the man's accent. "De been-a here ever since . . . bladdy skinheads."

"Dancing all night ye say . . . where they been doing that then?" Jimmy enquired.

"How do I bladdy know . . . bladdy hooligans, dey scaring off-a my customers ain't dey?" Jimmy smiled.

"Ye want me to tell em to leave?" The cafe owner looked puzzled, Jimmy reached inside his leather jacket. He searched the inside pocket and pulled out a small, black wallet. Jimmy threw the leather wallet down on the counter. The cafe owner was shocked to see the brown, leather shoulder holster beneath the man's armpit with the wooden handle of a revolver sticking out of the cradle. Jimmy flipped the wallet open with one finger to reveal a large, silver police badge. "I'll tell em te feck off if ye like." Jimmy raised his eyebrows and smiled. The cafe owner's face dropped, his belligerent manner becoming instantly subservient. He shook his head and tried to say something but the words just didn't form, until he eventually murmured,

"No I don't-a want any trouble Mr . . . no trouble, dey just-a kids." Jimmy gave a sinister laugh.

"Oh don't ye worry Mr, it's no trouble." He picked up the wallet then reached across the counter to where the steaming hot run off water from the coffee machine had collected in an old grey, aluminium tea pot. He wrapped a teacloth around his hand grabbed it by the handle and turned to the group and screamed at the top of his voice.

"HEY! . . . ye . . . ye feckin skin headed bastards . . . time to feck off home! Ye filthy bastards!"

The cafe owner watched as the Belfast man walked into the back of the cafe and out of sight. He could see the shadowed figures behind the frosted glass panels at the rear of the service counter, he could make out the Belfast man's form in its brown leather jacket and blue jeans, standing in the midst of the group of teenagers. He saw the group rise from their seats and turn from the pinball machines to the sound of the aggressive Belfast accent. There was a short silence, then a splashing sound as the bald man threw the scalding hot water at someone out of sight. A high pitched scream from one of the girls in the group; the scream turned from one of shock to one of pain and finally, the sound of men shouting obscenities and smashing glass. The Mediterranean man stood frozen behind his huge, silver coffee machine. He knew he should raise the counter shelf and go and stop the horrific sounds coming from the back of the cafe, but his instincts told him not to. This resulted in him just standing motionless, dirty, damp table cloth in hand, muffled thumping sounds now as flesh hit flesh and more glass breaking. Two of the skinhead girls stumbled around the corner of the frosted glass panels that hid the rear of the cafe. One of the girls had her arms wrapped around the other. At first he couldn't see anything wrong with the pretty blonde skinhead girl, until she turned to him, *then* he could see the damage the scalding water had inflicted. The skin on the left side of her face was just a white slab hanging uselessly from her cheek where it had separated from under the eye, exposing the top part of her jaw and tooth roots. Her once sky blue eyes were now different colours. One had a look of fear sparkling amongst the tears, the other, was now just a pale blue dull thing that sat dead in the socket in her head. The girls stumbled through the front door of the cafe and out into the falling sleet. The girl screamed again as the freezing air hit her wounds. The other girl began shouting at the passing cars, hoping one would stop and help. The Mediterranean man turned back to the chaos behind the frosted glass. He held the damp cloth up to his mouth as if to stifle a scream.

"No . . . no . . . no . . . day just kids!" was all he could mutter, he could make out two male figures lying motionless on the ground as the bald man in the beige jacket sat astride one of the teenagers and seemed to be pummelling something small and black into the prostrate man's face, *thump, thump, thump,* the sound of metal and wood against skin and bone. He watched, frozen, as the beating went on, too scared to get involved yet too horrified to look away.

Suddenly a screech of tyres came from the street outside. The man peered from behind his coffee machine and out of the large steamy windows. A light brown Rover had pulled up diagonally on to the pavement, almost touching the window pane. A man in a sheepskin coat leapt from the car. The Mediterranean man thought he was going to help the injured skinhead girl, but he totally ignored her and stormed into the cafe.

"FEENY!" he screamed before he was all the way through the door. The volume of his voice made the man behind the counter jump, "DCI FEENY!" he crossed the room, ignoring the man behind the counter. He stopped at the end of the frosted glass screen. There was a short silence as he took in the bloody scene. "Just what the fuck have you been getting up to?" Jimmy Feeny didn't move, he seemed to be exhausted and almost in a trance. The man continued. "FEENY I'm fucking talking to you!" The bald man turned towards the other man and smiled.

"I heard ye sir." The other man continued.

"What the fuck do you think you're doing?" He said confused. Jimmy sat astride the blooded and unconscious teenager for a second, unable to find the right words. He looked at the pistol in his right hand, its butt covered in gore from the faces, heads, noses and mouths from the skinheads he had attacked, the light brown handle was now a deep red, smiling he said,

"Just letting off a bit of steam . . . so I am sir." Jimmy gave a nervous laugh.

"Well get off your arse and let's get you the fuck out of here, before the uniforms turn up." The older man crossed the room and grabbed Jimmy's collar and pulled him to his feet. Feeny swayed slightly as the rage dissipated. The two men turned and walked towards the front door of the cafe. The older man stopped at the counter. He reached across the faux marble and grabbed the cafe owner by the throat.

"You didn't see anything . . . understand?" The man held his hands up and nodded, wide eyed. Jimmy stepped behind the older man and pointed his pistol into his face.

"If I ever hear anything more about this I'll be back to pay you a visit . . . understand?"

The man's jaw dropped and he began to shake, a damp stain began to appear on his groin, Jimmy and the other man began to laugh.

"Dirty fecking bastard." Jimmy grabbed the cloth from the Mediterranean man's hand. He wiped the pistol grip and threw the bloody cloth back into his face.

"Come on we gotta move!" the older man said, then, "Don't forget grease ball," Jimmy finished the sentence,

"we know where ye live."

The two men walked out into the cold day and climbed into the Rover. The girl with the injuries was still sobbing as she sat in the gutter. Her friend had run along the street to the red call box Jimmy had used fifteen minutes before and was phoning for an ambulance. The older man clunked the Rover into gear and reversed at speed across the pavement almost hitting the skinhead girl who sat clutching her disfigured face. She screamed, Jimmy gave a short laugh before the car lurched forward into the traffic and full throttle raced down the middle of the road, in between the opposing lanes of traffic to a cacophony of car horns.

Fennel turned towards Fletcher and asked

"How did you know I was in the cafe?"

"Oh I dunno," he replied sarcastically "maybe it had something to do with the girl outside with half her face hanging off. I was warned about your aggression from your colleagues in Belfast.

That's one of the reasons they wanted you out the way, but untruth it's one of the reasons you're perfect for this operation."

"We are fighting a fecking war out there in Northern Ireland so we are, the British government won't beat the IRA with one hand tied behind its back." Jimmy took a cigarette from a packet on the passenger shelf. He pushed in the electric cigarette lighter and waited for the little black knob to pop up. "Sometimes you have to fight fire with fire." He became impatient grabbing the black lighter and holding it to the cigarette.

"Calm down DCI Feeny.! You don't have to convince me. That's why I requested you for the job." Jimmy seemed surprised.

"You requested *me*?" Fletcher gave a short laugh.

"Your name got flagged up for an operation you did in the Republic of Ireland." Jimmy suddenly seemed uncomfortable.

"Oh aiy and what operation would that be then?" Fletcher just smiled.

"You know the one where you went *illegally* into the Republic and took the battle right to the heart of Dublin and executed an IRA general and his whole family." He turned to look at Feeny before continuing. "Then covered the scene to make it look like a drugs deal had gone wrong." Jimmy said nothing, he just stared through the side window. "Tommy McGuigan . . . so called IRA general . . . you . . ." Jimmy spoke up cutting Fletcher short.

"Yeah I know the fecking name . . . you don't forget the name of a man you shot in the face in front of his whole family." Fletcher watched to see if there was any regret in the other man's face. There was none and that pleased him.

"You crossed the line Jimmy . . . you deserve a fucking medal for that operation, a fucking medal." His mood changed. "Fucking politicians don't realise that we have to do bad things just to maintain the status quo." Jimmy wasn't listening, he could see the faces of the two young children he'd shot that night. He could hear the screams of their mother as she watched her little son and daughter die and her begging him to kill her as well but his heart being filled with hatred for the Irish, he just left her to sit in her apron surrounded by her family, lying in pools of their own blood. But his days as a member of the paramilitary were over he would be able to do his job better without the restrictions of such organisations.

"FEENY!" Jimmy snapped out of his daydream. "Feeny are you up for this operation?"

"What operation sir . . . ? To be honest, I don't even know why I'm here. I was asked to infiltrate the Birmingham IRA, *which I have* by the way, but apart from that I don't know what the feck I'm doing here." Ronnie Fletcher gave a grin.

"I'm taking you to meet a gentlemen that's going to help us achieve both of our needs. All you need to know right now is that you're on a deep undercover covert operation against the IRA, you answer to *me* and me only." The older man let the words sink in before continuing. "If this goes to plan then you and I will be personally responsible for destroying the Birmingham IRA forever." Fletcher could hardly contain himself.

"*And* rid Birmingham of what I consider one of the biggest crime families in the United Kingdom!" Feeny smiled.

"Let me guess," both men looked at each other, "the Fewtrells?"

Dodgy Motors

Chapter 7

Chrissy Fewtrell stood outside the *Cedar club* drumming his fingers across the black vinyl roof of his new pride and joy, he was waiting for Eddie to show up. Chrissy had always wanted a sports car and this fitted the bill nicely. MGs, Mercs, Spitfires were all just a bit effeminate for Chrissy, he had his image to consider. He stood in the early March sunshine in his dark brown, sheepskin jacket, a black polar neck, jeans and sunglasses looking more or less like a dark haired Steve McQueen. While he was considering his image, watching himself in the window of J.Grey's furniture shop Eddie pulled up behind him in his sky blue Rolls Royce. Chrissy didn't notice the silent behemoth of a car slide into its parking space.

"Alright our Chrissy?" Eddie voice made Chrissy jump out of this self indulgent posing.

"Ehh, alright Ed," he said smiling, turning back to his car, "well what do you reckon?" Eddie walked passed Chrissy and looked the car over.

"It's nice . . . what is it?" Chrissy laughed.

"You're out of touch bruv, this . . ." he paused for dramatic affect, "is an Alfa Romeo GTV 1600, otherwise known as the poor man's Ferrari." Eddie was impressed, but he wasn't going to let Chrissy know that.

"Why didn't you just get a fucking Ferrari?" Chrissy became defensive, Eddie was considering getting himself one just to see the look on Chrissy's face.

"Fuck off Ed . . . they're about two or three hundred grand." Eddie's day dream evaporated.

"Very nice our Chrissy, very nice." He nodded and gave an exaggerated smile. "Where did you get it?" Chrissy wasn't ready for the question.

"Err, our Bomber gave it to us."

Bomber or Roger Fewtrell, was the youngest of the brothers, although that never stopped him from throwing himself into a fight whenever he was needed or helping out with the running of the clubs. Being the youngest of the seven brothers he had had the best education and so was good with figures, on top of that he was a bit of a wizard on the golf course. Eddie would never admit it but Bomber could beat him on the golf course, eyes closed. Eddie liked to make out he'd cheated but Bomber really had a talent for the sport. Chrissy knew that Eddie would never admit he was the better golfer and so Chrissy had his alibi for the car.

"Bomber won it in a round of golf," he waited to see what Eddie's reaction would be. "He needed the cash so I bought it off him." Chrissy voice trailed off. He couldn't tell if Eddie had believed him or not. Of course Bomber knew nothing about the car or indeed the round of golf in which he'd won the Alfa Romeo.

"Well as long as you didn't buy it off our Gordon." Eddie gave a laugh. Gordon Fewtrell had managed to extricate himself from the night clubs and had opened a second hand car dealership which had become quite successful, although it must be said that at the time, some of the cars that sat on the forecourt of the dealership had let us say, an *interesting* past life. Chrissy suddenly felt too hot in his sheepskin, the beginnings of a cold sweat starting to climb his spine.

"Oh, what's wrong with Gordon's cars then?" Chrissy said frowning.

"Well if they ain't bent they're broke." Eddie burst out laughing.

"Fuck off . . . our Gordon wouldn't rip me off." Chrissy knew Eddie was pissed off about the fact that Gordon Fewtrell had branched out on his own and Eddie had lost his hold over his younger brother, he also knew that Eddie didn't like the fact that Gordon was doing ok for himself without his help, so Eddie was quite happy to cast aspirations about the quality of some of Gordon's stock.

Eddie opened the driver's door and peered in at the black, leather bucket chairs. He was secretly impressed. The walnut dashboard and matching steering wheel gave the car a feeling of speed and almost James Bond flashiness.

"Very Italian our kid . . . no really it's a little beauty," Eddie continued, "but if you did buy it from our Gordon which of course you didn't," Eddie smiled at Chrissy and savoured the moment, "then it's gonna breakdown within the month." Chrissy dug his hands into his jacket pockets.

"Well what do you know about cars?" Eddie rested his arm against the black vinyl roof.

"You're right I know fuck all about cars, *but,* I don't need to know anything about cars do I?" He stopped and let Chrissy think through his puzzle. Chrissy was none the wiser and just looked confused. He took off his sunglasses suddenly feeling foolish.

"Explain?" Eddie continued.

"All I need to know about is *Gordon* and our Gordon could sell ice to Eskimos. He sold me a gold Rolex watch the other week . . . I had it two weeks before someone pointed out the X in the Rolex was upside down." Chrissy was dumbfounded.

"The X was upside down?"

"Upside fucking down." Eddie said holding his open hands up. Chrissy pressed him.

"Oh and who enlightened you to this *forgery*?" Chrissy couldn't work out if Eddie was joking or not, he wasn't

"Do you remember Jacques Diamond, the French jewellery fence from Dudley?" Eddie laughed, Chrissy could see where this was going.

"Let me stop you there Ed, Jacques told you that the Rolex wasn't real because the X was upside down?"

"Yeah that's right, clever lad our Jacques."

"Very clever. The weight of the gold watch and hallmark didn't sway you though Ed?"

"Nah . . . !" Eddie was watching two girls about nineteen years old approach them in mini skirts and high boots, Chrissy turned his attention to where Eddie was staring.

"An X is the same one way as it is the other Ed, Jacques Diamond's pulled the wool over your eyes bruv."

"Yeah but this X *was* upside down." Chrissy shook his head in disbelief and turned his head to the two girls who were drawing nearer. This was typical of Eddie, he thought, he could be a sharp as a pin if he wanted to be but if he knew you and more importantly *liked* you then he could be duped very easily.

"Hello girls . . . fancy a ride in me new motor?" The teenage girls giggled. Eddie and Chrissy scanned the two young beauties in their short coats and long legs.

"Yeah alright then," said one with a cheeky laugh, she turned to her friend who looked horrified. "Come on he's cute!" They both gave Chrissy a good look over. Chrissy stood straight, enjoying the attention of the two girls. "Ok then where you gonna take us?" Chrissy's smile dropped, he hadn't thought for a moment the girls would actually say yes.

"I . . . eh well we could go to . . . eh?" He turned around to the little red car and peered inside. "Eh . . . sorry girls but it's only got two seats." He turned back to them, smiling.

"He's got cold feet," they both laughed, "can't handle us." Chrissy felt embarrassed. Eddie saw Chrissy's cheeks redden.

"E Ar girls you can have a ride in me Rolla if ya like." The girls turned to look at Eddie. He smiled and spread his hands out, inviting the girls to step into the luxurious cream leather interior of the Rolls Royce. The smiles dropped from the girls' faces.

"You dirty old man!" both girls laughed, enjoying the opportunity to ridicule the rich man. "Yeah, you're old enough to be me granddad." They burst into laughter again, this time joined by Chrissy. Eddie was taken a-back. Chrissy had rarely seen Eddie stuck for words but was enjoying the moment. Anyway at least it had taken the attention away from himself, but Eddie didn't do humiliation. He turned on the girls, his mood darkening in an instant.

"Yeah well fuck off then you pair of lesbos." The girls realised the fun was over, turned and walked away.

"Pair of silly old *wankers!*" One of them shouted over her shoulder, Chrissy turned to Eddie.

"Well she's got that right," he said with a snigger. Eddie just shrugged hiding his embarrassment and humiliation and changed the subject.

"Stanley Kay phoned me this morning, jabbering on about something or other he needs to talk to me about, but you know Stanley, once he starts he can't stop, so you go and see him for me will ya, cos I got club stuff to sort out for this ITV party at the club tonight."

"ITV lot?" Chrissy enquired, anything to do with show business always caught his attention.

"Yeah they're making a new kids TV show on Saturday mornings and they've asked me to lay something on for them every Saturday; early evening after the day's filming has finished. Eddie rubbed his hands together indicating there was plenty of cash being put behind the bar.

"Any stars I know?" Chrissy asked.

"Nah." He thought for a moment. "That black bloke, eh . . . Lenny Henry . . . and that bloke with the guitar and funny nose?" Eddie tried to recall the name. " You know . . . something to do with vegetables?" He said shaking his head.

"Jasper Carrot." Chrissy said enthusiastically, Eddie nodded, smiling. Chrissy raised his eyebrows, disappointed there were no film stars. "Is that it ?"

"Nah . . . there's loads of em apparently, I don't know who they are but they've got all sorts going on, clowns and stuff." Eddie's explanation left Chrissy even more in the dark than he was before. Chrissy turned to lock the door of the Alfa Romeo.

"Where's Stanley Kay now then?" Eddie pointed at the Club entrance.

"He's waiting for me in the back office . . . said it's important." Chrissy patted Eddie's shoulder.

"I'll sort it, see you tonight at some point," he said climbing back into his Rolls Royce, smiling.

"Let me know wh . . ." Eddie slammed the car door, he continued to talk but Chrissy couldn't hear him through the glass, the sound of passing traffic drowning out his words. Chrissy made a rotating motion with his hand. The glass slid down effortlessly, Eddie was finishing off his sentence, ". . . got to say for himself . . . anyway . . . tara." With that the big car floated away, almost silently and merged with the other traffic along the busy road. Chrissy stood and watched the sky blue Roller until the buses and cars obscured it. He turned and walked through the entrance to the Cedar club and went through the empty building, calling for Stanley Kay.

Stanley Kay appeared at the rear fire door to the club. He had been bringing in the beer towels from the washing line from outside at the back of the club and seemed shocked to see Chrissy there instead of Eddie.

"Where's Ed?" Chrissy smiled.

"He's busy Stan, he sent me . . . what's so important?" Stanley looked uncertain.

"I really need to talk to Eddie . . . it's er . . . personal." Chrissy sat on one of the barstools and gestured for Stanley to put the beer cloths down and join him.

"There ain't no secrets in our family," he lied, "come on spill the beans."

Stanley sat next to Chrissy looking embarrassed. Chrissy waited for a few seconds.

"Come on Stan I ain't got all day, what's on your mind our kid?"

"I don't know where to start really . . . I mean I don't really want to get involved." Chrissy gave a little laugh.

"Bit too late for that mate." Stanley searched for the right words then decided it was best to just come out with it.

"Hazel's having an affair," he blurted. Chrissy just stared at him. At first the sentence didn't register but after a second the words hit him.

"What do you mean Hazel's having an affair . . . our Hazel?" His voice raised in pitch as he started to unravel the meaning of what he was saying. "Hazel's having an affair? With who?" Stanley didn't want to talk, he knew Eddie had a habit of shooting the messenger but Chrissy continued to press him.

"What the fuck are you talking about Stanley . . . you can't just say something about our Hazel like that and then just shut the fuck up . . . WHO?" He shouted.

"I don't know . . . he's got a beige Ford Capri is all I know, young, blonde, good looking bloke." He stopped to see Chrissy's reaction, there was none so he continued. "I saw them across the road from the *Wheel club*. They were in the car park of that old hotel that has been shut for years across the road," Chrissy nodded that he knew the place, Stanley carried on, "they were parked next to each other and chatting." Chrissy gave a snigger.

"That don't mean fuck all Stan, they could've just bumped into one another, stopped for a chat." Stanley continued.

"They were holding hands." Chrissy smile dropped. "And they both got in the back of the Capri."

"Then what?" Chrissy said, a look of dread replacing his smile.

"Well they just stayed in there, I didn't hang around I had business to sort out for Eddie, but they were in there for quite a while Chrissy, I mean it's fucking obvious what was going on ain't it . . . ? We should tell Eddie." Chrissy jumped off his bar stool and grabbed Stanley by his collar.

"No, that's exactly what we *shouldn't* do. If we tell Eddie then it's gonna fuck everything up for *all* of us." He stopped to think for a second before continuing. "Who have you told Stan?" Stanley shook his head.

"What kind of a question is that?" Chrissy sighed, he knew Stanley Kay was a good bloke and had always had the Fewtrells' best interests at heart.

91

"Yeah sorry Stan," he said softly. Stanley could hear desperation in Chrissy's voice as if the wind had been knocked out of him. "Look we gotta keep this under wraps. If Eddie gets to hear about any of this there will be bloody murders. We got to think of Hazel and the kids." Stanley nodded.

"Yeah but who's the bloke in the beige Capri then? I've never seen him before." Chrissy frowned.

"Don't worry about him, you leave him to me!" Chrissy stood up indicating the meeting was over. "And Stan," he patted the other man's shoulder, "not a fucking word, understand?" Stanley nodded. "There's only the four of us that know about this; you, me, Hazel and lover boy . . . let's keep it that way!" With that he turned and left the club the same way he'd entered.

Battle of the Little Big Fellas

Chapter 8

Humiliation comes in all shapes and sizes: the humiliation of the cuckolded, the humiliation of the ignorant, love spurned, the financially disgraced and so on. But for Tony Merrick it came in the form of six dwarfs. That's right, dwarfs.

Tony Merrick was one of about fifty door men that worked the Fewtrell doors around the city. He was a hard guy but funny with it, as were almost all of the Fewtrell door men. He came from a stable of boxers trained by head door man and gym owner Nobby Nobbs, Eddie's most loyal enforcer. A huge contradiction of a man standing six foot six in his stocking feet, as hard and fearless as they come. Nobby had two jobs given to him by Eddie which were no drugs on any of the Fewtrell premises and no trouble, that is unless it was in the Fewtrells' favour. He carried out both tasks with zeal and a humour rarely found in modern times.

In the last few months of 1973, the ATV network commissioned a small group of ex radio DJs, would be TV personalities and a TV announcer by the name of Peter Tomlinson to come up with a children's TV show that would be totally original and break new ground for children's entertainment in the United Kingdom, working under the name *This is Saturday, watch and smile* which was abbreviated to *Tiswas*. After the initial pilot at the end of 1973 the show was broadcast in January 1974 and became an instant hit. Its ad-lib approach to TV presenting gave the children of Birmingham something they had never seen before, a slice of anarchy. Kids, parents, teachers, together with TV personalities in three hours of none stop, slap-stick sketches and on the spot chaos that left the studio almost destroyed and the crew looking to carry on partying. Anchorman Chris Tarrant and co presenter Sally James suggested they hire a club for the after show parties and Eddie was only too happy to oblige.

Normally drunk when they arrived, the TV crew would continue at the club where they had left off at the studio. Champagne, cocktails, beers and spirits were passionately consumed by the fifty or so crew and guests until the exuberant and sometimes belligerent TV crew and stars had to be contained in the VIP area, to prevent them causing offence to the normal punters, starting to arrive for their regular Saturday night out. Sometimes keeping a lid on the group became a problem, especially when they had guests from out of town,who didn't have anything to lose by going on an bender for the whole weekend especially seeing as ITV were picking up the bill.

One such group was a gang of dwarfs who had been taking part in some of the *Tiswas* sketches. Many of the little fellas had played parts in major film and TV for several years and were used to the goings on at celebrity dos. One of the group David Rappaport, had been born into one of the toughest areas in London, which was only made tougher for David because of his debilitating dwarfism. Rappaport developed many talents including a fine singing voice, acting, playing the accordion, he even had a degree in psychology from Bristol university and although small, even by dwarf standards he could also deliver a knockout punch to a man, *literally* twice his size. On this particular evening he was eager to show off his abilities to his fellow dwarfs.

The evening had started with about thirty of the cast and crew showing up, already pissed at four thirty in the afternoon. ITV cash was put behind the bar and the drinks and buffet were laid out for the guests as they arrived. Eddie, who always stood watching events from a safe distance, couldn't help but give a little laugh as the troupe of dwarfs arrived en masse at the front doors to the club, still in the Roman centurion costumes they had worn in their TV sketch, filmed only a few hours before. The little fellows came marching through to the VIP lounge, past the sniggering doorman Tony Merrick, followed by the voluptuous Sally James in her skin tight, yellow *Tiswas* T-shirt, black leather mini skirt and thigh high boots. Tony gave her his best, flirty smile and he showed her through to the rest of the guests. With the cast and crew being made up of mostly drunken men and of course six very horny dwarfs, Sally James, or rather her tits, became the centre of attention amongst the group. Instead of doing his job watching the door and patrolling the club, Tony was star struck or maybe *tit* struck by Miss James and was unable to take his eyes off her for most of the evening. He stood on the sidelines of the group watching the shenanigans getting wilder and wilder. On top of that, the club had started to get busier and now groups of regular everyday punters were trying to infiltrate the TV crew and join the party. The dwarfs were having none of it and, standing on tables and chairs began to give plenty of verbal to these club goers, who in turn were giving plenty back.

"Where's Snow White?"

"Fuck off ya lanky wanker!" This was the level the cat calls had sunken to and as the tension began to build, a confrontation between the TV group and club regulars looked inevitable. Tony watched on as Sally James, who it must be said was a little worse for wear and up for a good time, was bombarded with sexual innuendos from all and sundry. As the drink flowed, so wandering hands wandered, mainly little dwarf hands and a little too close to a certain leather skirt. Sally took it all in her stride though with sexy Barbara Windsor style giggles. Tony, however, who by now saw himself as Sally's knight in shining armour began to feel jealous and irritated. He approached Eddie and Nobby who were sat at the front of the club chatting about boxing techniques.

"Those little bastards are getting out of hand Eddie." Tony seemed at his wit's end.

Eddie, caught by surprise mid sentence didn't know what he was talking about. Both men came to attention, always on guard and expecting some form of trouble from a local hard man or gang inside the club.

"Who's that then?" Tony gestured the two men to follow him.

"There's six of em . . . but don't worry I can handle em." Eddie and Nobby followed Tony through to the VIP lounge expecting a stand off of some sort. Instead they found Sally James screaming laughing hysterically and covered in dwarfs whist Chris Tarrant and the rest of the gang watched on, tears rolling down their cheeks.

Tony didn't wait for Eddie's permission to stop what seemed to him like a mini Roman orgy taking place and just dived in.

"Oi take your hands off that lady!" he shouted to no one in particular as he strode into the room grabbing one of the dwarfs who was sprawled prostrate over Sally James, his face buried in her bosom. Tony pulled on the Roman centurion costume expecting to be able to lift the little fella as if he were a child. Eddie and Nobby took two bar stools to watch the show about to take place. Eddie leant across and shouted over the DJ's music into Nobby's ear.

"E ar Nobby watch this! That David Rappaport is a right stroppy little fucker when he wants to be, he won't stand for that." Nobby gave a gravelly laugh.

Tony had realised too late that the dwarfs, although small, weighed the same as a fully grown man, not only that, they also had the same core strength as their fully grown counterparts. Tony continued to pull the little man out of the nest he'd made for himself in Sally James's tits. Obviously the horny midget was having none of it and was putting up a hell of a fight by grabbing whatever he could, which included her T-shirt, ripping the yellow cotton and nearly exposing her breasts completely. Tony lost his cool.

"You little bastard. Get the fuck off her . . . *now*!" At this point it was already too late for Tony Merrick to back out of the situation. He was committed, he knew it, and now so did the dwarfs who had started to group together, some behind David Rappaport, the others behind the unsuspecting doorman. The first Tony knew about the little gang was when Rappaport threw a champagne bottle at him. The Moet bottle simply bounced of Tony's head without too much damage. But damage wasn't the point in the thrown bottle, it was a distraction to prevent Tony realising that the troupe of the little fellas were surrounding him. Tony still didn't grasp the trouble he was in, even when Rappaport stepped forward and offered the bouncer a fight, man to man. Eddie sat laughing uncontrollably. Nobby had run back into the corridor and told all the other bouncers in the club to come watch Tony's battle. They came running and along with nearly everyone in the club at the time, they watched the bizarre gladiatorial event about to play out before them. Tony held his open hands up.

"I ain't gonna fight a fucking midget am I?" Tony laughed, "I fight men not little boys." He said arrogantly, Rappaport physically bristled at the words, he came in closer to the bouncer and pointed his little fore finger at the towering man in front of him.

"You obviously don't know anything about dwarfs do you ... *meat head?*" Rappaport said with his squeaky voice, he grabbed his groin, "Cos I'm big where it counts ... ain't that right lads?" Tony laughed nervously, he looked around the room for support, glancing at Sally James who looked at him as if he were mad. He turned back to the dwarf. Once again Rappaport had caused a diversion, as two of the other little fellas stepped in behind Tony each one grabbed a trouser leg and pulled down on the black material for all they were worth. The trousers came down easily, leaving the six foot hard man standing in the middle of the club with his C&A underpants, which were also dragged down along with his trousers, gathered in a pile around his ankles. There was a weird few seconds of silence that fell over the whole club. Tony, shocked at his sudden nudity, took his eyes off David Rappaport to see who was responsible. Then everyone watching burst into howls of laughter, Eddie sat screaming at the bar, tears rolling down his cheeks. At that very moment Rappaport sprang forward like a cat, teeth bared and locking his arms around Tony's knees he trapped the unfortunate bouncer. Before Tony could react Rapport sank his teeth into the bouncer's genitals. The sound of breath being drawn in filled the whole club. Eddie and Nobby sat frozen, lips pursed and faces screwed up in disgust.

The bouncer stood there looking at the snarling, mad dog hanging from his balls for exactly the same amount of time his brain took to process the bizarre image in front of him into one of ultra high pitched scream. It was a high pitched, female squeal that every single man in the building not only heard, but *felt* right down to their core. He bent slightly over trying to protect his groin, eyes and mouth wide. He began hitting Rappaport around the head, and then . . . they were on him like a pack of wolves. Little Roman centurions streamed over the doorman, their combined weight bringing him to his knees. The howls of laughter started again but this time with surprise in their voices. Rappaport had let Tony's balls drop from his vicious bite and climbed on the bouncer until he was face to face with the opened mouth, hard man. Little fists pounded Tony's head and shoulders left and right, the poor doorman didn't know which way to turn.

"You fucking big bastard!" called out one of the dwarfs.

"Lanky twat!" another shouted over the screaming laughter as he sank his teeth into the door man's ear. Then, in a tiny window of clarity, the two men's eyes met. Tony's aggression had been replaced by one of humiliation, Rappaport's drunkenness with one of triumph. In that tiny second Rappaport brought his head back and with all the power and determination of a man that had put up with this type of shit his whole life David Rappaport brought his forehead into Tony Merrick's nose with such force that the doorman's nose exploded in a fountain of bright crimson, that showered the swarm of tiny centurions. Tony dropped to the floor unconscious. The blood soaked tribe of dwarfs stood in a tightly packed circle around the fallen bouncer. The laughter had stopped now and even the DJ had become silent. David Rappaport climbed onto Tony's chest and stood with his hands on his hips like some kind of tiny, victorian, big game hunter. Eddie, Nobby, the TV cast and crew all held their breath, waiting for his words.

"It's a small step for mankind, but a giant *leap* for dwarfs," and with that he gave a little jump off the unconscious man's chest.

He landed, one arm raised, a huge grin on his face. The whole club came to their feet and gave him a rousing cheer, Eddie fell of his bar stool laughing.

* * *

Amid all the confusion and comedy, nobody noticed two Irish men walk through the front doors of the club. Whilst the whole place was laughing at the slap stick shenanigans, the Irish men had paced the club, checked the fire escapes and counted the door staff, until finally, Jan McGowen, head of the Birmingham IRA was satisfied that he could rule out this venue as the target for the upcoming campaign. The young Irish lad with him was dead against bombing anywhere that might involve injuring the general public and although McGowen agreed with him, Belfast Jimmy had insisted that this club *was* the best target. They left as they had entered, unnoticed.

A little Piece of Peshawar

Chapter 9

The brown, V8 Rover flew across Birmingham's wet streets, Ronnie Fletcher and Jimmy Feeny in deep conversation on its dark brown, leather tuck and roll seats. The purr of the engine easily outpacing the Morris Minor's and old Austin trade vans, that seemed to be from a different century. Jimmy felt pleased with himself, following his altercation with the skinhead kids his adrenalin was still pumping and the frustration he'd felt since he'd arrived in the city had finally dissipated. Now here he was with the boss of the Serious Crime squad about to bring down the largest cell of IRA terrorists in the British Isles.

"Deep under cover." The words made him tingle. Of course he'd already made in roads within the IRA and these Fenians seemed to trust anyone that could speak a bit of Gaelic. "Where we heading boss?"

"Moseley." Fletcher smiled but said nothing more, as if the word would explain everything. Jimmy shook his head.

"Sorry boss but that means fuck all to me." Fletcher drew on his cigarette and blew a cloud of smoke out of the little gap at the top of his driver's window.

"Moseley, it's where my contact, *our enabler* is based." He turned to Jimmy, raising his eyebrows. "He's the man that's going to get us what we need to bring down those Fewtrell fuckers." Jimmy nodded.

"But how does he fit in with the Irish, boss?" He questioned.

"All will become clear DCI Feeny, all will become clear." Fletcher gave a little laugh. "Today we're going to combine business and pleasure, DCI Feeny, business and pleasure." The men didn't speak again until the car had reached the outskirts of Moseley village.

* * *

The beautiful village of Moseley has alway been the avant garde centre of Birmingham. Artists, musicians, left wing activists and university lecturers filled the huge Georgian and Victorian houses that stand side by side on its oak tree lined streets and boulevards. One person that *didn't* visit Moseley was Adolf Hitler. The war didn't make so much as a mark on the village, and, as if by some miracle the Birmingham city planners of the 1950s seemed to overlook the place too. This left a beautiful village that time had forgotten, with original Victorian and Georgian fronted shops and pubs, a gothic church and a cast iron Victorian sunken public toilets that acted as a busy cottage for some of Birmingham's homosexuals.

Jimmy sniggered at the psychedelic freaks wandering around the village in their out of date, hippy clothes as he was chauffeured through the winding streets. The Belfast man had never seen anything like it. Fletcher slowed the car down as he reached the higher end of the village, on the Wake Green road. The road was lined with huge houses in many styles from Gothic to Edwardian. He seemed to be looking for something but Jimmy couldn't make out exactly what that was. Then, after around half a mile or so, the Rover slowed to a crawl. A magnificent house came into view on the opposite side of the road. Victorian in style, very grand if a little run down, the house was cut off from the street by a thick set of thorn and bramble bushes that had been allowed to grow wild around the taller trees that lined the frontage of the house. A set of ten foot high, stone pillars that in better days had held massive iron gates, blocked the only entrance into the front courtyard of the house. They stood like sentinels topped with lion heads and had seen too much weather over the hundred or so years they had kept guard over the property. Parked in between the two pillars and acting as a makeshift barrier was a light blue transit van, a young Pakistani man sitting at its wheel. Fletcher gave a short toot on the Rover's horn. The asian man seemed to jump in his seat as the car horn woke him from his slumber. The man reached for the van's keys and gave them a turn, bringing the transit van to life. The clunk and grinding of gears engaging could be heard from inside the Rover as the man, who obviously couldn't drive, tried to reverse the van out of the way. Slowly the van crawled backwards and the gateway into the front courtyard was clear.

"Come on Abdul!" Jimmy shouted from the passenger window. The unamused Pakistani man stuck up his two fingers in a V, both policemen gave a sarcastic laugh, but Ronnie Fletcher became suddenly serious again.

"None of that racist shit here Feeny!" Fletcher gave Jimmy a stern look. "This ain't Ireland son. These bastards will literally skin you alive if you fuck them over." The car pulled up in front of the big porch that led into the grand hall within. Fletcher turned off the engine. "Now DCI Feeny," Ronnie twisted in his seat towards Jimmy, "keep your fucking mouth shut and let me do the talking." He seemed suddenly wary but tried to hide his feelings with a thin smile. "I think you're going to be very impressed by what you're about to see . . . but leave the talking to me." Both men climbed out of the car. Jimmy noticed the blue transit van had been placed back in front of the gateway so any quick escapes were out of the question. The young Pakistani man opened the front door to the van and slid out of the cab. He looked scruffy in his cheap, black leather jacket and shoulder length, ruffled hair. He yawned, stretching his arms above his head, the action made his jacket fall open and Jimmy got a glimpse of a small, black sub machine gun hanging from a canvas strop around his neck. In all his time in the war zone that was Belfast, he had never seen such a modern weapon being so openly shown.

"Hey boss." He said turning back to Fletcher. "Did ye see that?"

"What did I just say to you Feeny?" Ronnie spat. "Keep your eyes down and shut your fucking mouth. From now on don't talk unless you're spoken to . . . get it ?" Jimmy nodded.

"Yes boss." The two men went to the huge red front door. Jimmy looked up at the building. The once white, lime stone had now turned a rusty red set against the black key stones that gave the building its unusual design. The place seemed even bigger now they were out of the car. The frontage was framed by two pointed gothic style turrets that perched on the corners of the building, windows with curved glass spread out over three levels sat within the turrets. The front door sat under a large porch held up by two, ten foot high, roman style pillars. Even in its current level of decay it was still a magnificent piece of architecture. Ronnie grabbed the large, brass button that was counter sunk in the wall and pulled it. The action set off a wire pulley system that rang a bell somewhere in the house. The sound came from deep within the building and created an echo that rang around the panel lined corridors. The men stood there for a short while waiting for an answer. Billy turned and looked towards the young man by the van, he was leaning against it smoking and watching them with disinterest. Billy turned back to find his boss had pushed the door open and was stepping into the front hall. A rush of pungent air with the sweet smell of coriander hit them instantly, making both men hungry. The hall was far bigger than he'd expected. A beautifully hand carved, elm staircase swept down from the first floor on to the black and white ceramic tiles that lay on the ground floor. The men walked in to the middle of the hall. They could hear what sounded like lots of sewing machines and people moving around the house, speaking Urdu.

"HELLO!" Ronnie called out. Suddenly there were people everywhere! Little brown asian faces peaked from doorways, a look on panic on their faces. Voices became raised. Neither Jimmy nor Ronnie understood a word of the Urdu as more faces continued to appear. Jimmy estimated maybe thirty people had shown their faces but still no one had answered them.

"Hello, anyone speak English?" Ronnie shouted again. The front door behind them opened with a loud clunk as the metal latch lifted. Both men turned around to see who had entered and came face to face with a huge Pakistani man, who seemed just as shocked to see two white men stood in the hall. The man had another small sub machine gun on a strop over one shoulder. He slid it behind him out of sight. There was a silence for a few seconds as the men weighed each other up. Ronnie spoke up,

"I'm here to see Mr Khan." He searched his jacket pocket and produced a little black wallet. He held it up so the man could see it and let the flap of the wallet flop open revealing a silver police badge. The big man smiled a huge tooth filled smile.

"Oh praise be to Allah . . . I thought you were here to rob us." He said in broken English, laughing at his own joke. Ronnie and Jimmy smiled, both of them feeling the release of tension. "I am Haroon, I'm afraid you have come in the wrong entrance gentlemen. Mr Khan is in the basement." His grasp of English seemed to improve the more he talked. He stepped back and opened the front door. "This way gentlemen." He gestured politely for them to step back outside. As Fletcher stepped through the large front door behind Jimmy, Haroom shouted something in Urdu at the faces in the doorways who suddenly vanished and the sounds of the machines started again. He let the door slam shut and gestured for the men to follow him. He walked around to the side of the building and stopped at a set of steps that led to the basement. "Here gentlemen, if you please."

"Oh the tradesman's entrance." Jimmy said sarcastically, Fletcher gave him a dark stare. Jimmy shrugged. Both men stopped at the top of the stairs and looked down into the dark stairwell. There was music coming from behind a thick oak door with a small, metal grated, spy hatch at its centre.

"This way please, Mr Khan is waiting." Fletcher nodded and began descending the stairwell followed by the other two men. He reached the door and gave it a push. The door was heavier than he'd thought and he had to give it a hard push to open it. The door swept back with a swoosh and the same smell of coriander and spices hit him as he stepped through the doorway. Soft sitar music was playing from somewhere within. The men walked into a short, dimly lit corridor, off of which ran several small rooms with curved vaulted ceilings. Unlike the grand rooms above, these rooms each had a bed or chaise-long draped in a variety of oranges and reds, to match with the soft reds and muted browns painted on the brick work. All the rooms had lava lamps of different colours pulsating on small, Moroccan style tables. Mirrored tiles on the walls created strange, shifting shapes that gave the whole basement a feeling of movement. The whole space felt exotic and mysterious to the two policemen, as if they had somehow been transported to an ancient hareem in Peshawar.

They walked along the corridor until they came to a door. Haroom gestured that they should stop. He slowly opened the door and put his head inside. Jimmy looked at Ronnie, a look of confusion on his face. Ronnie smiled.

"Wait for this Feeny, you're gonna like this." Haroom said something to whomever was in the room followed by the sound of shuffling, he turned back to the men.

"Wait here please gentlemen!" With that he disappeared into the room completely, allowing the door to shut behind him. The two men stood like school boys outside the headmaster's office, both stared at their feet, hands in pockets listening to the sounds coming from inside the room.

"Come on you little bitches!" Haroom's muffled voice sounded impatient. "You've got clients to entertain." The sound of a hand slapping something, then a female crying. Eventually Haroom held the door wide open so the two men could see inside.

He made a sweeping movement with his hand, "Please gentlemen come and meet the pretty ladies." His big smile illuminated by the lava lamps gave him a bizarre caricature-like appearance.

Fletcher and Feeny stepped through the doorway. The dimly lit room had the same feel as the smaller rooms but was much larger, one of decadence and Peshawar luxury. Twenty or so Moroccan lamps hung or stood on shelves around the room. Candles flickered inside the multi coloured lamps making the smoky air flicker red, blue and green. The sitar music was coming from a reel to reel tape player on a shelf on the far wall and a huge red Persian rug lay on top of the stone floor. Along the wall were two, long, red leather settees scattered with cushions and on the settees were ten or twelve girls. Billy couldn't make out how many there were as they were all flopped on top of one another in various states of undress. None of the girls looked at the men as they entered. Haroom ushered the men through the door and began slapping the thighs of the girls as he walked past the sofas. One by one the girls rose from the red leather and formed a line along the room. They stood there, swaying in their little, baby doll nighties or just underwear. All of them appeared to be drunk. Jimmy looked at his boss who had a big grin on his spiteful face. He was rubbing his hands together and it became clear to Feeny that Ronnie Fletcher had been here before.

"Drinks gentlemen?" Haroom had stepped behind a little, semi circular bar. He flicked a switch and a small, florescent light came on under the bars top shelf, its yellow light illuminating the bottles of brandy, cognac and whisky that sat behind the plexiglas.

"Whisky?" said Ronnie without taking his eyes from the girls. Haroom's eyes shifted to Jimmy.

"Not for me." Ronnie turned to Feeny.

"He'll have a whisky too." He turned back to the girls. He reached up to his head and swept his greying waxed hair back until it sat slick on his head and licked his lips, savouring the girls.

"Hello darling, what's you name then?" He was addressing a young girl who seemed oblivious to the fact that he was right in front of her, it was at that point that Jimmy realised just how young the girls were. He could see several were in their late teens but some of them were much younger and one, the one Fletcher was talking to seemed to be about fourteen.

"You like her sir?" Ronnie nodded. Jimmy thought of his nieces back home in Belfast.

"She's a bit young for you sir ain't she?" Jimmy laughed nervously.

"How would you know what I like or not?" Fletcher almost spat the words, lust taking over him. Haroom came from behind the bar with the drinks and handed it to the two men. Ronnie grabbed his drink without taking his lustful gaze from the young girl and licked his lips as he drank in the golden liquid and the girl's figure. Haroom opened the door back into the corridor.

"Take her sir . . . she is yours. Choose any room you like." Unlike his boss, Feeny felt embarrassed by the sight of the girls.

"I thought we came here to see Mr Khan?" He said to Ronnie. Haroom answered.

"Mr Khan will see you after you have enjoyed yourself, he is in a meeting and he'll be with you directly sir."

"Just fucking relax DCI Feeny . . . that's an order!" Ronnie gave him that thin smile before grabbing the swaying girl by the arm and dragging her from the room and out of sight.

"Which one do you like sir?" Haroom smiled. "Maybe you like two girls . . . or three?"

Jimmy shrugged. "Let me choose for you sir." Jimmy nodded.

"Yeah that's a good idea." Haroom walked along the line of girls and pulled two of the older ones from the group. He clicked his fingers and the other girls began to file out of the room and into the corridor outside. Jimmy caught a glimpse of his boss closing a curtain in one of the small rooms, the early teenage girl in the background. The door shut behind the last girl and he turned back to the girls Haroom had picked out for him.

"Drink . . . drink enjoy yourself, sir!" Haroom made a drinking gesture. "The drinks are there, help yourself. I will leave you now and the girls know what to do. I shall be back in one hour." With that the big Pakistani left the room.

Jimmy caught sight of himself in a large mirror that sat on one of the walls. Was he really going to do this with these girls? As he took a sip of the whisky and stared into his own eyes in the reflection of the mirror, one of the girls came behind him and draped her arms around his neck. He drained the large whisky.

"What harm can it do?" He thought to himself. The girl took his jacket from him and let it fall to the floor, then pulling down the collar of his shirt she kissed the nape of his neck. Her hands ran along his chest as her mouth worked its way around his skin with feather light kisses. Jimmy closed his eyes and let the girl do her work. Her other hand ran down to his groin.

"Ooo do you like that baby?" The girl said into his ear in a barely audible whisper. "Just let yourself go Mr . . . forget about everything . . ."

Then Jimmy felt hands fumbling at his belt. He opened his eyes slightly and looked in the mirror opposite. The other girl had come around in front of him and was knelt down in front of his groin busily freeing his manhood. The older girl at his ear seemed far more experienced than the one on her knees but he wasn't about to start complaining. Jimmy gave a low gasp as the girl on her knees freed him from his trousers. Jimmy couldn't tell if there was something in his whisky or not, but his head had begun to swim with lust and sexual energy. Whatever it was that Haroom had spiked his drink with, it did what it was supposed to do and released a sexual cruelty in him he never even realised he possessed. The next few hours swept in front of him like a devil's shadow; images of nakedness mixed with groans of pleasure and pain. All with the taste and smell of the young women that filled his living fantasy. His blood soaked orgasms washed over him, again and again. Then after what seemed like an eternity of sexual blood lust, a darkness came over him and the images, smells and pleasures were gone.

* * *

Two hours had passed before Jimmy Feeny regained consciousness, he heard voices, raised voices, in the distance. He was aware of a coldness creeping through his limbs and realised he was naked. Images began to flutter in front of his closed eyes. At first one or two, then hundreds of images, uncontrollably flickering in front of him like some out of control movie clip. Slowly the memories of his sexual exploits returned to him and a feeling of confusion turned to one of self loathing.

"Mr . . . Mr." Harroom's voice, then a soft slap around his face. The pain brought him out of this horrific movie show. He opened his crusty eyes, painfully accepting the soft light of the basement. The music had stopped.

"What the feck happened? . . . I . . . I" Haroom placed his hands upon Jimmy's bald head.

"My friend you have done something very bad." Haroom let the words sink in. "Very bad sir!" He rocked backwards and forwards on his haunches as he stroked Jimmy's head. Feeny's head began to clear, he pushed the Pakistani's hand away. He sat up and took a deep breath. "*Very* bad, but I'm sure Mr Khan can sort it out sir, yes."

"Where's my boss?" He enquired looking towards the door, Haroom shook his head and gave a smirk.

"He's still passed out in the corridor." The big man laughed. "He never even enjoyed the girl, ha ha . . . just passed out." Jimmy tried to stand but fell back on to the Persian rug. The rug was wet, he felt the dampness in the rug and held his hand up in the dim light; blood stained his fingers, he examined the stains curiously then smelt his hand. The unmistakable smell of urine. Feeny jumped up off the rug, he nearly fell but Haroom had stood up with him and stopped him collapsing. His knees felt soft and unable to take his weight but after a few seconds he found his balance and the room, which a few seconds before seemed to have been slowly rotating, it remained stationary now. Jimmy looked back at his hand, blood, he checked himself over but couldn't find any wounds. Haroom watched him, a false look of concern on his face. Feeny started to pick up his clothes that were scattered around the floor. They were damp and smelt of piss. His shirt had blood stains all over it too. Jimmy began to see a lot of blood, too much blood for a small injury. Haroom could see Jimmy was confused.

"The blood," he paused, "belongs to the girl." He said earnestly.

"Sir," he searched for the right words, "Sir you did something to one of our girls, well it wasn't just you, the other girl helped you." He stood and approached Jimmy. "But do not fear sir, I have dealt with the situation and you should not worry." Jimmy stood in front of the huge man, incredulous.

"What situation?" He asked, forgetting his nakedness as the seriousness of the incident began to dawn on him.

"Yes sir, the girls won't talk so there is nothing for you to worry about . . . after all these things happen in our business and it isn't the first time I have had to clear up a mess like this." Feeny shook his head trying to release the memories of what had actually happened but his memory refused to return. He just raised his hands to Haroom, his piss soaked clothes in hand.

"Mr Khan has asked me to give you this." Haroom crossed the room and took a black, plastic bag that was hanging on a coat hanger on a nail in the wall. He held the bag out to Feeny. "Please sir, some clean clothes." Jimmy took the black, plastic bag from the hook on the hanger cautiously and ripped the top of the bag open. He looked back at Haroom for an answer. "New clothes for you sir, from Mr Khan. Very nice suit sir. I will get you some coffee sir, maybe that will clear your head?" Haroom turned to leave.

"Wait!" Jimmy ordered. "The whisky . . . it was spiked wasn't it?" Haroom nodded.

"Yes sir." Jimmy was shocked by the big man's honesty.

"Why?" Haroom smiled.

"All will become clear sir. Now please dress yourself, I will wake Mr Fletcher and then you can talk to Mr Khan, ah . . ." he said remembering, "first coffee, yes?"

"Yes!" Jimmy replied. The fact that he had been well and truly stitched up began to dawn on him. He was experienced enough to know when someone had him in their pocket, and this Mr Khan, whoever he was, had done a good job. Jimmy peeled away the black plastic to reveal a grey two piece suit and a new, cream shirt and tie. He carefully took the suit from the bag and began to dress. As the clothes went on he began to feel a little better. A shuffling came from the corridor and Fletcher stumbled into the room. Feeny ignored his boss and carried on dressing himself.

"Those bastards did it again!" Fletcher was wearing the clothes he'd arrived in. He suddenly looked very old, Jimmy recognised the look of self loathing on the older man's face. "Fucking dirty Paki, drugged me." Jimmy couldn't resist.

"Now now sir, no racist stuff here, remember?" He said with a sarcastic laugh.

"Fuck you DCI Feeny!" He slumped on to one of the sofas, then leant forward, head in hands. Jimmy ran his boss's words through his head.

"What do you mean a*gain*?" He turned to the older man. "Don't tell me you've done all this before?" Fletcher still held his head in hands but nodded. "And you came back for more . . . for feck's sake boss!" Fletcher had had enough.

"Shut the fuck up Feeny!" He searched for the right words but his mind was still awash with whatever drug Haroom had used to spike him. "Just shut the fuck up . . . let me think." Jimmy laughed.

"Well there ain't too much to think about is there boss?" Feeny searched the floor for his shoes and socks. "This Mr Khan . . . who-ever he is, has got us." He stopped and thought things through. "Well . . . he's got *me* over a barrel at least, you might have got off with it because apparently you just passed out." Jimmy turned to look at his boss. Fletcher just sat on the sofa, rocking backwards and forwards, head still in hands.

"Nah," he said suddenly, looking up at Feeny, "nah they got me same as you . . . but *why*?"

"Well, I've got a feeling that will become apparent very soon, sir." Jimmy said, pulling on his shoes. He checked his appearance in the large mirror. The image of the girls jumped into his mind, he shook his head to release the memory.

"Very smart Feeny, courtesy of Mr Khan I take it?" Jimmy nodded but continued to stare at the large mirror. The situation becoming clearer. He waved at the mirror.

"Thank you for the suit." He shouted at his reflection, Fletcher stared at him as if he'd gone mad.

"What the fuck is wrong with you Feeny?" Jimmy just pointed at the mirror. At that moment the door to the corridor opened. A tall thin but elegant man stepped into the room followed by Haroom carrying a tray with two Moroccan coffee pots and cups on it. The man was dressed immaculately in a golden mohair, mandarin collared suit. He had an air of royalty about him. Haroom stepped around the man.

"Gentlemen please let me introduce . . ." Jimmy finished of his sentence.

"Mr Khan I presume?" The man nodded. "Why?" Jimmy pointed at the mirror, the man smirked, impressed with the policeman's intuition.

"Insurance, DCI Feeny." He answered. "We all need insurance in this business, surely a man of your experience realises that?" Feeny nodded raising his eyebrows resigned to the fact the Pakistani man had him. Fletcher just looked on, unable to make sense of anything that was being said. "Do not worry DCI Feeny, you are not the only one who has unwittingly partaken in my insurance policy," he let the words hang. Jimmy shook his head. "Oh I have many, many people included in my plans and I must cover myself on all sides, police superintendent . . ." he nodded towards Fletcher and smiled, " . . . judges, politicians, headmasters, doctors . . . even a pop star." He gestured to Haroom to pour the coffee. The big man nodded and began to pour the strong coffee in to the delicate, gold etched coffee glasses. "It is a very *exclusive* club gentlemen and thanks to my insurance policy we are all obliged to protect one another."

"Mr Khan . . ." Jimmy began.

"Please call me Zafa." The Pakistani man smiled. Haroom brought the silver tray over to Feeny who looked at the glass of steaming coffee. Zafa laughed. "Do not worry DCI Feeny, you are quite safe . . . it's just coffee." He picked up one of the other glasses and took a sip of the dark liquid to prove the point. Jimmy put the drink gingerly to his lips and took a sip, the coffee was strong and he pulled his head back from the glass. Haroom noticing the look on his face, stepped forward and poured two heaped teaspoons of sugar into the coffee, Jimmy tried again.

"Mmm that's better." Fletcher, who until now had been sitting, head in hands feeling disgusted with himself jumped out of his seat.

"Well . . . that's just fucking great . . . at least your fucking coffee's ok, now would someone explain to me just what the fuck is going on?" Jimmy was shocked at his boss's inability to work out the situation. Jimmy turned to Fletcher.

"Well," he said pointing at the mirror, "unless I'm off my mark, I'd say that there's a an 8-mm film camera behind that mirror and Mr Khan here has just filmed me getting up to no good." Fletcher's face became flushed.

"You fucking bastard Zafa! I trusted you !" Zafa laughed.

"Really?" He shook his head "Then you're a fool inspector." He turned his attention back to Jimmy. "And in answer to you DCI Feeny, yes there are cameras but they are 16 millimetre . . . better quality you see," he looked around the room, "better in dim lighting conditions.

"I thought we came here to talk business." Fletcher said agitated.

"And so we shall gentlemen, I am just . . . as you say, levelling the playing field."

Fletcher was still none the wiser. He wasn't used to being dictated to, after years of throwing his weight around he had become used to people being subservient to him.

"Follow me gentlemen!" With that Zafa crossed the room and stepped out into the corridor. Jimmy grabbed his old, leather jacket but left his jeans and piss stained shirt on the floor where he'd dropped them. He helped Fletcher to his feet and the two men followed Zafa through the door, Haroom bringing up the rear.

Zafa was at the end of the corridor holding open a door next to the entrance that neither men had noticed as they had entered a few hours before.

"This way please." Zafa held the door as both men entered. The room was adjacent to the one they had just been in, only this room was painted matt black that was everything apart from a large window that looked into the room they had just left.

"The mirror." Jimmy said, Zafa nodded. Either side of the window were two *Bolex* 16 millimetre film cameras. "I fucking knew it." Zafa laughed.

"You are to be congratulated on your instincts Mr Feeny." The coin had finally dropped with Fletcher but all he could do was mutter curses under his breath.

"Now to the business at hand." Zafa gestured to Haroom. The big man reached up to the ceiling of the basement and pulled down a large, white screen. Zafa clicked his fingers and Haroom crossed to the other end of room to where a film projector stood on a high trestle table. He clicked the large dial on the side of the projector and the machine suddenly burst into life. The men turned from the projector to the screen. A hollow feeling filled Jimmy's stomach, he didn't want to watch. The film rolled around the big discs either end of the projector as the celluloid fed into the bright light. An image appeared on the white screen. The image was that of the room next door and three people. Jimmy could plainly see that whoever was in the film wasn't him. They watched as the man was undressed by two girls and the sex acts began. He didn't recognise the girls in the film, or at least he was sure they hadn't been there when he had seen the line up earlier. The man seemed familiar but neither Jimmy nor Fletcher could place his face. Slowly the sex became more extreme.

"You see how the 16 mm camera catches everything in such detail." Zafa said to himself thoughtfully.

"Hold on isn't that . . . ?" Jimmy pointed at the screen and crossed the room to get a closer look, suddenly he knew who the man was, "That's fucking Gary Raven!" Fletcher shook his head.

"Who?" Jimmy sniggered.

"Gary fecking Raven . . . the durty bastard." He could see the name meant nothing to his boss. "Gary Raven, the pop star . . . that fucker was on *Top of the Pops* last Thusday."

Fletcher joined him by the screen.

"Pop star?" Jimmy nodded. Zafa interrupted.

"Suffice to say gentlemen, I have films of both of you doing pretty much the same thing . . . well," he addressed Jimmy, "*almost* the same." He gave the policemen a wink. Jimmy enquired about the girls.

"Do not worry DCI Feeny, Harrom will . . ." He searched for the right words, "deal with the situation in his usual *delicate* way." Jimmy was eager to change the subject.

"Ok what's Gary Raven got to do with all this?" Zafa smiled.

"Well DCI Feeny, Mr Raven is going to be very useful to all of us . . . in many ways he will be the lynch pin for our plans." The two detectives looked at each other.

"Ok we're all ears Zafa." Fletcher said. Zafa signalled Haroom to turn the projector off. The big man turned the dial and suddenly the noisy machine was dead. Haroom flicked the light switch and Zafa sat at a small table. He gestured the others to join him.

The men talked for hours, reluctantly at first, not trusting the Pakistani but their experience and corrupted principles made it easier for Zafa to win both men over. Zafa spoke in his calm, matter of fact manner setting out the objectives of their collaboration and encouraged the officers to talk freely about their ambitions within the force, as he did about his ambitions for Birmingham.

Zafa spoke about what he wanted to achieve from this deadly collaboration. He explained that he wasn't going to spend his whole life as a whore master. He had higher ambitions but firstly he needed money, far more money than his whores or his clothing manufacturing upstairs would ever bring in. He needed big money and he knew how to get it but there was one family standing in his way, the Fewtrells, Fletcher bristled at the name. He had tried to put a stop to Eddie Fewtrell's businesses years before, but his constant police raids on Eddie's clubs had come to nothing. He suspected the Fewtrells had been tipped off about the raids by one of their bent coppers. In the past he had pressurised other Birmingham gangs to cause trouble, but once again the Fewtrells always came out on top. You might get an individual hard man from out of town that wanted to have a pop at one of the brothers, but as they found out too late, if you hit one of them you've got to hit *all* of them. They had even tried using the taxman, but all Eddie's businesses, at least the ones they had looked into, were legitimate. Zafa changed the subject, explaining how his contacts in Afghanistan could procure a never ending supply of the purest heroin to be found anywhere in the world. Furthermore, he had already organised a shipment line via Birmingham airport and everything was waiting and ready to go. He already done a run with a small amount of the substance and everything went smoothly, if he could get it into the country in quantity, he could cut the pure heroin and triple his profits. He went on to point out that he was more than willing to give the two policemen a percentage of the business, so as long they did their bit to make the operation work, without any nosey police intrusions.

"So what's the problem?" Jimmy asked, Zafa and Fletcher smirked at each other.

"The Fewtrells," Fletcher said sarcastically, "have you not been listening? Eddie Fewtrell runs this town, at least the night life anyway, it's a well known fact the Fewtrells don't allow drugs into the city." He stopped to see if this was sinking in.

"Well we got plenty of muscle ain't we? So why can't we just . . . ?" Zafa stopped him.

"That is all very well if you have nothing to hide, but we do not have that luxury. We can't use muscle against an enemy if we are in a covert situation, we can't bring attention to ourselves, we must use guile and cunning to trap a man like Eddie Fewtrell. We need someone else running the nightlife in this town. Someone a bit more openminded to my products!" They all agreed.

"The London gangs tried to open up the city back in the early 1960s. The Krays, The Richardsons, Lambrianous all tried to take the place over to start a drug trade, but the Fewtrells got wind of it and kicked the shit out of anyone that stepped foot in the Birmingham. Even if we could use muscle, we'd need the fucking army to bring that lot down." Fletcher shrugged and took a sip of coffee. Khan replied,

"We must gather information about the Fewtrells, the more we know about their movements, the better we can prepare their downfall." Ronnie nodded in agreement, taking over the conversation again.

"Yes but if there's nothing to report back where do we go from there? I mean if they're not getting up to anything dodgy . . . well I can't nick em can I? I've been here before Zafa!"

"Everyone does *something* dodgy boss." Jimmy spoke up, Zafa agreed.

"We all have our secrets inspector, if we watch long enough the skeletons will fall from the closet, as you British like to say." He waited to see if Fletcher agreed but the older policemen just sat looking at his feet. "I will *create* a reason for you to raid these clubs and we will bring these Fewtrells down together." Zafa said, trying to improve Fletcher's mood.

"How?" Jimmy asked.

"Our little pop star, I have a way to put him to good use gentlemen," he gave them a few seconds for his ideas to sink in. "Leave all this to me. I will call you when the pieces are in place and when we are ready . . . *checkmate!*" Fletcher liked the sound of that, suddenly becoming more positive about the whole scheme. Zafa continued.

"Are we agreed? Good. In the meantime Haroom and some of my other men," Zafa gestured to the big man, "will watch the Fewtrells and discover any weak points we can exploit to our favour. Sooner or later we will find something to bring this Eddie Fewtrell down." Jimmy nodded, he was thinking about the meeting with Jan McGowen and the Birmingham IRA he'd had earlier that week at the Irish Centre. If everything they planned went ahead then *the IRA* would deal the killer blow to the Fewtrells' empire and all of this would be irrelevant, but he wasn't about to share this information with these two.

"Just one more thing Zafa, this money, drug money," Jimmy questioned, "what is it you need it for?" Zafa smiled raising his index finger.

"That is the million dollar question DCI Feeny," he laughed, "but seeing as we are all partners in this business I shall share my dream with you." Both policemen perked up. "There are around fifteen thousand Pakistanis and Indians in Birmingham, some legally here other not so legal, but all of them need a voice; a political voice, a *Pakistani* voice, someone to represent them when they can't represent themselves." Fletcher sniggered.

"You want to go into *politics*?" Zafa became serious suddenly.

"That is such a bad thing?" He replied quizzically. "Apart from the heroin money gentleman, I shall be collecting money from almost every one of those fifteen thousand immigrants. Each one of my fellow country men legal and illegal . . . especially the illegal, shall pay for my voice to protect them from the British establishment." His eyes glowed, "Think about that! Fifteen thousand, five pound notes coming to me every pay day! Fifteen thousand votes on election day! Fifteen thousand today . . ." He let the words hang, then continued triumphantly. "Tomorrow it will be twenty thousand and every year it will become more and more." Feeny shook his head doubtfully.

"That's a lot of money Mr Khan, why bother with the heroin at all?" Zafa frowned.

"I need the drug money to pay the hundred or so Pakistani men to collect the protection money from my people around Birmingham. I must be a gold giver if I am to have loyalty DCI Feeny." Jimmy thought he could see a tiny flicker of shame in the Pakistani man's eyes. Zafa continued. "Every politician has to get their hands dirty at some point in their career and if I'm to be a king to my people, I must do the same." Belfast Jimmy looked at the Pakistani man in his shiny, golden mohair suit, looking like some kind of eastern king and he wondered if the man knew just how dirty his hands were going to get.

The Shadow

Chapter 10

The BBC weather forecasters had been predicting a heatwave for quite a while. After the news at 9pm every night, the weather girl would stick small, yellow suns all over a map of the United Kingdom of England, Scotland, Wales, and Northern Ireland. The BBC left a big, blue gap on the map, almost as if the Republic of Ireland didn't exist and the decision to do so illustrated just how bad the feelings between Great Britain and its Celtic neighbour had become. Nevertheless, the beginnings of summer were glorious; so hot in fact that the black tarmac along the roads of Birmingham began to melt in the rising temperature. The soft surfaces tripping would be sidewalk surfers who were taking their first steps in the new craze of skateboarding that was spilling over the Atlantic from the USA. The parks were filled with mass football games made up of hundreds of kids from the many housing estates throughout the city, the kids escaping the grime of home in the little slice of nature the city parks offered to them. Pop music blaring from transistor radios filled the air accompanying young lovers that strolled hand in hand through the early summer blooms and tree lined footpaths that ran through the ornately planted parks, Hazel Fewtrell and Brendan Hodgson were two such lovers.

Hodgy had done well in the *Grapes bar*, just as Eddie had predicted he would. The bribes had proved a good investment too; he stayed open serving alcohol just as long as he wanted and this had almost doubled his predicted bar takings. This gave him a surplus and with the advice of his father, he had taken the first steps towards following in the family tradition and starting up an undertaking business. His clandestine meetings with Hazel Fewtrell were becoming more passionate as the days rolled on and his emotions floated somewhere between passion and pure fear.

Hazel on the other hand was far more confident about the situation. Her optimism encouraged Hodgy to feel almost as confident in the future as she did. Unfortunately for Hodgy though, Hazel's confidence came from a sheer refusal to see things as they really were. Her motivation for the affair had its roots in revenge rather than aspirations of love, revenge for the clumsily covered up rumours of Eddie's indiscretions. Hazel had lost sight of the fact that, after all, the rumours were just that, *rumours*, spread by the jealousy of enemies, friends and family alike, who all had their own reasons for spreading such maliciousness. Of course Hazel knew Eddie, and she also knew what he was capable of and without doubt, somewhere at the back of her mind, Hazel knew she was playing with fire. Nevertheless the liaisons continued. An anonymous phone call to the Fewtrell home in Harborne was usually followed by Hazel deciding to 'go for a walk', usually down to the local phone box where the two lovers would arrange a venue for their love making. Sometimes the passions were so high Hazel would bring Abigail, her toddler daughter along, her pram left at the end of a hotel bed, the sleeping child within, as Hazel and Hodgy made love only feet away. The arrangement had gone almost unnoticed for months, that is until Stanley Kay had spotted them, purely by accident and had told Chrissy Fewtrell who had in turn sworn him to secrecy. Chrissy now watched the pair from a distance, waiting, choosing the right moment to intervene. Chrissy loved Hazel as if she were his sister and understood the pressure she was under. She had never been a wall flower, far from it. Hazel had been an integral part of the Fewtrell operation during the early days and here she was now, in her prime, yet pushed to the sidelines as Eddie's empire grew and grew. Far from being part of the action she was now expected to stay at home with the kids and be the perfect mother and housewife. He also knew about her constant back pain that was causing a growing dependance on strong pain killers and valium. Chrissy wondered if the drugs helped her escape the frustration she felt about being excluded or maybe, they had just softened the picture concerning the affair. Either way Chrissy couldn't bare the idea of Hazel and Eddie separating just when the businesses had begun to become so successful. A divorce would ruin everything and Chrissy had decided from the first moment he had heard about Hazel's *mistake,* that he would go out of his way to deal with this delicately. The red Alfa Romeo had shadowed their every move, the little car hadn't broken down as Eddie had predicted. Gordon Fewtrell had given Chrissy a great deal on the car and had stood by his word, as he always did where Chrissy was concerned. The little red car had driven all over the West Midlands trailing Hazel's green Mercedes; hotels, parks, pubs, anywhere the two could find a secret spot. Chrissy had sat in the black leather seats watching and waiting for the right moment. Hodgy on the other hand would have to be dealt with, just how badly depended on what Hazel had to say for herself. Hodgy's beige Ford Capri was easy to spot with its silly whippy aerial standing six feet high wherever it was parked.

* * *

As Chrissy sat in the ever increasing heat of the early summer, something else had come to his attention. A light blue, transit van had started to show up at these liaisons too. Chrissy had thought it was just a delivery van at first, dropping off its goods around the same restaurants and hotels and purely a coincidence. However the regularity of the blue van's appearance now made such a coincidence very unlikely. No, whoever was driving the van had an unhealthy interest in either Hazel or her boyfriend, no doubt about it.

To combat the stifling heat in the Alfa Romeo, Chrissy had parked under the shade of a willow tree that not only shaded him from the sun but also from any attention he may have drawn from the happy couple as well as whoever was driving the blue transit. Whether it was the heat in the car or just pure curiosity he couldn't tell, but as he sat outside of the *Holiday Inn* in the leafy suburbs east of Wolverhampton, waiting for Hazel to reappear with her lover boy, he couldn't help but get out of the car and casually stroll around the car park to where the light blue van had appeared a few minutes earlier. He honestly expected the van to be driven by a private detective hired by his brother Eddie. He couldn't believe Eddie had no idea about Hazel's secret affair. Eddie rarely missed a trick but maybe but this particular situation had gone under his radar.

The van had parked with its rear doors facing the hotel. Chrissy left it a minute or so then strolled past the transit van's cab but to his astonishment the cab was empty. He had witnessed the van pulling up but hadn't seen anyone leave it, yet the cab was empty. Chrissy peered inside expecting to see someone lying along the floor to the van hiding. The bulkhead that blocked off the rest of the van from the cab was intact as far as he could see. Yet he had seen the van pull up only a short time before and no one had got out. He walked around to the rear of the van, its rear windows were covered in mirrored glass. Chrissy suddenly felt as if *he* were being watched. He walked back to the willow tree and stood under its over hanging branches and watched the scene through the golden leaves. He waited for nearly two hours, as did the blue van, until Hazel reappeared at the hotel doors alone, and walked across to her car without looking back at the young man in the reception in hotel, waiting for her to leave. Hazel's eyes darted this way and that, searching for a face she might recognise. Chrissy stepped further under the branches until she had climbed into her Mercedes. Usually he followed Hazel back to her house in *Harborne* but this time he hung on, waiting for Hodgy and more importantly the blue van driver to return. As Hazel left the car park, Hodgy appeared at the doors to the hotel, a small travel bag with him. He'd changed his clothes since arriving and seemed less concerned about looking around the car park to see if anyone was watching. Hodgy opened the Capri and climbed in. The beige car started with a roar. Hodgy gave the throttle some gas and the car left the car park in a dramatic squeal of rubber and smoke. Still Chrissy waited. He knew where to find the lovers, now he wanted to see who the van driver was. He watched, smoking from under the branches enjoying the light breeze and waiting for the return of its driver. He looked over the Alfa Romeo, following its lines, mentally comparing it to other Italian sports cars. He took a drag on the cigarette, lost in the sunshine and his thoughts, then glancing back at the van he was astonished to see it moving. He had only taken his eyes off the vehicle for a few seconds and somehow the driver had returned to the van without Chrissy seeing him. Chrissy threw the cigarette butt away and climbed into the Alfa. The blue van was already leaving the car park and seemed to be in a rush, either to catch up with Hodgy or to get away from Chrissy. He watched the van pull out on to the main road and race along behind him. Chrissy turned the key expecting the Italian engine to burst into life. Nothing. He turned the key once more. Nothing. He watched the blue van disappear in the busy traffic. He turned the key once more, this time hammering his foot on to the throttle.

"Come on you bastard!" The conversation with Eddie months before running through his mind.

"It'll break down. All Gordon's cars break down."

"Fucking hell *come on!*" he roared as he turned the silver key again. This time the starter motor caught. VROOOM. Chrissy pushed the gear lever into first and the car lurched forward which took him by surprise. The wheels screeched on the hot tarmac and the car wheel spun out of its hiding place beneath the golden willow tree. He had some catching up to do. Chrissy had always been a good driver and the Alfa's 1600 GT engine gave him plenty of torque in which to indulge himself. He raced on to the main road and squealed up the road, still in first gear. He slammed the car into second gear and the car instantly upped its pace, the rev counter jumping in and out of the red as he shifted through the gears, racing through the traffic. The blue van came into sight around half a mile ahead. The van was easy to spot with its baby blue paintwork. It was stuck in the rush hour and Chrissy began to slow down and join the ambient traffic, whoever was driving the van had seen Chrissy following and it suddenly turned off the main road and drove the wrong way down a one way street on the right. Chrissy reacted instantly, mentally working out the road grid system and then *he* too turned right onto a parallel road, before becoming stuck in the same traffic the van had been caught in. He raced along the road trying to outpace the transit. The little 1600 engine enjoying the race, giving him everything he needed to catch the other vehicle. As he sped along the road through the narrow space left between parked cars, he hoped he wouldn't meet any on coming traffic as it would certainly block the road ahead. The appearance of school children in small groups wooing and clapping their hands, excited by the sports car's speed and this was making him even more anxious. He passed various t-junctions on the left and saw that the smaller roads linked the two bigger roads together. Every time he drove through one of the t-junctions he glanced at the road on the left hand side to see if he could spot the other vehicle travelling on the road that ran parallel to the one he was on. The long lines of parked cars fled past him in a myriad of colours. After the third junction he spotted the blue van which was also speeding as fast as it could go. Chrissy came to the fourth junction and he turned the steering wheel left and raced along the adjoining road, as he approached the road the van was on, he pulled up at the edge of the T-junction. Suddenly the van appeared from his left, racing past at sixty or seventy miles an hour. Chrissy caught a glimpse of a huge asian man at the wheel of the van, their eyes locked for a second. The sight of the big man added to the confusion Chrissy felt about the day's events. He gave the Alfa full throttle and the sound of the exhaust filled the street, VROOOM! The car wheel spun again and Chrissy took up the chase. The driver of the certainly knew how to drive and Chrissy had a job just to keep up with the transit's 2 litre engine.

"Who was this guy and what the fuck was he doing watching Hazel?" Chrissy ran through questions as he shifted up and down the gears. The Alfa began to make ground as the two vehicles approached the outskirts of Birmingham. The van driver knew where he was heading and this slowed Chrissy down as he had to react to the other driver's whims, the Alfa Romeo need to be shifting gears continuously in order to get the best out of the engine. The blue transit zig zagged through the tight streets, Chrissy catching up one second, then loosing ground the next. He was wondering how much longer the transit driver intended to keep this charade up; there was no way he was going to loose Chrissy. The Alfa out gunned the transit every few hundred yards. As soon as there was a straight run Chrissy brought the little Italian sports car a hair's breath behind the chrome bumper of the blue van. Suddenly the transit turned right into an old service alley between two terraced houses, vanishing at high speed. Chrissy pushed the smooth accelerator down with his right foot and turned the steering wheel with one hand and one movement so that the car wouldn't lose any speed in its turn into the tight alleyway. The red car almost effortlessly glided exactly where Chrissy wanted it and he put his foot down as the long bonnet swung in to the gap, the rear wheels drifted on the hot gravel of the road.

He hit the gap at around sixty, which was way too fast for a normal car but the little Alfa GT made it seem easy. As the car screeched on the pavement and entered the alleyway Chrissy could see the transit only twenty feet in front of him. He put his foot down. Unfortunately for Chrissy and even more unfortunately for his little car, the van wasn't trying to escape any more. Instead it was reversing towards him at full speed. Chrissy's reactions were just too slow. As his foot came off the throttle the rear of the Ford transit hit the Alfa, sending Chrissy's head into the wooden steering wheel and almost knocking him out cold. The throttle of the sports car stuck open. The sound of the engine that had only a few seconds before been such a joy to hear, was now making an awful, out of control noise and was spewing out steam from its shattered radiator and smoke from its exhaust. Chrissy was dazed. He shook his head, trying to free himself from the punch drunk feeling he'd experienced many a time in the boxing ring as he had sparred with his brothers as a younger man. He could see the transit which had begun to pull forward again, its rear, chrome bumper hanging off and making a jangling noise as the van moved down the alley dragging it behind itself. The front of the car was like a concertina, its crumple zone wrapping around what was left of its radiator. Chrissy gave the accelerator a kick and the engine stopped its revving and began a normal, if somewhat spluttery-sounding idle. The steam rose from the crushed bonnet and Chrissy could see through the broken windscreen that the van had stopped at the end of the alleyway. Blood had started to run down from the cut on his forehead, he felt its damp warmness soak into his dark eyebrows. Through the steam and broken glass he could see a man climbing from the van. Chrissy wasn't sure if he was seeing things correctly. The blow to the head would have floored another man. He tried to shake away the fog that was building up in his field of vision. *Yes* he *could* see a man, a huge man and now another, smaller man. He was holding something short and black. The smaller man pointed it at Chrissy and walked towards the car. As the man came nearer, Chrissy could see the black shape was some kind of machine pistol. The man held it in his two hands, its short, black barrel was lined with holes and the man gripped the barrel. He came right to the front of the Alfa's crumpled bonnet and levelled the gun. Chrissy's head swam with pain from the impact but he knew what was about to come. He closed his eyes. He heard the loud click of the gun spring being pulled back and cocked and knew he was only seconds away from certain death. The questions of who and why forgotten in his final moments of terror. Apart from his thumping heart and the distant hum of the city, the world had fallen silent. He waited, listening, what was this guy waiting for? Then he heard it, children talking, laughing, doing what kids do. Chrissy opened his eyes. The man was still there, gun in hand, the big man standing next to the van at the end of the alleyway. A movement in his rear view mirror caught his eye. There were children gathering at the end of the alleyway, where seconds before, Chrissy had made such a perfect turn in the little sports car. They were standing pointing at the crumpled mess of smoke and steam. The gun man turned, Haroom shook his head and gestured that he should get back in the van. Chrissy watched as the smaller man backed away then turned and sprinted back to the blue transit van as ordered. Haroom opened the back doors and the gun man skipped in. As he did so Chrissy caught a glimpse of a wooden bench in the back of the van and what looked like a small hatch between the cab and the rear of the van cut into the bulkhead. The hatch had been left open and a patch of light shone through from the front cab illuminating the back of the van. The blood had started to trickle down into Chrissy's eyes but he still had the clarity of mind to work out that the asians had used the hatch to climb into the back of the van from the cab without ever leaving the vehicle, explaining why he hadn't spotted them earlier. The big Pakistani pulled what was left of the van's rear bumper from its brackets and passed it to the gun man. He slammed the rear doors to the van, their mirrored windows glinting in the sunlight. The big man turned to look directly at Chrissy, raising his finger he pointed at Chrissy then drawing his finger across his neck, he turned and climbed into the van and with a cloud of summer dust, he was gone.

Talking Treason

Chapter 11

The phone in the hallway of Belfast Jimmy's digs gave a shrill ring that bounced around the cold, red, victorian tiled hallway. He stepped into the hall covering his nakedness with a grubby, grey towel.

"Yep." He answered sharply.

"Jimmy?" came the crackly reply.

"Ai."

"McGowen here. There's a meeting upstairs at *the Bull*, 7pm, make sure you're there!"

"A meeting?" Jimmy enquired. "What about?"

"Just make sure you're there!" McGowan hung up, leaving the hand set purring and Jimmy with a growing feeling of dread in his stomach. There was a tone in McGowen's voice, something that said he knew about Jimmy's real identity. Of course it may have been paranoia on Jimmy's side, but people in his position didn't have the luxury of paranoia, feelings like that could get you killed. He had honed his instincts over the past few years whilst working under cover in Belfast. He knew that it was far better to believe the worst and act on it, no matter how deadly, rather than convince yourself otherwise, because if you were wrong it would be you that ended up bound, gagged and about to get a bullet in your head, not your enemy.

Jimmy returned to his room. The room stank of the damp and mould that seeped from the walls in dark patches. The place was a dump, but Jimmy was past caring. He pulled on a pair of jeans and searched the pockets for a packet of cigarettes he knew were in one of the pockets. Turning the dial on the little, two ring electric cooker, he waited for the ring to glow before bending and lighting the fag on the glowing, hot metal. He pulled the curtains apart and looked out over the busy road. The streets were busy with cars and buses and he watched as a brand new Ford Cortina estate squeezed through the melee below. Jimmy pondered over Zafa's words, just how much cash was he in for and what would Fletcher and he have to do for the money. He stood blowing the smoke out of the open window, day dreaming about what kind of car he'd buy himself once the deals had been done. The British Small Arms factory stood opposite his window, its red brick chimney rising one hundred feet high above the run down, inner city suburbs of *Bordesley Green*. B S A was written in ten foot high letters down its side, just to remind the working class residents where they had to trundle to, every working day of their lives, as if they needed reminding.

* * *

Jimmy shaved, dressed, then stepped out in to the hallway to check in with the office. His handler was a man called Monk. Monk's job was to take down anything Jimmy Feeny reported and to pass it on to Ronnie Fletcher. He had been given specific orders not to talk to anyone else about anything, just Fletcher. He was to report anything unusual, such as the meeting tonight and he was only to blow his cover if things got life threatening. He talked to the faceless voice in a low, monotone voice and Monk answered in the same way. Every time Jimmy talked to the handler he had an image of a medieval monk sitting at his desk, quill in hand writing down everything he told him. After the call, Jimmy placed the receiver down and checked around the hallway and the other doors to the other bedsits to make sure no one had listened in to his conversation. After he was sure he'd been alone he stepped out on to the pavement outside. He strolled down the tree lined street towards the busy Stratford road, enjoying the light summer breeze that wafted the exotic smelling, eastern food in his direction. He had a few hours to kill before the meeting so decided to walk to James McDade's place. McDade was a lieutenant in the IRA and had confided in Jimmy about a collection of hand guns he had stored. Jimmy had asked if he could see them and '*Jamesie*' as his friends called him was only too happy to oblige. The forty five minute walk had been a pleasure in the summer sun, the hot weather had brought out the mini skirted girls who strolled around the streets in twos and threes going here and there, the sight of their long legs and little jiggling breasts taking Jimmy's mind off the long walk. Jimmy came to a set of Victorian terraced houses with no front gardens, their doors opening directly on to the dusty street. Jimmy stopped at a large, badly painted, green door with a large, tacky, brass shamrock door knocker. He gave a little snigger at the irony of the IRA man's choice of colour and ornaments.

"Why don't ye just write it on the fecking wall . . . IRA lives here!" He gave the brass knocker a loud rap. The door was opened by a man in his early twenties, Jimmy was surprised to see this unfamiliar face, but James McDade appeared behind the man and ushered him in to the old house. Jimmy liked McDade, again he was in his early twenties and a likeable man from the *Ardoyne* area of Belfast, a small enclave of Catholic houses in the middle of a huge council estate with a one hundred percent Protestant occupancy. As you can imagine life was tough for the Catholics living in the *Ardoyne*. When Belfast Jimmy first heard that McDade was from the *Ardoyne*, he had reflected on his days as one of the hundreds of young football hooligans that would pay a visit to the area whenever the local football team were playing, not so much for the football, more for the stone throwing, street fights and petrol bombs that were thrown through windows of the houses in the narrow Catholic streets. The Royal Ulster Constabulary were only too happy to join in with the youth vandalism by arresting anyone Catholic that dared complain or respond to the violent apartheid. When a people can't turn to the police for protection they inevitably turn to each other and thus the modern IRA were born, out of fear and need for self preservation. James McDade didn't stand a chance. He was radicalised at the age of ten years old and it was just a matter of time until he became one of the Fenians that filled the cells in the H-block prison that housed political activists from both sides of the conflict. His doting mother decided to send him to her relative in Birmingham, so saving him from a future that could only hold misery, fear and repression. Little did she know when she bought his ferry ticket to England, she was actually signing his death warrant.

The three men went through to the kitchen of the house, a large room with an ancient, white, enamelled Aga upon which an old kettle was steaming. Jimmy noticed the men were halfway through their breakfast, bacon and eggs lay on white plates on the rickety formica table, cigarettes burned in the ashtray at its centre.

"Tea Jimmy?" McDade asked, already raising the kettle towards a tin mug.

"Ai, lovely." McDade poured the water into the mug and Jimmy sat down on one of the matching chairs.

"Oh Jimmy this is Ray ... Ray McLaughlin." Jimmy just nodded at the man.

"He's just a prospect." Meaning he was in the process of joining the IRA but still on the outside. The usual process was a drawn out affair but had been the same for years. The prospect was given a gun, something old but still usable. The gun would be left at the prospect's house for a week or two then picked up and removed for a week, then returned before the whole process started again. This could go on for months until the leadership could see there would be no problem and the prospect could be given something bigger to deal with. Ray was at the first stage of the process. Jimmy was concerned that he didn't know the man but didn't show it. McDade returned with the tin mug to the three men sat around the little round table.

"For feck's sake Jamsie, eat your fecking breakfast, don't let me interrupt, the guns can wait!" Jimmy lit a cigarette, sat back and watched the two men eating.

"Are ye going to the meet tonight Jimmy?" McDade said chewing greedily on the food.

"Ai of course." McDade smiled.

"It'll be a good craic, there's a session on downstairs so we can have a few jars and a sing song after the meet." Jimmy nearly burst out laughing. He remembered the man was a good singer and everyone he'd met through the IRA had mentioned that McDade had a rare voice. He couldn't help think that if the British government could see this young lad in front of him, who was more interested in singing a few songs and slugging back a few jars of the black stuff than blowing up the houses of parliament, they would surely realise just how amateur these IRA men were. Time would prove just how wrong he was.

McDade and Ray showed Jimmy the small collection of pistols that had been left at Ray's house as part of his initiation. Jimmy pretended to be impressed, but in reality, the guns were old and not very well looked after. Yes they would work and if needed and would be deadly enough, but the collection was a sign that the whole underground terrorist cell in Birmingham was underfunded and lacked direction, and if Jimmy was to get the result he wanted, then they would need to procure better weapons than this lot of out of date rubbish. As Jimmy sorted through the pistols Ray spoke for the first time.

"Do you like Jan McGowan?" Jimmy thought it a strange question.

"I don't really know him, why?" Ray suddenly felt embarrassed that he'd said anything at all but Jimmy saw this and encouraged him to speak up.

"I don't know him and I gotta say, I don't really like him." Jimmy left his words hanging like a fish hook, the negative words about their cell leader the bait and Ray took it like a hungry fish.

"I fecking hate him, he's an arrogant bastard so he is." Jimmy and McDade were both taken aback by the outburst. Jimmy laughed, deciding to bring the young man onside.

"Fecking hell Ray, don't mince your words." They all burst in to laughter, McDade spoke up.

"Yeah I'm not too keen on him either, he's too aggressive, picking on people all the fecking time, good Irish people too. I mean just who are we meant to be fighting for here?" Jimmy was surprised by the openness with which both men talked about Mcgowen. In truth, Belfast Jimmy didn't like the man either. He was both aggressive *and* dangerous. This was the type of man that the British *were* scarred of, intelligent and determined, plus he was well known for sniffing out people that didn't share his passion for explosives and death. If there was anyone that would uncover Jimmy's secret it would be Jan Mcgowen.

* * *

The Bull public house in *Digbeth* has been a drinking hole for the Irish for over two hundred years. The tall, Victorian, mahogany bar stretched around the room with its matching stock shelves lined with *Jameson's*, *Tyrconnell*, or *Red Breast Irish* whisky rising up to the beautiful, but tobacco stained, ornate plaster ceiling. During the 1970s the pub had taken on the role of a folk music venue, a place where many touring folk musicians would visit after their 'real' shows, the ones that actually paid cash, like the town hall or the Irish centre across the road, had finished. On any particular night, folk stars such as the *Dubliners*, *Chieftains* or *Christy Moore* could be found singing songs just for the sake of the music and a jar at the scruffy, old pub.

As well as the musicians, it was a place for men to skull a few pints after a long day on the site before returning home to their wives and children. Busy, always loud and with a dubious clientele, it had a character and charm that could have fallen from the pages of a Dicken's tale.

Thursday nights were special, the *Ian Campbell Folk club* came to town on a Thursday and the pub would be busy with folk musicians and singers, as well as fans of the folk singer himself, who would always start the evening's events with a few songs of his own, just to get everyone in the mood. Fiddles, guitars, whistles, banjos and accordions, jostled for dominance in the foot stomping reels and jigs that made up the glorious cacophony of Celtic music.

Upstairs the group of men sat around a long table with pints of beer or glasses of whisky in front of them. They all smoked in the small room and the cigarette smoke lay in a thin, blue cloud over the table like some long lost, ghostly spirit.

As the meeting began the men made small talk about their home or work. Jan Mcgowen sat next to Belfast Jimmy, he leaned in closely to Jimmy and half whispered.

"I'm afraid you'll have to sit this one out Jimmy," then stopping to make sure no one was listening continued, "I've heard a few things about you." He turned to look at Jimmy square in the face. "I won't be mentioning it to this lot tonight, but . . ." he glanced around again, "I'm gonna have to ask ye to leave." Mcgowen could see the look of concern on Jimmy's face. "Ai it's probably nothing Jimmy but . . . I'm gonna have to get your credentials checked out back home in Belfast before you can take any further actions with the IRA." He raised his eyebrows. "Sorry pal, as I said it's probably nothing, but I need to check you out properly." Jimmy gave a false look of confusion.

"What type of things have been said?' He asked, a deep hollow opening in his stomach.

"Well it's not *what* Jimmy it's *who!*" Jimmy shook his head, this time truly confused. Mcgowen continued, "all I know is the top brass in Dublin have had a tip off from someone and they want me to act on it. Suffice to say, they don't trust ye Jimmy and if they don't trust ye . . . *I* don't trust ye!" Jimmy shrugged, trying to look nonchalant about the comments. Mcgowen continued. "Look Jimmy we all go through this shit, as long as you are who you say you are, then there's no problem and I won't have to shoot ye!" He gave a short laugh and slapped Jimmy on the back. "Listen go downstairs, listen to the music and we'll be down in half an hour." He smiled "Go on, we'll have a few jars and talk things over in a while, downstairs, away from these bunch of gobshites!" Jimmy laughed and rose from the table, Mcgowen stood too, he leant across the table, "Belfast Jimmy's nah too well so he's gonna sit this one out, anyone got a problem with that?" He looked around at the ten other men, no one spoke up. "Ray McLaughlin," the young man perked up, "you go down and keep Jimmy company while we talk!" He handed the young man a five pound note. "Get yourselves a few beers boys, courtesy of the IRA." He gave a laugh and the other men joined in. Jimmy and Ray left the room and descended the dark stairwell to the sound of a young boy's voice coming from the bar below. Jimmy heard the click of the door locking behind him and wondered if Mcgowen would keep to his word about not telling the others about the doubts over his credibility. If he didn't, Jimmy knew it was just a matter of time before he felt the cold barrel of a gun against the back of his head.

Chapter 12

Chrissy came round after only three or four minutes. The young, giggling child rapping on his driver's window brought him out of his semi consciousness and back to the moment. He turned towards the boy who instantly stopped giggling and ran away excitedly to the group of kids that stood at the corner of the alleyway, daring each other to open the driver's door. The blood had caked around his eyes and he had to blink a few times in order to open them fully. He felt his forehead, the gash was small and had stopped seeping blood. Chrissy searched the small pocket inside the driver's door for his handkerchief, finding it he spat on the white material and wiped his eyelids with the wet cloth. He turned the small, rear view mirror towards him and looked at the gash and his blood caked eyes. He could see the reflection of the children becoming more daring behind him. Pulling back the chrome handle on the Alfa's door he gave it a shove with his shoulder, the bent metal of the front wing had been driven back into the door seal by the impact and the door refused to budge. He slammed his shoulder into the door frame angrily. The heavy, red door dropped opened with a loud clunk. Chrissy climbed out of the car, his neck already stiff from the whiplash he suffered during the collision. Turning, he looked at the kids who instantly disappeared like surprised cockroaches, sprinting out of sight. The car was a mess, the bonnet was totally smashed in which was *bad* but the radiator wasn't burst after all, the cap had just popped off during the smash. The steam he'd seen earlier had been escaping through the hole it had left. He looked in to the radiator top and saw the glimmer of oily water indicating the radiator was indeed intact. Turning, he looked around the cobbled alleyway until his eye caught the glint of the silver cap twenty feet away in the gutter. He searched under the car, nothing; no oil, no water, he smiled. This meant the car was still drivable as long as the steering rack was ok. Climbing back in to the car he turned the key, nothing, again he turned the ignition and again, nothing. Maybe the smash had disconnected some wiring on the starter motor. He pondered and kept turning the key, again and again until finally, without warning the engine burst into life as if nothing had happened. Chrissy's shoulders were becoming stiff and the tight seat made him uncomfortable so he sat there for a second, playing out the incident in his mind, whilst listening to the engine for any tell tale knocking sounds that would indicate bigger mechanical problems inside, there was none. It all seemed ok. He put the car in gear and pulled forward. As the car moved, he spun the wheel first left, then right, testing to see if there was any play in the steering rack, everything seemed as it should. He was just beginning to pull away when suddenly Chrissy became aware of someone watching him. He turned to the high wall on his right and met the man's gaze. It was a Rastafarian, his old faded blue and yellow, woolly, tea cosy hat standing two feet above his head stuffed with dreadlocks. The man was saying something to Chrissy but the engine drowned out the Rasta's words. Chrissy wound his window down and held his hand up to his ear. The man spoke again but the Alfa Romeo's engine noise was bouncing around the alleyway. There was not a chance in hell of hearing the fellow. Now the Rasta began pointing at the front of the car. Chrissy began to worry in case he'd missed something or maybe the radiator *was* leaking after all. The Rastafarian began to point at the car bonnet and shout. He was gesturing for him to turn off the engine, his tea cosy wobbling precariously on his head. Chrissy reluctantly turned the key, shutting the Alfa's engine down. The silence in the alleyway was deafening and both men savoured the moment. Chrissy leant out of the window of what was left of his little Italian sports car.

"You were saying something?" The Rasta smiled.

"Ya mon, some blood-clot smashed da front of da car in mon. Ya need to git a new one." He nodded approval, either to his own words or to some music that was out of earshot to Chrissy. Chrissy sat there opened mouthed, the Rastafarian continued.

"Ya need to git a . . ." Chrissy finished off the sentence.

"NEW ONE . . . yes I fucking know!" He said angrily "You made me turn the fucking engine off to tell me *that*." The Rasta just nodded, unsmiling and sucking air through a gap on his two front teeth, he spoke again.

"If ya gonna git a new one I'll av dat one. It's fucked mon, someone's smashed in the front of it, it's no good to you, give it to I and I . . ." Chrissy couldn't believe what he was hearing.

"You want me to give you my car?" The Rasta nodded.

"Give it to I mon!" he said a big grin climbing across his face, his yellow teeth making his smile look more like a grimace. He began nodding in time with some unheard music again. "Come on, mon gi me da car mon!" Chrissy leaned as far out of his window as he could and shouted two words separately and deliberately so the Rastafarian could clearly hear him.

"FUCK. OFF!"

The Rasta disappeared behind the wall with a loud shout.

"RRRASTAFARI!"

Chrissy turned the ignition key . . . nothing.

"BASTARD!" His voice echoed around the cobbled alleyway as he turned the key again and again and again.

* * *

By the time Chrissy got going, the yellow street lights were starting to flicker into life. The Alfa Romeo had finally fired up when Chrissy had convinced several people to give the car a shove out of the alleyway and bump start the car, whilst Chrissy sat inside and threw the car into second gear. The car spluttered away from the group of neighbours that had come to his rescue, he waved his hand from the open window and drove into the muggy evening.

He pulled into the long drive that wound through the impressive front gardens of Eddie's house in *Harborne*. He let the car slow, its tyres digging into the soft gravel. Parking at the rear of the large house he reluctantly turned the engine off and went in to the house. He wasn't looking for his brother, Eddie would be at one of the clubs, probably wondering where Chrissy was. He was here to talk to Hazel. The fact she was having an affair was bad enough, but the run in he'd had with the blue van driver put a whole new perspective on her secret indiscretion. He wanted to talk to Hodgy too, but that could wait. He didn't knock, he never did, walking through rear conservatory he found Hazel in the huge kitchen. Whenever he came to Eddie's house he couldn't help but think of the poverty they had come from only fifteen years before, from the back streets of *Aston* to one of the biggest houses, in one of the most affluent parts of the city. Hazel looked surprised but happy to see him.

"Alright bab?" She was feeding her new born son Daniel whilst Abigail her two year old toddler was sat on a blanket, playing with various toys. Chrissy looked at the happy scene and wondered what the hell she was thinking having an affair with a chancer like Hodgy. Yes, he was a good looking lad, but so was Eddie, on top of that Eddie was successful, powerful and he doted on her. True, he was probably knocking off the odd barmaid or someone or other, *but*, Hazel was the one he came home to at the end of the night.

"Maybe you should get the nanny to look after the kids Haze? We need to talk!"

She stood slowly from the high chair, the little lad protesting about the removal of the plastic spoon from his greedy mouth.

"What's up Chrissy?" She could see the serious look on his face.

"Call the nanny Haze." Hazel looked perplexed but obeyed, not because she had been told to but because she was curious to hear what Chrissy had to say. She went to the door to the large hallway and called the nanny to come downstairs. She stood by the door, arms folded and turned to look at Chrissy. She had known Chrissy since he was a young lad and loved him like a brother. A mixed race girl appeared at the doorway to the hall.

"What's up Hazel?" Hazel smiled.

"Just keep an eye on the kids for a few minutes will ya Nettie?" She nodded her head to Chrissy and they both went into the lounge.

"What happened to your head bab?" Chrissy just shrugged it off.

"Never mind that." He searched for the right words but just decided to come out with it. "How was Wolverhampton?" Hazel was shocked by the question but hid it well.

"Wolverhampton . . . what about it?" Chrissy frowned.

"Come on Haze, don't play coy with me." Chrissy sat on the arm of one of the big leather sofas. "I know about you and Hodgy." Hazel nearly swooned, she went to say something but couldn't find the words. Chrissy could see the rising panic in her face as she looked here and there, like some kind of trapped animal.

"Look Haze, no one knows except me." He decided not to mention Stanley Kay as he knew Stan could be relied on to keep his mouth shut. Hazel covered her mouth with her hand, the look of panic still with her. Chrissy repeated his words.

"Only me . . . Eddie doesn't know." Hazel began to pace back and forth. Chrissy stood up and grabbed her softly by her shoulders. He turned her towards him. "Eddie doesn't know . . . yet!" He said the words as a warning. "He will find out though, it's just a matter of time Haze. You've been lucky so far but someone's bound to see you and that someone will say something to Eddie and you'll have a right load of shit from him." He let the words sink in. "Never mind you Haze, think about what Eddie will do to young Hodgy." She suddenly became suspicious.

"What's in it for you then Chrissy, what do you want from me?" She said the words spitefully. Chrissy felt hurt but understood her reaction.

"I don't *want* anything Haze, just you and Eddie back on track, I mean you've got to think of the kids for god's sake." Hazel began to feel angry at being cornered.

"So Eddie can do just what he wants with who he wants and *I* have to sit here like a good little wife, keep me gob shut, and look after the kids . . . is that it?" Chrissy looked around him. He swept his hand around the room.

"Fucking hell Hazel get a grip . . . look where you live for fuck's sake." He turned and walked to the drinks cabinet. "Do you mind? I've had a fucking strange day." Hazel just nodded towards the drinks.

"Help yourself." Chrissy picked up a brandy decanter and poured the dark liquid into a cut glass. They both relaxed, Chrissy sat back on the arm of the chair.

"Look Haze I know what it's like for you. I know, trust me ." He was referring to the affair he had started with a female singer he had met through the clubs. He continued. "Look if you and Eddie divorce then the whole thing's gonna be ruined just when we're starting to make some real cash." Hazel bristled at the word divorce.

"I ain't gonna divorce him am I?" Chrissy shook his head.

"Well if Eddie finds out, you might not have a choice in the matter. Did you think of that?" Hazel sat on the sofa her head in her hands and began to cry.

"But he make me happy." She was talking about Hodgy. "He makes me feel like I'm worth something." She burst into tears, Chrissy was exhausted and his patience began to wear thin.

"Look I didn't come here for this shit, so stop ya blurting and promise me you'll knock Hodgy on the head." She sobbed in to her hands silently. The fantasy life she had planned for herself and her lover finally crumbling with every word Chrissy said.

"Promise me Haze." She nodded, knowing there was no way out.

"OK . . . OK . . . I'll tell him." Chrissy's mood changed instantly. He came across to where she sat and knelt down in front of her, wrapping his arms around her shoulders he hugged and rocked her.

She lifted her face and looked at his handsome face. She looked at the cut on his forehead. "Who copped it today then?"

Chrissy stood up and turned to look in the large mirror over the fireplace. He still had blood caked in his eyebrows and the cut on his forehead looked swollen and angry.

"Shit I didn't realise it was that bad!" Hazel went into the kitchen and returned with a damp paper towel. She wiped the towel across his eyebrows and was surprised by the amount of blood the dark eyebrows contained. She examined the cut and fetched more paper towels. She placed the damp paper on the gash and told Chrissy to hold it there.

"The cold water will take the swelling down ... what happened or don't you want to talk about it?" Chrissy began to run through the whole episode.

"Do you know any Pakistani's?" Hazel was confused by the question.

"What?" Chrissy continued.

"Have you had a run in with any ... ?" Hazel interrupted.

"Pakistanis ... no ... why?" Chrissy thought for a second before answering.

"What about Hodgy?" Hazel shook her head.

"Nothing he's mentioned, I mean I know a few but, not really, why?" She enquired, her curiosity about the strange question growing. Chrissy didn't reply. He drained the glass before walking through to the kitchen. Hazel followed.

"There's a couple of Pakistani blokes taking a massive interest in you and Hodgy." Hazel frowned trying to work out some connection but couldn't.

"What do you mean Chrissy, paying big interest?" Chrissy told her about the blue transit van, the huge Pakistani and the smaller one with the gun, how he believed they would have shot him if it hadn't been for the street kids in *Handsworth* earlier. Hazel just listened but was still confused about any connection with the Asians and wondered if Chrissy was making the whole thing up just to scare her. Chrissy saw her doubt and he turned to leave.

"If you don't believe me about the big Pakistani Haze, then go and take a look at what they did to my Alfa, it's on the drive. Anyway, just do as I said, tell him the affair's over . . . because if you don't, I will and you know what that means." Hazel became angry.

"Don't you fucking dare touch him Chrissy . . . he's just a young bloke." Chrissy turned on her.

"Yeah a young bloke that's shagging my brother's wife. You're a fully grown married woman and a mother . . . you need to start acting like one Hazel." He walked to the rear door of the house and stopped in the doorway. "I won't touch him, I promise, but if Eddie finds out . . . and he will find out, you know what'll happen to Hodgy, now get it sorted, Haze, before it's too late." Chrissy let the door slam behind him, he walked down the drive to the road and began the short journey to the Hagley road where he could hail a cab. That was one problem sorted out, but just who the Pakistani gun men were was a question that still played on both their minds.

The Micky Finn

Chapter 13

Zafa and Ronnie Fletcher had been running through ideas about Eddie Fewtrell for a few weeks now. Ronnie had being paying visits to the big house, combining business and pleasure with every visit. Whilst on one of these trips he had come up with the idea of putting pressure on some of the Fewtrell's old enemies from the Birmingham Meat Market to come on side and cause Eddie as much shit as possible. Fletcher explained to Zafa about the bad blood between the Fewtrells and the old Meat Market Mob, and how it had flared into bloody violence ten years before. He went on to explain how he could put together a gang of the hardest men there that still held bad feelings towards Eddie and his brothers. Zafa said he had his own contacts in the Meat market amongst the fledgling, Halal meat abattoirs that could be found in warehouses that ran behind the main market. He could probably muster another ten men, not so hard with their fists perhaps, but vicious nonetheless. Unlike Fletcher's men, Zafa's would be paid to fight rather than threatened. Being Pakistani, it was always hard to integrate with other gangs throughout the city; the Greeks, Italians and Irish all kept themselves to themselves. But Ronnie Fletcher seemed more than willing to be the go between in this strange alliance. Whilst Ronnie and Zafa were running over the plans Haroom came in to the room talking of an important phone call. Zafa stood up and crossed the room towards the phone in the dingy, brick corridor outside, Haroom stopped him.

"Sorry sir, but it's for Mr Fletcher." He pointed at the detective who was sat in his beige, grubby shirt and tie.

"Me?" he sounded concerned, trying to work out who knew where he was. Haroom nodded.

"Yes sir, it's DCI Feeny sir." Ronnie let out a sigh of relief.

"What the fuck does he want?" Fletcher said to himself. He crossed the room and followed him through the door and into the corridor beyond. Haroom led him into the main house. The never ending noise of the many sewing machines making a cluttered, metallic sound all around him as he stepped into the hall.

"Feeny?" There was a short silence.

"Yes sir." Fletcher couldn't hold in his anger at being telephoned there.

"Well?" Jimmy's voice sounded desperate.

"They're on to me sir, well, *Jan McGowen's* on to me." Ronnie perked up.

"Jan McGowen's on to you?'

"Yes sir . . . I think so." Fletcher snapped.

"Well is he or isn't he?" Belfast Jimmy snapped back.

"Well either way I'm not taking any chances, it's me that's gonna end up with the bullet in my head now isn't it *sir?*" Fletcher didn't like his tone.

"Don't get fucking snotty with me sonny!" but Jimmy interrupted.

"Right the main members of the IRA are in a meeting at the moment, Mcgowen pulled me to one side and said that he'd heard rumours about me and that he's going to check them out. You know as well as I do, that if he does, I'm a dead man and you've lost your undercover man in the IRA . . . *me.*" He let Fletcher take the words in before continuing, "I've got to act tonight or I'll miss my chance." Ronnie answered.

"We can't afford to lose you Feeny, we've put too much effort into getting you inside." Jimmy continued, thinking out loud.

"Look, I can sort it but I need two things from you, and I need them to happen *now*."

"Ok, name them." Jimmy took a breath.

"Ok, that stuff that Zafa Khan gave me . . . I need some of it, enough to knock a man out." Fletcher was about to tell Feeny that he was stood in the Pakistani's hall, but decided against it.

"Ok that shouldn't be a problem, but you said *two* things." Jimmy continued.

"I'm at the *Bull Tavern* on Digbeth high street. I'm downstairs with a young lad that's trying to join the IRA. They said neither of us were allowed in the meeting but I think they said that to the lad, just so he could keep an eye on me." Jimmy took a drag on his cigarette, then continued. "I told him I needed some fags, that I was nipping out to the coach station to buy some and he stayed in *the Bull*."

"OK . . . OK." Fletcher interrupted, letting Jimmy know he was making sense.

"Well I need some of that stuff. Tell Haroom to drop it off, they'll never suspect a Paki. When he drops it off I'm gonna give him a notepad."

"Ok, carry on." Fletcher said.

"Are ye getting this down? I can't stay here much longer I have to get back to the pub before the meeting's over." Fletcher became irritated.

"Well fucking get on with it then!"

"In that notepad are the names and addresses of almost every IRA member in Birmingham. The only ones I've left off the list are the ones I'm gonna use. You have to nick everyone of them tonight . . . get that?" He said the word again driving the urgency of the situation home. "*Tonight!*"

"That's not much notice." Fletcher added.

"It's all the notice I have to give you, the situation is fluid to say the least. I'll deal with Mcgowen, you deal with rest of them. Tell Haroom to come in the pub and go to the toilet. I'll follow him into the bogs when I see him . . ." With that Jimmy dropped the receiver and the line went dead.

When Ronnie returned to the basement of the house Zafa was sat on the small table, watching the film of Gary Raven again.

"Trouble?" He enquired.

"No . . . far from it." Ronnie seemed pleased with himself, he explained Feeny's request for the knockout drug and Zafa put Haroom on to it straight away. Then Fletcher made his excuses and started to leave. "Things are taking on a life of their own Zafa, it won't be long now until we are enjoying the fruits of our labours. Anyway, I've got some nasty bastards to arrest."

* * *

Jimmy Feeny stood at the bar with Ray McLaughlin watching Davey Keogh taking his turn amongst Ian Campbell and the many other musicians and singers, to sing a ballad called *The Wild Mountain Thyme*. Belfast Jimmy knew the song, it was one of those rare songs that crossed the divides of culture and religion, and for a few minutes, the troubles were forgotten, as the young lad sang the song with a passion that made almost everyone in the *Bull Tavern* join in with the chorus. Jimmy enjoyed the lad's voice. Maybe he thought, it would be this lad's generation that would finally put an end to the sectarian violence and then there would be no need for men like himself. He stared at the blonde haired boy enjoying the moment, his mind taken away from the problem that was about to come downstairs from the meeting above, in the form of Jan Mcgowen and the other members of the Birmingham IRA. As the song finished in a loud round of applause, Jimmy saw a Pakistani man poke his head nervously around the door. Jimmy recognised him as the bad van driver in the gateway to the house in Moseley. He was expecting Haroom but was glad that Zafa had had the sense to send this fellow instead. Haroom's size and stature would have brought too much attention from the mainly Irish crowd in the pub. Jimmy gestured to the man to follow him, turning to Ray he made his excuses and went to the toilet. The Asian skirted around the crowd so as not to bring attention to himself. Jimmy reached the toilet first. There was an old man swaying in the latrine, peeing and singing an inaudible song to himself. Jimmy stood next to him and waited. The Pakistani joined them but went into one of the two filthy cubicles. The old man rested his head on the toilet wall behind the latrine and looked like he was about to fall asleep. Jimmy gave him a slap on the back.

"Come on old fella!" He said in a friendly voice. The old man came to with a drunken smile and burst into a rousing chorus.

"OOOOHHHH some say the divil is dead . . . hic!" Jimmy laughed, he slid his arm under the old man's and pulled him away from the latrine and over to the second cubicle.

"AAANNDDD buried in Killarneyyyy !" He continued. Jimmy turned the man around so their eyes met, Jimmy's smile dropped.

"Go to sleep ye filthy Fenian bastard!" With that he drew his arm back and punched the man square on the jaw. The man took the punch without even noticing. He just stood, his happy eyes locked on Jimmy's as if nothing had happened,

"OOOOHHHH some say the divil is dead . . ." he continued to sway and sing drunkenly. Jimmy scowled, confused that his punch didn't even register with the drunk. Bringing his elbow up in a lighting fast second strike, he hit the man across the jaw, sending the man's head sideways and knocking the poor fellow out cold. He dropped like a sack of Irish spuds on the piss covered tiles of the toilets. Jimmy picked up the old man's legs and forced them into the cubicle, then pulled the door shut behind the unfortunate drunk. He knocked on the cubicle where the Pakistani was hiding. The man poked his head through the doorway, smiling nervously.

"Come on Punjab, hand it over, I ain't got time for this shite!" The man held out his hand, it had a small glass vial in it with a silver screw top. Jimmy looked at the object for a second then snatched it, he reached into his underpants and pulled out a small notepad. He slapped it in the asian's hand.

"Make sure Superintendent Fletcher gets this . . . understand? It's a matter of life or death!" The man nodded, his big innocent looking, brown eyes shining against their ivory coloured background then Jimmy turned and left the toilet without a word. The little Pakistani man still hiding in the cubicle gazed at the notebook. Although he couldn't speak a word of English he sensed that it was important.

Jimmy returned to his place at the bar. Ray McLaughlin had bought him another pint of Guinness and had been joined by McDade. Jimmy checked around the bar for the other members but couldn't see them in the crowded room. Jimmy was just about to ask McDade where they were, when McDade was called up by someone to sing. The room became very quiet as the young man walked to the centre. Jimmy realised that *this* was the real reason McDade was here, not the IRA meeting, and judging by the crowd's reaction there were plenty of people who had travelled into the city centre from the outskirts of Birmingham, just to hear him sing. Jimmy hadn't realised the lad was so popular. James McDade sang three song. His voice captivated the audience as the charismatic Irishman touched the hearts of everyone in the bar. The cigarette smoke clouding the room full of hard drinking men who for a few minutes gave themselves over to the poetry of songs written before their great-grandfathers were born. The silence was broken by the the door behind the bar opening as the IRA men entered the room, chatting noisily. As the men stepped into the room they began hushing each other, members of the audience turned angrily, giving the men dark stares, protesting about the disturbance. Mcdade ignored the intrusion and continued to sing. Jan Mcgowen came alongside Belfast Jimmy at the bar. He nodded to McLaughlin and the younger man moved away. Jan came in close to Jimmy and whispered.

"We need to talk Jimmy, there's something about you that just don't make sense." Jimmy smiled.

"Ai no problem Jan, let's have a pint first, it'd be a shame to miss McDade's fifteen minutes of fame." Mcgowen turned to the young man in the middle of the room and shook his head dismissively. Jimmy felt for the vial in his jacket pocket, he unscrewed the lid whilst it remained hidden and pulled the small glass vial from his pocket. He checked to see if Mcgowen or anyone else could see him, but the man had fully turned towards Mcdade and was leaning with his back against the bar, arms folded. When he was

David J. Keogh

satisfied that all eyes were on the singer, Jimmy brought his hand up to the pint of Guinness that Ray McLaughlin had bought him earlier and spread his fingers over the top of the glass letting the vial with the *Micky Finn* knock out drops empty into the pint of beer, without anyone seeing what he was doing. Placing the vial back in his pocket, he tapped Mcgowen on the shoulder, the IRA captain turned towards Jimmy. He looked into Jimmy's face without expression and took the Guinness. Jimmy turned back to the bar and ordered two whiskies. Jan Mcgowen was going to appear very drunk in the next half an hour or so, Jimmy knew he had to make it look realistic. After thirty minutes the music became far more upbeat. Banjos, fiddles, bodrhans and pipes reeled away and the Micky Finn Mcgowen had drunk had started to do its work as the man began to sway at the bar. Belfast Jimmy handed him another whisky, which Mcgowen threw back, slamming the glass on the counter. Jimmy could see his eyes begin to roll and threw his arm under Mcgowen's and said loudly.

"Come on big fella it's time to go." He said, so everyone around him could hear. "Jesus I thought a big man like you could handle ye drink." Mcgowen looked like he would pass out there and then, unable to focus never mind talk. Jimmy began to shuffle the man towards the door. "God bless lads, I'll get him in a taxi and be back when he's on the way." At that moment another man stepped from the crowd. Belfast Jimmy only knew him as Kelly, another Northern Irish man. He stepped to the other side of Mcgowen and lifted him from under his shoulder. Jimmy protested.

"It's ok I've got him." The other man took no notice and just carried on carrying Mcgowen towards the door. *"I said I've got him Kelly!"* The man gave him a stare then gestured towards the door. Jimmy was confused but decided to just go with it. No point in bringing attention to himself. The three men stumbled through the door and on to Digbeth High street. The fresh air of the night hit them and Mcgowen seemed heavier all of a sudden.

"Kelly you go back inside with the lads, I have him, I'm only gonna throw him in a taxi anyway." Kelly gave a little snigger. He looked over his shoulder to see if they had been followed onto the road. When he was sure they weren't, he stopped walking and pushed Mcgowen against a wall, pressing against him so he wouldn't slide down the wall on to his backside, leaning towards Jimmy he whispered.

"God save the Queen." He stood back and watched Jimmy's face, he smiled and raised his eyebrows. Jimmy stood dumbfounded, various scenarios running through his mind. Did Kelly know he was an under cover policeman and by saying *God save the Queen,* letting him know the game was up?

"God save the Queen." He said it again, only this time with a little laugh. Jimmy didn't know whether to make a run for it or stay and try and talk his way out of the situation. Before he could say anything, Kelly continued. "Did you think you were the only undercover cop on the job Jimmy?" He held his hand out, Jimmy looked at it without saying anything. "Don't worry Jimmy your secret's safe with me, I've been involved with this cell for two years." He still held his hand out and gestured that Jimmy should take it. "I'm a *protestant* . . . like you," Jimmy didn't seem convinced. "Look, I'm a member of the Grand Orange Lodge for fuck's sake, ex British army that's why they chose me." Jimmy spoke.

"They?"

"Ai they . . . the police." Jimmy shook his head.

"Who's your handler then . . . *Fletcher*?" Kelly looked at Jimmy, a blank expression on his face, the name obviously meant nothing to him. Kelly smiled again.

"No I'm being handled by . . ."

"I don't want to know. All I want to know is if you're gonna help me deal with this gobshite." He looked towards the now, almost unconscious Mcgowen. Kelly turned and stepped back under the drugged man's shoulder. Jimmy did the same. They half shuffled, half walked down the dark streets behind the *Bull Tavern.*

The canal was only half a mile behind the pub but it took nearly thirty minutes to drag the man to the canal's edge. They lay Mcgowen down beside the water, he lay snoring on the dusty cobbles. Jimmy began to remove the unconscious man's shoes and socks. Kelly looked on, sweating from the exertion of having to carry the big man so far. Jimmy dragged Mcgowen until his feet dangled in the dark water. He pushed the man up to a sitting position and to anyone that passed, it looked as if three drunken friends were simply enjoying a cold, refreshing dip of their feet on a unusually warm September night.

The John Doe

Chapter 14

Throughout the late summer and early autumn that year, almost every active IRA man in Birmingham and the surrounding areas were arrested in early morning raids in the city and beyond. A rake of small arms, such as automatic pistols and revolvers were recovered in the raids, along with ammunition for the weapons. The West Midland Crime squad swooped on the known bomb makers too, recovering a large amount of a certain type of explosive that had been smuggled into England from across the Irish sea, in the backs of cars and lorries on the many ferries between Rosslare and Pembroke, or Dublin and Holyhead. The IRA had, at the time, used this particular type of explosive in many bombings in Northern Ireland and had begun using it on an increasing scale throughout the UK. According to one of the bomb makers, the police had wiped out the IRA's supply of the explosive in the city and Ronnie Fletcher was happy to take full credit for doing so himself, giving press interviews to all and sundry, quoting,

"We've got them on the run now!" So it was with some surprise that at the beginning of October, an IRA bombing campaign started within the Birmingham area. Aimed mainly at property, Conservative clubs, banks, police stations and the like, the targets were generally hit out of hours and amazingly, injuries were few and far between. Ronnie Fletcher could be seen on local news TV making promises he couldn't keep and incredibly, no one was asking the big questions. If the police had shut down the IRA and confiscated all their explosives, then just who *was* making the bombs and *where* were the explosives coming from. The latest bombs had the familiar alarm clock timing mechanisms and wiring set ups. No one checked to see if the detonators or the explosives themselves were of a military grade.

Fletcher only heard from DCI Feeny once more, immediately after the arrests. Feeny had called in to ask about Kelly, he wanted to confirm Kelly was who he said he was, so Jimmy Feeny could bring him on side. Ronnie told Feeny he'd never heard of him and furthermore, DCI Feeny needed to come back in, as Ronnie considered it a

'job well done'. He pressed him a little further on Kelly but Fletcher would neither confirm or deny any knowledge of the man. He did on the other hand mention Kenneth Littlejohn, who, Fletcher insisted worked for MI6 and was to be avoided at all cost as he was sure Littlejohn was a double agent and would give away their scheme. The IRA in Birmingham were over, and as far as he could see there was nothing left for Jimmy to do. Feeny just laughed at the suggestion he should come back in.

"You asked me to destroy the IRA and bring the Birmingham Irish to their knees, well, that's exactly what I intend to do!" Ronnie ordered his plant to come in, but Jimmy was now well beyond working within the law, Feeny continued, "I've got my own crew around me now, real IRA men who are willing to kill not just talk about rebellion. You said destroy them once and for all, well I've got something planned, something big, even by the IRA's standards." When DCI Feeny went on to tell him that he was also "head of the Birmingham terrorist group," Fletcher immediately realised his agent had gone rogue and must now be brought in, one way or another, preferably the other, dead.

Belfast Jimmy hung up, Ronnie was dumbfounded at first, he threw the phone across his desk, it fell towards the floor and then bounced on its white, curly cable, its ring tone buzzing. He had never been in this situation before, he had been cornered before, yes, but nothing that couldn't be sorted out by framing someone or by paying a low life to get rid of the situation. Of course, once the low life had done the job, he would be arrested for murder, thus killing three birds with one stone a) the initial problem would be sorted b) the low life would be off the streets and c) Ronnie Fletcher would receive a commendation from the top brass. He took a bottle from the desk drawer and poured himself a large glass of rough, cheap whisky. He ran over the situation in his mind. The fact that DCI Feeny was *his* agent was bad enough, but the films Zafa Khan had of both of them in, shall we say, compromising positions, made him realise that something drastic must be done before the whole house of cards came tumbling down around his head.

* * *

Five days had passed before they found the man in the canal. His bloated body had become lodged in a weir and rats had enjoyed his company, feeding greedily on his arms and back. The John Doe remained in the police morgue for three weeks before being cremated. Nobody missed him, there was no one to miss him. The members of the IRA that were arrested during the purge in September just assumed that Jan McGowen had been arrested too and had been sent to another jail for questioning, lost in the justice system. The police had no idea who the man in the canal was, no identification, no fingerprints came up on the system, nothing. He had been living off the money he had been taking from the collections made around the city for the families of the internees in Northern Ireland, only taking enough to live on, so as not to raise suspicion with the IRA command in Dublin. No income, no social security number, no name, nothing, just a John Doe that had drowned whilst swimming drunk in the dirty, brown canal that ran parallel to the Irish quarter of Birmingham.

A Matching Pair

Chapter 15

Hazel had been looking at the phone all day, but couldn't bring herself to make the call to Hodgy, God knows, she had left it well over a month to do it, avoiding Hodgy and Chrissy alike. Her summer affair had been a distraction, but now it was autumn. Eddie had returned home from work at his usual time around 4 am, he was still sleeping in his room, they had slept separately since the children were born. Hazel didn't like it, but since having the kids she had found it hard to put up with being woken up early in the morning when Eddie arrived home. Often drunk, he would wake the whole household, fumbling around, banging into this and that. She had become increasingly reliant on sleeping pills and between these and the heavy pain killers for her back, Hazel spent most of her mornings in a confused fog and this certainly contributed in taking away the motivation needed to make the call. Eddie rose around midday. He cooked himself a fried breakfast and ate it with his children playing around his feet, he made small talk with Hazel and their nanny Nettie, but really his mind was on the night ahead. November was always a slow month so he had organised something big on all three floors of *Rebecca's*. There was a big northern soul night that evening which always pulled around a thousand or so dancers and onlookers. The scooter boys, suede heads and skins turning up on their cut down scooters in large groups from all over the West Midlands to dance into the early hours. Bernard Manning, the Manchester comedian, was also giving one of his infamous performances on the top floor of the same club. Bernard was one of the few performers who was a real friend to Eddie. He realised the extent of Eddie's control over the city, even making fun of the Fewtrell's gangster reputation by joking that,

"If Eddie Fewtrell says it's Christmas, then everyone starts singing carols!" A joke he made whenever he played gigs in Birmingham. Even though Bernard was well known for his racist comedy material, his shows would, somewhat surprisingly always attract a large number of Pakistani and Indian punters from the growing Asian population within the city. During the show, the overweight comedian would often make fun of minority groups within the audience, aimed mainly at the Pakistani's, Indians and Irish who, it must be said, gave the impression of enjoying the experience, during the early 1970s anyhow. Tonight would be no exception. The middle floor was hosting another show by the pop star Gary Raven. Eddie didn't want much to do with the teen idol but the gig had been offered to him for expenses which had seemed very unusual to Eddie. Whatever his reasons, they were none of Eddie's business, his business was making money and tonight business was going to be good.

He finally left the house around 2pm when Kenny, Eddie's driver, arrived to collect him in his pale blue Rolls Royce. Hazel watched the two men standing by the red Alfa Romeo on the driveway, Eddie was laughing at the crumpled front end of the car and she thought she heard Eddie laughing the words,

"I fucking told him!" as he walked around the little Italian sports car. Kenny and Eddie climbed into the Roller and glided out of the driveway and out of sight, Hazel stayed at the window taking in the falling, golden leaves. Autumn was well and truly underway. She ran her mind over the past few months, the summer seemed to have flown by in the blink of an eye. Her mood seemed to reflect the dying trees that lined the road around her house. She sat in the window for ages, lost in her thoughts and the drowsiness the drugs had provided, until finally she turned and picked up the golden phone that sat by the side of her bed. Still gazing through the lead beaded windows she dialled the *Grapes Bar*. The phone was answered by one of the bar staff.

"Can I speak to Hodgy please?" The barmaid held the receiver to her ear without any reaction to the request, she seemed lost in a world of her own.

"Hodgy . . . ?" the voice said again, the barmaid's trance broken.

"Hodgy's in hospital luv." She let the words hang for a second.

"Hospital?" The voice repeated.

"The Q.E Hospital luv, they nearly killed him . . . the police have been here asking questions all day." The girl began to cry as she started to open up. "I said it was them gangsters, the Fewtrells, he was mixed up with them he was . . . I said there's nothing good coming from knowing them Fewtrells, Hodgy. I tried to warn him." Hazel felt a pang of jealousy as she imagined the relationship Hodgy had probably enjoyed with the barmaid and she hung up without saying anything more. Her blood ran cold, a shiver of cold sweat began to creep along her spine and the feeling of being trapped began to take over her once more. Chrissy had obviously betrayed her, but why? Maybe Eddie had found out and paid someone to beat Hodgy up, but if he had he certainly didn't show any emotion whilst he was sat talking to her and Nettie earlier that morning. Then again, Eddie Fewtrell was well known for his poker face and she knew that he was more than capable of organising someone else to do the beating if he so wished. She threw on her clothes in a panic and wrapped a long, leather coat over herself to cover the mis-matched outfit she had hastily thrown together. Without saying anything to Nettie, she grabbed her car keys and began to run out of the house, but as she did so, she caught sight of the phone in the hallway and changed her mind. She picked it up and dialled the office to the *Cedar club*. Chrissy, who was covering the office, answered.

"Hello, *Cedar Club*." Hazel's head swam in a growing rage,

"You fucking arsehole Chrissy," the outburst didn't explain anything, but she wanted to say it again. She wanted to insult the man, to hurt him for the the way he had fooled her into thinking she had a way out without anyone being hurt, "you fucking bastard, you said you wouldn't touch him!" Chrissy didn't get a chance to answer, Hazel slammed the phone down and ran out to her green Mercedes on the drive and floored the accelerator pedal. The long sports car spun its rear wheels on the gravel drive, spraying a shower of stones onto the red sports car that sat behind it.

She drove across town lost in a flurry of thoughts, not really concentrating on her driving. The powerful sports car wheel spinning at traffic lights as she became angrier about Chrissy's betrayal and Eddie's intervention in her happiness. The journey only took ten minutes to the Queen Elizabeth hospital. She didn't bother to park the car properly, just leaving it askew across the large hospital car park. She ran through the main entrance to the victorian hospital and the staff on the reception could see by her dishevelled appearance and disturbed manner that she needed help. She lied that she was a member of Brendan Hodgson's family and a nurse ushered her through to a ward where the young man lay in his hospital bed, in a confusion of tubes and machines.

The room smelt of bleach and seemed sterile. It was painted in a light blue that seemed to match the early evening sky outside the large window that gave a bird's eye view of the surrounding area. Hodgy lay on the bed motionless. His face was bandaged diagonally across one eye and he had tubes coming and going out of each nostril. The skin that wasn't covered by the bandages was a myriad of blue bruises that ran from turquoise under his eye, fading from deep blue to black, as the bruise ran down his cheek and on to his neck.

The nurse stood in the doorway for a second, watching Hazel, she could see that the woman was beautiful but tired and stressed, her body bent and small.

"If there's anything you need I'll be outside, ok?" Hazel nodded blankly. The nurse shut the door softly. Hazel ran her fingers along the bandages delicately, tears began to well up and she sobbed quietly, wondering how Eddie had found out. Chrissy just wasn't the type of man to go back on his word. She picked up his hand, as she did she noticed that even his hands had dark bruises that ran up his arms. Hodgy opened his eyes, or at least the one that wasn't covered by bandages. Hazel let go of his hand, she had assumed he was unconscious.

"Hazel!" he croaked. She picked up his hand again and held it to her lips and kissed it softly, it was stone cold.

"I'm so sorry Hodgy, I didn't realise he would go this far, the bastard." Hodgy looked confused. He shook his head and immediately wished he hadn't, sharp pain ran up his neck and into his hidden eye socket. He grimaced. "Stay still, don't move. This is all my fault, I should never have got involved with you Hodge."

"No." He mumbled, she shook her head.

"I'll get Eddie back for this . . . or was it Chrissy?" She searched his bloated face, he tried to smile but just managed a painful grimace again.

"No . . . it wasn't Eddie." He managed, Hazel nodded.

"So it was Chrissy then, that bastard." Hodgy shook his head tentatively. "Nobby then?" Hazel continued. Hodgy began to run through what he could remember from the night before in his mind, which wasn't much; the beautiful asian girl that had thrown herself at him in the *Grapes bar*, the taxi ride to the party at the big house, the dream like music in the basement club. There were other people there too, men and women. He could remember the writhing, naked bodies all over the floor, he had wanted to leave straight away but the asian girl insisted they stay, serving him drinks, undressing, and obeying his every need, and then the sex, which was beautifully painful and extreme, almost in slow motion. He remembered his head swimming from the drinks and the man in the golden suit, walking amongst the softly moaning lovers as he filmed the events, laughing at the exploits of the ten or so young people indulging in each other's bodies on the rough Persian rug. Different coloured lights making strange ink splat shapes around the walls, the smell of incense mixing with the smell of sex. The images were still fresh in his head.

He looked at Hazel, her large, brown eyes set in her beautiful face. How could he have done this to her? She thought this had all been her fault but the affair, as far as Hodgy was concerned anyway, had always been about getting revenge on her husband for ripping him off with his business venture at *the Grapes*. Of course he couldn't tell Hazel that, if he'd had any true feelings for her he wouldn't have been so eager to go back to the party with the Asian girl, although right now he wished he hadn't. Then there was Trudy the barmaid at the pub, that's who he really fancied. The past six weeks without any contact with Hazel had been a relief if he was honest, yet here she was at his hospital bed. Hodgy shook his head again, this time he let out a little whimper of pain.

"No it wasn't Eddie or Chrissy or any of them," he replied impatiently, Hazel looked at him blankly, he continued, "it was two Pakistani blokes, one of them was huge, I didn't stand a chance." He omitted the part of the story he could remember, where the two asians had cleared the room of young lovers and began beating him mercilessly for no apparent reason, as the others watched on, laughing and occasionally joining in themselves. Whatever he had in his system, presumably from the drinks the girl had given him, hadn't let him pass out, even though his head had taken enough pummelling to knock out a heavyweight boxer, his heart still kept pumping. So he had taken the beating with his mind fully conscious until they had dumped his body on the cold, wet tarmac on a nameless Birmingham road. He had lain there for almost an hour until the dawn clatter of a milk man trundling along in his electric milk cart had awoken him from this semi conscious state and he had managed an agonising call for help.

"Pakistani's?" Hazel suddenly lost her remorse. "You said two Pakistani's Hodgy?"

He nodded, "Did you know them Hodgy?" He shook his head. "Did you owe them money Hodge, seriously?" Once more he shook his head. "Chrissy said that two Asian blokes were following a while back, that's why I've been lying low Hodgy, that's why I haven't been in touch ... I'm sorry." She burst into tears. "You see ... this is what happens if you get involved with me." She searched for the words. "I can't see you any ..." The door to the room opened, Hazel turned to see a young blonde girl standing in the doorway, a look of confusion on her face.

"Who are you?" The girl asked, Hazel turned back to Hodgy. He had closed his eyes again. "Oh you're that old woman Brendan has been telling me about." The girl said spitefully. Hazel turned on her, weighing the situation up instantly.

"I'm thirty five years old luv . . . hardly an old woman am I?" The girl gave a snigger as she shrugged her shoulders.

"Thirty five looks old enough to me *luv.*" The girl answered. "He's too young for an old bird like you." She continued, Hazel looked at Hodgy and gave a sarcastic laugh.

"Well you certainly pulled the wool over my eyes bab . . . well maybe she's right, I am too old for you." She turned to leave but stopped and turned back. "I won't mention this to my husband, because if I do, he'll make the beating you've just had look like a soft body massage." She turned gathering as much dignity as she could. "Goodbye Hodgy." She turned and crossed the room and the girl in the doorway stepped to one side.

"Best get back to the old people's home . . . *luv.*" Without any warning or hesitation, Hazel brought her fist up and punched the girl square on the nose. The girl's face exploded in a fountain of blood that showered her mini dress and knocked her over in the doorway. The girl lay there gurgling pathetically, eyes rolling in her head. Hazel turned back to Hodgy.

"There ya go bab, now you and your little tart are a matching pair." Triumphantly she turned and walked down the corridor back towards the exit and her car. The nurse who had left her in the room didn't recognise her as she approached. The woman she had left next to the injured man was obviously troubled, tired, almost shameful, but this woman was proud, strong and beautiful, she walked through the hospital doors and out into the city as if she owned it.

Tick Tock Tick Tock

Chapter 16

The stolen, white, Cortina van trundled across the back streets of *Bordesley Green* towards the line of council owned, lock up garages. Belfast Jimmy was satisfied that it was now time to step up the game. The smaller explosions the other cells of the IRA had set off had been causing negative publicity for the Irish, but nowhere near as much as he wanted. Anyway thanks to Jimmy's notepad of names, Fletcher had taken almost all of the IRA off the streets of Birmingham and had raided two of their bomb factories, shutting them down for good. But Jimmy had something else in mind.

As the van pulled up in the dingy November twilight one of the garage doors opened slightly, a tall, dark haired, middle aged man peeked out from the shadows. Jimmy turned the van around so that it faced the way it had come in and now faced back towards the only exit to the car park. He got out, leaving the engine running. The man didn't step from the garage as Jimmy approached the door. He handed five white plastic, carrier bags to Jimmy without a word. He took the bags, walked back to the van and opened the back doors and carefully laid them side by side just inside the rear door, before closing it again. He returned to the garage door, the man still hadn't come outside.

"Is everything there?" Jimmy enquired casually.

"Ai . . . everything, the detonators and clocks, the package itself . . . they will need priming though, I take it you know what to do?" Jimmy nodded. "You'll need these too." He held out a small shoe box, lifting the lid. Jimmy looked inside. There were three watches. Jimmy looked at the man and nodded. "They're all synchronised. The package must be in place by five minutes to eight, the delivery man should be out of the way by five to, at the latest. All he has to do is connect the . . ." Jimmy interrupted.

"I know what to do." He said raising his eyebrows.

"Well that's that then." Jimmy held his hand out to the man in the shadows, the man didn't respond to the handshake. He came closer to the door and half whispered.

"Good luck . . . *Tiochfaidh ar la!*" With that the door slammed shut leaving Jimmy standing outside, looking at the peeling, green paint on the old, wooden shuttered door.

"Tiochfaidh ar la." Jimmy repeated the gaelic phrase to himself. "Our day *shall* come."

He climbed back in the van and headed to James Mcdade's house. As he left the housing estate, Jimmy pulled the van to the side of the road, he checked around to make sure he was out of sight of the garages. Then, taking the shoe box from the passenger seat he placed it on his lap and reaching inside he took all three watches. He looked them over, they were identical *Timex* watches, all telling the same time, ten minutes to six. Taking one of the watches, he wrapped the black leather strap around his wrist and looked it over, then he took one of the other two watches and pulled the timing mechanism and turned the minute hands back exactly eight minutes. Then placing the watch in his pocket he shoved the shoe box with the other watch under his seat and drove on.

The roads were still busy after the rush hour but the journey only took around ten minutes. McDade and Ray McLaughlin were waiting nervously for Jimmy. Jimmy had promised the two that they would receive a commission from the IRA top brass in Dublin for their participation in tonight's events. Jimmy knew the commissions were nonsense but it seemed to make the two young men very proud of themselves. McLaughlin climbed into the front seat, the other man sat on cushions that he brought from his house in the back of the van.

"This is it lads, this is the first of our cell's operations." Jimmy was letting the two men know exactly what their target was for the very first time. "You'll be hitting the tax office in Coventry lads." McDade laughed.

"Ai hit em in the pocket ey Jimmy." Jimmy looked at the young man in the rear view mirror. He just smiled and nodded.

The little van travelled along the Coventry road past Elmdon airport. The aeroplanes were lined up in long rows around the little departure lounge. Ray spotted an *Aer Lingus* airplane and gave Jimmy a tap on the shoulder, pointing at the shamrock on the tail wing of the plane, Jimmy didn't bother looking. His mind was on his objectives.

The journey took thirty minutes to the centre of Coventry city. The ruined Cathedral spire standing tall against the cold, starlit night sky, lit up by the yellow lights around its base. A flock of starlings swooped and dived around its great spire, giving the impression that the stone tower was moving in the dark sky. The building had stood witness to much death in its history, some happening inside its very walls, and tonight it would see yet more.

Belfast Jimmy parked the van on the outskirts of the town centre. McDade had been sat in the back of the van on the old sofa cushion and had started to complain about his back being stiff then he began singing softly, a tune he'd known all his life. Jimmy couldn't place it, probably because the song was a *republican* song, a soft Gaelic tune with a sadness in its melody, McLaughlin began to join in.

"Shut the feck up you pair!" Jimmy turned to McDade. "Do you know what you are about to do here sonny?" He gave James an astonished look. "This is no time for sentimentality Jamesy." He reached inside his tweed, sports jacket pocket and produced the watch. "Here take it!" McDade took the timepiece, looking over it. "Put it on son," Jimmy continued, "now that watch is set exactly to the time on the alarm clock connected to the detonator." He turned to Ray then back to McDade to make sure they were both listening. When he saw they were, he continued. "All you have to do is connect the battery at exactly three minutes to eight, then . . . the package is live." Both men nodded, serious looks on their faces. "Once the package is primed you've got three minutes to get clear . . . got it?"

Ray McLaughlin shook his head.

"Package?" Jimmy raised his eyebrows.

"Fecking package . . . the fecking bomb . . . Jesus, Ray." McLaughlin looked concerned suddenly.

"No one's gonna get hurt are they?" Jimmy shook his head in disbelief.

"No . . . no one's gonna get hurt . . . if you two pair of bollocks do the job properly." He pointed at McDade. "Right *Lieutenant* McDade." Jimmy let the title sink in, McDade's face lit up. "You're gonna prime it and you," he turned to McLaughlin, "you're gonna stand next to him and keep watch. Your job, Ray is the most important because you do not . . . want to be disturbed during the priming . . . understand?"

Neither men answered. McLaughlin was disappointed he hadn't received a commission. Jimmy pointed down the road towards the city centre. "Good, now feck off the pair of ye and go and cause some chaos!" James McDade looked at the plastic carrier bags.

"Which one Jimmy?" Jimmy just shrugged.

"That's up to you Jamesy son, choose any of them." McDade clambered across the plywood lined floor of the van and opened the back door, climbing out he took the first bag in the line and walked around to the driver's door. Jimmy wound down the window and McDade crouched down beside the driver's door.

"Just connect the battery . . . three minutes to eight?" He whispered, Jimmy nodded. "You'll be waiting here?"

"Ai, I'll be here . . . engine running." McLaughlin joined Jamesy and the two men said their goodbyes and walked off into the town centre.

* * *

The city centre was almost deserted as the two young men walked through the wet streets with their deadly package. Every now and then they passed an odd couple wandering hand in hand to one of the many pubs that sat at Coventry's heart. McDade searched the street names, looking for the name that Jimmy had told him. Glancing at the *Timex* watch he began to become concerned. The watch said it was fifteen minutes to eight, he was worried that they wouldn't find the tax office before the clock had gone past its priming time. McDade didn't know how to reset the alarm clock so the bomb would become live at a later time and he didn't want to make a fool of himself in front of Belfast Jimmy and Ray. Ray McLaughlin had crossed the road and was searching the brass name plates that gave the names of the businesses that lay on the first floors above the shop fronts that lined the high street. McDade did the same on his side of the road. As he searched for the address he couldn't help looking in the windows of the fashion shops along the road. The mannequins, dressed in the latest fashion of high waisted, flared baggy trousers and short, differently coloured, leather bomber jackets, their blank, expressionless faces stared from the large, pane glass windows. Their gazes seemed to follow him as he walked along the road, the only witnesses to his treason and once or twice he caught a glimpse of his reflection. The sight of which made him question what the hell he was doing and how had he got mixed up in all this, he had to stop himself from thinking about the situation in order to calm his nerves.

"Connect the battery and leave, you'll be reading about it in the papers by tomorrow morning." He said softly to himself. Suddenly a short whistle came from the other side of the street. McLaughlin had found the tax office. The whistle had snapped Jamesy out of his day dream and he crossed the road, carrier bag in hand. The tax office was in the middle of a terraced block, its entrance sat in a shallow recess that would give the bombers some cover whilst McDade primed the explosive. James glanced at his watch. He had three minutes before he had to prime the package. The two men stood casually in the doorway, adrenaline pumped through their veins and it was difficult to control the urge to just dump the bomb and run for it. McLaughlin lit a cigarette, took a drag and passed it to McDade who took it greedily and drew the smoke inside him in a long, deep breath.

"Go check the cross roads, make sure no one's coming, I'll set the primer and meet you back at the van." McLaughlin nodded and crossed the road, heading back the way he'd come towards the large crossroads that lay twenty yards away. Standing on the corner he searched left and right, his eyes scanned the high street but there was nothing. He turned back towards McDade who was crouched over the plastic bag. McLaughlin walked towards him. When he got twenty feet away he could hear Jamesy McDade humming softly, it was the same song he had been singing in the van earlier. That same sad tune from their childhood in Eire. McLaughlin took the fag from his mouth and flicked it into the gutter.

"I love that song Jamesy, what's it called?" McDade didn't answer, his expression had suddenly changed, a look of shock on his face as he looked at the time on the silver alarm clock that sat in the bag and then checked the watch on his wrist. He turned towards McLaughlin confused, he began to say something.

We shall never know what Lieutenant James McDade was about to say, because, instead of words came death. McLaughlin saw his friend's mouth open but the words were replaced buy a huge explosion that ripped the poor man to pieces in a cloud of smoke and body parts, mercifully it was all over in a second. A second that left a blood red mist floating on the air and a ringing in McLaughlin's ears. The man stood there, watching what was left of his friend float away on the cold breeze, his body parts filled the doorway which had turned from its limestone yellow to a mixture of black burn marks and blood stains. McLaughlin stood there for almost a full minute. Unable to tear his eyes away from the horror in the doorway to the tax office. His mind was having trouble processing the fact that, one second his friend had been there staring at him eye to eye, his whole life in front of him, and now he had simply vanished. The soft Irish tune replaced by a deafening high pitched ringing.

As the ringing in his ears slowly subsided, McLaughlin became aware that he was wet, he looked down at himself, his trousers were a deep red colour. He ran his hands over his soaking face. He drew them back and held them out in front of him, they were bright red, covered in blood and small pieces of a gristly matter, at first he thought that it was *his* blood, from some unknown injury, but after a few seconds he realised the dark red bloody matter that was dripping down his face, into his eyes and his mouth, was actually, his friend.

* * *

Belfast Jimmy heard the explosion, his *Timex* told the exact time the bomb was due to go off and he counted down the seconds 5.4.3.2.1 BOOM! He mouthed the words as what sounded like a clap of summer thunder broke across the cold November sky. He turned the key to the van and wound his window down. He watched the scene for a minute or so, he was just about to turn the van around and drive back to Birmingham, when, in the distance he saw a man running. He didn't recognise the man at first. He was tall and looked familiar, and as the man drew nearer he could see it was Ray, but this man was the wrong colour. In the yellow street lights he looked like a black man, or at least a white man with a blacked out face, almost like the black and white minstrel show buffoons that were so popular on British TV, ridiculous white rings around his panicked eyes. Jimmy watched as the man drew closer. Then blue flashing lights and the familiar nee-nah of police sirens came into earshot. Jimmy twisted the steering wheel and turned the car, putting his foot down on the accelerator he drove away in the opposite direction to the man. He glanced in the rear view mirror. The man had stopped running at the sight of the van leaving. Jimmy smiled as he watched Ray McLaughlin who just collapsed onto his knees pathetically, the blue flashing lights bearing down upon him.

* * *

As he drove back to Birmingham, he reflected on the night's events. He felt sorry about McDade, he was a nice guy, but sacrifices had to be made. Ray McLaughlin and McDade had to be removed from the situation one way or another. They were too worried about civilian casualties, and if he was going to complete his objectives and destroy the IRA grass roots support by discrediting them to the world, then things were going to get worse not better. The last thing he needed was two idealistic, soft hearted Paddies crying in his ear about innocent people getting hurt.

"You can't fight a war with one hand tied behind your back." He thought to himself. His boss Ronnie Fletcher understood that, but, seemed to have got cold feet as soon as Jimmy had become the lone wolf.

Ray's close encounter with death had created another problem. Ray McLaughlin wasn't a real IRA man. He was one of the dreamers that talked of the poetry of war, without ever wanting to get his hands dirty. Well now he was covered in the filth of the Irish wars and the police were going to have a field day with him. Unfortunately, McLaughlin hadn't been standing next to Jamesy when the bomb had gone off as he was told to, if he had of been, then Jimmy wouldn't have had any questions to answer to anyone.

"There's no fecking *way* he won't talk." Jimmy said aloud to himself, mulling over the problems created by McLaughlin's survival. The bombing campaign Jimmy had in mind would have to be brought about sooner than he'd planned. He didn't see it as a problem, more of a motivation to give the new IRA recruits he would use on the next job, a good kick up the arse. Of course there would be questions about what had gone wrong with the detonation of the bomb in Coventry, but that could be easily explained away with McDade's inexperience. By the time anyone would get to talk to Ray, be it the police or the IRA, Jimmy's mission would be over and he would be just another faceless name to the IRA command and a bad, unmentionable memory to Ronnie Fletcher.

"There was an English bloke, Irish bloke and a Paki . . ."

Chapter 17

Bernard Manning arrived at Rebecca's night club around six pm. Eddie met him at the stage door and gave him a strong handshake and friendly slap on the shoulder.

"Good journey Bernard?" Eddie asked the large man as he stepped into the club backstage area.

"Fucking lovely Eddie," he turned and pointed at the baby blue Rolls Royce he had turned up in, "see that Eddie . . . that's British engineering at its best, I could've driven to Hong-fucking-Kong in that beauty and still got out fresh as a daisy." He turned back and continued inside to the dark, backstage area. "Many tickets sold Eddie?" Eddie laughed.

"You're fucking sold out . . . have been for weeks, since you been on the telly we've sold loads, done the world of good for you lot, that *Comedians* show." They both walked through the club, making small talk and jokes until Eddie reached the plush VIP dressing room on the top floor. The venue was a horseshoe shaped affair with the stage in the middle of the room and a dance floor in front of the stage. Eddie had covered the dance floor in tables, each of which had a candle in the centre, giving the place an intimate, Vegas style atmosphere cleverly disguising the disco it really was.

After Bernard was made comfortable Eddie returned to the front door of the club where Nobby, the doorman was giving his market stall spiel to the growing crowd lining up to enter the club.

"Come on girls and boys!" Shouted Nobby above the busy noise of the traffic. "Three floors of fun, a pound per floor, three floors: three quid." His loud, cheeky voice, huge frame and massive smile gave the front door a carnival feel as he entertained the waiting crowds. To the good looking lads he made vulgar double entendres which usually embarrassed his young victims and gave a good laugh to everyone else queuing. Eddie often joined him on the door and tonight was no exception. Eddie looked down the line which was already stretching around the corner towards the Navigation fish bar and on to John Bright Street.

The line for the northern soul night wouldn't get busy until gone 10 pm so the scooter boys, skinheads, blacks and pill popping dancers wouldn't be showing up for a while. The queue for Gary Raven on the other hand, much to Eddie's surprise was nearly non existent, made up of only about thirty or forty girls and the odd embarrassed boyfriend. They were all wearing Raven's tell tale, glitter outfits and ridiculously high platform boots. Some of the young girls were of questionable age but as there was no laws about checking IDs their entry was down to the doorman's discretion. The Bernard Manning show was going to be a relatively early one, starting around nine thirty. The man was an old, show business trooper and would probably continue for at least and hour and a half maybe even two, depending on how pissed the audience were, and Eddie was going to make sure they were totally hammered. Eddie expected his crowd to be the first to show up and he wasn't disappointed. Small groups of older, middle aged men and women arrived in taxis and pig nosed, Ford transit mini buses from all over the city. Eddie was always there to meet and greet.

Birmingham on a Saturday night in the 1970s had a certain buzz about it. The city didn't have the glitz of London's West End, but it did have a charm that came from the fact it was so compact; over a million people in the surrounding areas all came into the city on a weekend to celebrate. Old friends weren't hard to bump into and with the Brummy temperament the way it was, new friends weren't hard to make. The fact it was the second city gave its population a defensive, protective nature towards the city, a 'we're all in this together' approach to life, as it were. Eddie, Hazel and all the other Fewtrells knew this and used it subconsciously to their best advantage. The friendly handshake and big smile on the door from the famous Eddie Fewtrell was something the working man wouldn't forget and it brought the punters back week after week.

"Where's our Chrissy, Nobby, he's meant to be here tonight?" Nobby just shrugged.

"Ain't seen him Ed." Was his short reply.

"Probably that fucking car our Gordon sold him ... broke fucking down again ain't it!" Eddie said laughing, the fact that Chrissy had sold the motor on after it had been written off in September didn't make any difference to Eddie. He knew it was a sore point with Chrissy and any chance to have a pop at Gordon's self reliance was fair game to him.

Nobby just shrugged again, hands dug deep inside his Crombie pockets. The crowds began to arrive in bigger numbers now and the night had become increasing colder. The clear, black sky showed bright stars between the high rise buildings, it looked as if they would get the first frost of the year before dawn.

"Let em in Nobby," Eddie ordered, "they look fucking freezing." Nobby reached down to a red cord that hung between two silver stands and gestured the Gary Raven fans to enter the club. Normally the customers would have been let in as they arrived but Gary Raven had insisted they shouldn't be let in until the sound check had finished. Eddie had noticed that the musicians and roadies were more interested in drinking their free beer and food rider than setting up any equipment. He had intervened when one of the roadies tried to drag one of the barmaids into the band's dressing room by grabbing the man's greasy long hair and slapping him open handed around his face a few times, before giving him a kick up the arse and a warning never to touch his staff again. The roadie had scampered off to the dressing room not to emerge again until well after the show got under way.

* * *

Hazel drove through the busy town centre towards *Rebecca's* Club. Hodgy's betrayal had been a shock and made her feel like a dumb school girl but there was nothing she could do about that now, she would swallow her pride and go and see Chrissy to apologise about her outburst. Hazel had jumped to the obvious conclusion about Hodgy's beating, blaming it squarely on Eddie or one of his henchmen and now she must set things right with Chrissy. She prayed that her brother in law hadn't got the hump with her and as a consequence informed her husband about her indiscretions. There was also the matter of the real perpetrators, the men in the blue transit van and especially the big Pakistani, Chrissy would *certainly* want to know about that. The roads were busy with buses and taxis bringing people home after their Saturday excursions around the *Bull Ring* shopping centre and early drinkers being brought into town from the outskirts. She pulled on to Hill street and swung the Mercedes into the old bomb site behind the *Navigation fish bar* that had acted as a make shift car park for nearly thirty years. Chrissy was standing beside the entrance to the car park, half hiding behind one of the large, blue bus stops that lined both sides of the road. He was peering into the car park but kept ducking behind the bus shelter. She gave a short beep on the car's horn. He turned with a little jump, she pulled alongside him and wound her driver's window down.

"Looking a bit suspicious there Chrissy." She smiled. "We need to talk bab." He ducked low and left the cover of the bus shelter and came around the other side of her car and climbed into the passenger seat.

"Don't park in there . . . stick it in one of the parking spaces under the flyover over there!" He pointed to the new, council car park which was virtually empty, underneath the flyover that carried the beginning of the Bristol road, sixty feet above. She looked at him like he was mad.

"I'm gonna park where I always park Chrissy, behind the fish bar . . . it's free there and won't get vandalised." Chrissy slammed his hand on the dash board.

"Just do it Haze . . . do it now or they'll see us!"

"Who'll . . . ?" she asked. Chrissy shouted.

"Just fucking do it Haze . . . *now!*" Hazel looked at him incredulously, then pushed the automatic gear lever into drive and pulled the car around, she drove back along the way she had come and into the council parking spaces.

"It's gonna get broken in to here." She said, Chrissy stopped her.

"Remember I told you about the blue transit van a couple of months ago?" Hazel butted in.

"I know Chrissy . . . the big Pakistani bloke." Chrissy turned his attention away from the car park.

"What do you know?" Hazel put her hand on his.

"I'm sorry about calling you those names bab. I thought you and Eddie had done Hodgy over and I . . ." Chrissy turned to her.

"What . . . what do you mean done Hodgy over?" Hazel turned away from him, she just stared out of the front windscreen.

"I finished with him Chrissy." She was more upset than she thought she'd be by saying it but managed to hide her feelings, she chose to omit the part about Hodgy and the barmaid. "I was stupid and I should've known better, he was just a kid and I shouldn't have got involved . . ." Chrissy stopped her.

"Someone beat up Hodgy?" Chrissy said with a confused scowl. "Well let me tell you Haze, that was fuck all do with me or Eddie . . . as a matter of fact Eddie hasn't got a clue about any of this, I haven't said a word . . . I promised you and I never go back on my word . . . you should know that. Anyway Hazel, this is all gonna have to wait. I've just spotted those Pakistani blokes who smashed up my car and threatened to shoot me." Hazel continued.

"Well that's what I'm trying to tell ya, it was those bastards that beat Hodgy up. They put him in hospital. He's in a right state Chrissy." Chrissy shook his head.

"Why . . . why would *they* beat him up Hazel?" She shook her head. "Why would they beat him up and more importantly why are they now waiting here in the car park around the back of *Rebecca's*?" Hazel opened her door. "I'm gonna have it out with these bastards!" Before Chrissy could say anything she had stepped from the car and was walking across the car park towards the old bomb site. Chrissy leapt from the car,

"Stop Hazel!" She turned back towards him arms folded.

"Come on let's get these bastards Chrissy!" He came beside her and put his arms on her shoulders.

"No Hazel, stop! . . . there's more to this than meets the eye, I mean first they're following you and Hodgy, then the bastards are threatening to fucking shoot me! Somethings going on Haze, I've got a real bad feeling about this." Hazel shrugged and raised her eyebrows in frustration.

"Yeah . . . so let's go and fucking have em." Chrissy ran his eyes over the woman in front of him, her beautiful dark eyes, olive skin, long jet black hair and slight figure belied the wolf within. He knew she could give as good as she got, but this Pakistani gang were different from than anything he'd seen before. Yes he'd had guns pulled on him, God knows how many times, mainly by local villains and on the odd occasion, by a full blown East end gangster or two but this lot seemed to be vicious, organised and had cash behind them; sub machine guns don't come cheap, even the IRA had stopped using them due to the costs and easy traceability. In truth, the Pakistani gun man had scared him and Chrissy Fewtrell didn't get scared too often.

"Let's just watch and see what they're up to." He gestured with a nod of his head. "Follow me!" He grabbed Hazel by the elbow and guided her across the empty brightly lit, council car park to the darkness of the old bomb site behind the Navigation fish bar.

At first they couldn't see anything in the dim light. The Victorian buildings that surrounded the bomb site stood tall in silhouette against the yellow street lights on Hill street, causing the old buildings to cast long shadows across the muddy ground. Chrissy and Hazel stepped into one of these shadows and waited for their eyes to become accustomed to the darkness, slowly the layout of the car park became clearer and the blue van could be seen along the old, brick wall to the rear of the car park. They waited and watched in the growing coldness.

"Have you spoken to Dixie about any of this?" Hazel whispered, she looked at Chrissy, she couldn't actually see him but could tell he was shaking his head. She continued. "Well we should get him to put a trace on the number plate of that van then at least we'd know where they're based." As she said the words a black, long wheeled based Mercedes Ambassador rolled silently into the car park and pulled up beside the blue van.

"Who's that then?" Chrissy whispered, as the car stopped the light came on in the cab of the transit van and both of them could make out Haroom's huge frame. Hazel tugged on Chrissy's elbow. The car's door opened and a man in a sparkling, silver suit got out of the passenger door. As he did Haroom climbed from the transit. At first Hazel and Chrissy couldn't see who the sparkly man was until he stepped in front of the car headlights. His silver suit jacket and trousers burst into light. The shiny, silver material reflected the car's head lights, the sequins sending tiny beams of light into every corner of the car park.

"That's Gary fucking Raven!" Chrissy said in a stifled cry, they watched as the silver man crossed to Haroom and the two men talked together for a minute.

"Come on let's get closer." Hazel said as she began to shuffle along the shadows, Chrissy grabbed her coat collar.

"Woah, where do you think you're fucking going? We're just gonna stay here."

"But I can't hear em!" She complained.

"It don't matter Haze . . . just watch." After a minute the big man turned back to the van, he reached inside of the cab and after a few seconds retuned to Gary Raven with a small brown package. He handed it to the silver man who in turn looked the package over and bounced it in his hand a few times. When Haroom saw him doing this he stepped forward and grabbed Gary's hand.

"NO!" Hazel and Chrissy heard that!

"What the fuck is in that package?" Chrissy half whispered. Just then a plump man with a short, grey beard stepped out of the black Mercedes and said something to the Pakistani. Hazel and Chrissy couldn't see who he was but Gary Raven turned towards the plump man and gestured for him to get back in the car and leave. The man stood silently for a second before climbing into his car and starting the engine of the long, black Mercedes reversed it out of the car park. As he did so the car's head lights swept along the old, brick wall and Hazel and Chrissy became illuminated. Chrissy saw it coming and grabbed Hazel around the waist and pulled her into him. He wrapped his arms around her, pulled her against the wall and kissed her. The car stopped as the head lights caught the couple in their glow. Hazel began to struggle away from Chrissy.

"Ear . . . what's your game?" She asked angrily.

"Shut up and kiss me!" He ordered her and realising why, she did as he asked. After what felt like an eternity but in reality was only a second or two, the car reversed out onto the busy street and was gone. Chrissy let her go, "Sorry Haze." She giggled,

"Fucking hell our Chrissy, that was a bit awkward!" He laughed, then stopped as he noticed that the men beside the van were on the move. Gary Raven took the packet and slipped it inside his jacket pocket and leaving the Pakistani beside the van he turned and walked across the car park, dodging the muddy puddles as he went. They watched him walk out of sight on to main road towards *Rebecca's*. Chrissy turned to Hazel.

"Follow him Hazel, find out what he's doing with that package! I'll watch this big arsed bastard." Hazel nodded and followed the shadow along the wall until she reached the yellow lit road where she took up the Gary Raven trail.

Chrissy remained in the hiding spot and waited, Haroom crossed to another car, one he hadn't noticed before. Chrissy couldn't make out what type it was because the shadows along the opposite wall were just as dark as the one he stood in himself. Haroom bent down to the driver's window, a light came on inside the car to reveal two men; one white, one asian. Chrissy crouched down and scampered across the car park, making sure to keep a car between him and the other men. He managed to get three cars away without being seen, slowly he poked his head over the long bonnet of a ford Capri enabling him to see the men talking, only twenty feet away. The big man blocked the driver from sight but he could see the other man quite clearly. He was an older man, maybe in his early forties, his hair immaculately combed back in a black quiff that had turned slightly grey at the ears. He wore a shiny, mohair, mandarin collar jacket that gave him the appearance of an asian prince. He was talking dismissively to the big man who seemed subservient to his master. The Asian prince waved his hand towards the van and with that the big Pakistani had stood up and crossed to the van. Chrissy's gaze followed him until the engine was started on the other car. As the head and tail lights came on, Chrissy could see it was a brown, Rover saloon and to his amazement he recognised the man in the driver's seat.

"Ronnie-fuckin-Fletcher!" He said to himself, he needed to see no more than that and he began to retrace his steps, creeping back the way he'd come towards the main road. Suddenly he heard the unlocking and metallic creek of a door behind him, then another, he turned towards the sound. He could see that the big man was holding the rear doors to the transit van open, gesturing angrily at people to get out. Slowly, men began to climb stiffly from the back doors of the transit, until there was a group of maybe eight or ten men standing and stretching their legs in a huddle at the back of the van. To Chrissy's amazement one of the group was naked girl. At first he thought she was prostitute, but the big Pakistani came behind her and grabbed her hair. The men started to laugh, Haroom slapped the poor girl who started to sob. Chrissy could see by the headlights of the Rover she was covered in bruises. The big man slapped her around the face and dragged her back to the van where he pushed her, unceremoniously into the back of the van, before slamming the doors. Haroom turned and offered cigarettes to the group, passing the white packet from man to man. Chrissy began to head towards the main road but the Rover pulled forward towards the men, stopping just in front of them. Chrissy could see the asian prince in the passenger seat roll his window down, he addressed the man,

"You all know what to do," the men all nodded subserviently, including Haroom. He continued, "you will be paid handsomely." He smiled, Ronnie Fletcher butted in.

"And if you *don't* do what Mr Khan has asked you to do . . . I'll be calling at your houses with my friends from Her Majesty's immigration services with some deportation papers on each and every fucking one of you . . . and your fucking families . . . so don't fuck around!" The two men sat and watched the group walk across the car park. Chrissy couldn't move because the car head lights were shinning on exactly the spot he was hiding in. Chrissy sat there helplessly. The two men were smoking and talking in the Rover for around five minutes when finally the grind of gears signalled the car was leaving and as soon as the head lights shifted from Chrissy's hiding place, he was gone, racing around the corner to the club, hoping it wasn't too late to warn Eddie.

* * *

Hazel ran along John Bright street trying to catch up with the pop star. She could see him turning left at the end of the road into crowd that were waiting at the doorway to *Rebecca's*. He stopped in the doorway and began to sign autographs for the young girls who squealed with excitement at the sight of him. Nobby and Eddie ushered the pop star through the growing crowds through the small double front doors that led to the receptionist and the cloakroom. Gary Raven shook himself free from grabbing hands and sprinted up the stairs two at a time. Hazel took advantage of the crowd, head down, she managed to walk right past Eddie and the doorman into the reception to the club, without being noticed. She wasn't avoiding her husband for any other reason than that she just didn't have time to explain everything and had to keep up with Gary Raven. She nodded at the receptionist who smiled and tried to make small talk with her but she held her finger up to her lips and winked at the young girl through the little hatch before continuing upstairs. Raven had vanished into the labyrinth of corridors and rooms around the club. Customers were to-ing and fro-ing around the floors in excited moods, large groups were gathered around the bars, chatting and smoking. The cigarette smoke added to the atmosphere which was electric with anticipation for the live acts that were just about to start. Hazel walked through to the main room which was only half full, she stood in the doorway, watching the northern soul dancers spin and float across the talc dusted, dance floor before scanning the room for the tell tale glittery suit. The northern soul boys wore an unusual dress code of long leather coats, brightly coloured vests above super wide, high waisted trousers and flat nosed rouge shoes or trainers.

"No silver suits here." She thought turning she went downstairs again and into the smaller room where Gary's band had just finished sound checking. She crossed the room as the young girls crowded around the front of the stage. The roadies walked around the black stage self importantly, showing off in front of the young teeny boppers. She walked around to the side doors that led back stage and pulled the door. There were two, scruffy roadies there, sat on flight cases smoking and drinking from brown bottles of pale ale.

"Nah I don't think so love!" One of the doormen blocked her access with his arm, Hazel's head swam with rage.

"Move your fucking arm you little bastard before I rip your greasy, fucking head off!" The roadie stepped aside, shocked at the slight woman's instant aggression. She continued through to the back stage area where she started to check the dressing rooms. She saw the familiar face of John Tully, one of Birmingham's best band promotors, he was sat on a plastic chair writing something on the back of an old beer mat. "John." Hazel said over the music being played through the PA system out front of the club, he turned with a start.

"Hazel." he said smiling. He rose from the chair and gave her a peck on the cheek.

"Have you seen Gary Raven?" She half shouted.

"Nah ... I'm trying to work out the band's performance slots." He pointed at the roadies who had started drinking again following Hazel's outburst. "These lot are fucking useless Haze ... they've been here all fucking day and done fuck all, it's like they've never seen a PA rig before." He said, shaking his head.

"Yeah they seem useless enough . . . but where's Gary Raven?"
she asked again. Tully just shrugged.

"Your guess is as good as mine Haze . . . he didn't show up for
the sound check, not that that was any fucking good with this lot!"

"So he's definitely not here?" Tully just shook his head.

"Sorry Hazel . . . ask Eddie, he might know?" She just smiled,
turned and left the way she'd came past the roadies.

"You're here to work, not fucking drink . . . useless bastards!"

There was only one more floor. She retraced her steps to the
back of the venue. The crowd had grown whilst she had been back
stage. As she walked through the room the sight of the glittering
kids dancing to the DJ under the light beams that shone from the
huge glitter ball hanging from the ceiling above the dance floor,
gave the place a surreal feel, like something from a cheap, science
fiction movie. She continued along the corridor and then climbed
the stairs to the top floor that was acting as the cabaret room for
the Bernard Manning show. The room was full, standing room
only. Large groups of laughing men and women sat around the
tables or stood at the bar waiting for the big man to appear on the
small stage. Bernard's band were playing a selection of hits from
the sixties on the Hammond organ and drums. The background
music sounded old fashioned but somehow seemed to fit the event
perfectly. Hazel scanned the room, nothing, she wandered along
the bar front, searching the large crowd, recognising the odd face
here and there, saying hello but avoiding conversation. As she
reached the far end of the room there was still no sign of the pop
star. She racked her brain as to where he could be. Hazel decided
to start from the bottom of the building again and work her way
up through each floor, step by step until she found him, but just
as she turned to walk back along the bar, something caught her
eye which stopped her in her tracks. There was a group of around
eight men who had just entered the venue, eight Pakistani men
led by the big brute she had seen ten minutes ago in the car park
with Chrissy. She stepped back into the cover of a group of men
who were chatting.

"Belle!" She smiled knowing who it was, even before she turned to face him. The voice belonged to the youngest Fewtrell brother, Bomber. He always used that name when addressing Hazel and was the only person that ever did. They had a relationship akin to that of mother and son as she had known him since he was a wee lad. She breathed a sigh of relief.

"Bomber, thank God!" Hazel grabbed his arm "Have you seen that Gary Raven bloke around?" Bomber was chatting with the doorman Tony Merrick, who was still smarting after his run in with the six dwarfs the previous week.

"Gary Raven?" he said, "He was stood outside the office Haze . . . I thought he was waiting for Eddie or something." Hazel nodded then glanced back at the big Pakistani and the group of men who had followed him into the room. They had grouped around Haroom and were checking out the audience and bar area. They seemed more interested in each other than what was going on around them.

"See them over there Bomber?" Hazel gestured over her shoulder towards the eight men. Bomber looked across the room,

"Who, the Pakistanis?" Hazel nodded.

"Keep an eye on them for me, there's gonna be trouble tonight!" Tony looked across at the asians.

"Jesus . . . look at the size of that big fella, he's even bigger than Nobby!" Bomber nodded. "Fucking hell . . . if it kicks off tonight, Nobby can deal with that bastard!" He said astonished at the man's size. Bomber quipped.

"He's a bit too big for you ain't he Tony, I've heard you're only good with dwarfs." Both men laughed before returning to their drinks and Bomber promised Hazel he would keep an eye on the group. Hazel followed the wall around the club until she came to the entrance to the corridor that ran along to the office space at the top of the club. As she walked towards the offices, Gary Raven stepped out of the office door. She turned away instantly and began reading a poster on one of the corridor walls. The man in the silver suit stepped out of the office cautiously and walked past her, then descended the stairs to the first floor where he was due onstage. As soon as he was out of sight Hazel stepped into the office. The door was usually locked but by chance was left unlocked. She expected to see Eddie in his big, leather arm chair behind his desk as that's the only reason she could think of as to why Gary Raven would be in the office, and so was surprised to see the room empty.

"What was he doing in here on his own then?" She said the question out loud to herself. The image of the big Pakistani handing Gary the package ran through her mind and it didn't take too long to put two and two together. Crossing the room she stepped behind the old, oak desk and looked around the room at the messy filing cabinets, shelves, desk and draws. "Fuck this I'm gonna have it out with this little *pop star.*"

She stormed out of the office and began to half run down the stairs after the silver suited, glam rock star. The club was full of people arriving and milling around, chatting and drinking. She pushed through the throngs of customers and was about to take the second set of stairs down to the ground floor when she caught a glimpse of something shiny at the end of the first floor corridor. She stopped, trying to peer through the milling people. Then she saw him clearly, leaning against the wall under the large, transparent, fibreglass bubble, that covered the customer pay phone. Hazel strode through the crowd, her gaze unbroken. He was standing with his back to her, speaking into the black handset. She slowed her approach and came in close behind him and leaning her head around the bubble she listened in to the man's animated conversation.

"Yeah . . . all done . . . no, top floor . . ." The man turned to face the opposite wall, Hazel shifted herself back against the wall and tried to look casual as if just waiting to use the phone. He was looking at a picture of himself on a poster, advertising tonight's show. He crossed the narrow corridor and stroked the picture, leaving the privacy of the fibre glass bubble. "I ain't fucking bothered about playing the show anyhow . . . it's not like I'm getting fucking paid is it!" Hazel didn't need to lean in anymore she could hear him easily, she turned away from him and looked down the corridor towards the busy stairwell, as she did Gary Raven turned to face her. He ran his eyes up and down her body, taking in her slim figure. He had no idea who she was, so continued his conversation, "Yeah like I said, top floor, in the green filing cabinet at the back of the middle drawer and listen . . ." She noticed a change in his voice, "I've done what you wanted me to so now I want them fucking films, understand?" Whoever he was talking to began laughing so hard that even Hazel could hear the thin, crackly voice on the other end of the receiver. "What's so fucking funny Fletcher?" Hazel flinched at the name. She had trouble stopping herself from snatching the receiver away from him and pummelling the handset into his head.

"The bastard's setting us up!" She said to herself. She turned back towards the stairs, as she did so Gary spoke again.

"Look it's there, all you got to do is find it. The sooner you show up, the sooner I can get back to London and out of this shit hole. She crossed the room to the stairwell and began to walk down the steps towards the front door just as Gary Raven passed her, hurrying down to the ground floor venue to the safety of the backstage area. She followed him to the bottom of the stairs but turned towards the front door of the club. She looked through it and out into the street, Chrissy was outside, talking in an earnest manner to his older brother, Eddie. She joined them outside and Eddie looked shocked to see her,

"Haze what you doing here, who's looking after the kids?' She completely ignored his question and anxiously addressed Chrissy.

"I've just heard Gary Raven on the blower to Ronnie Fletcher . . . we're gonna get raided!" Chrissy could see the look of concern on her face. Eddie kept his usual cool.

"Fuck him Haze, let em raid us there's fuck all anyone can do . . . we've got all the licenses and . . ." She butted in.

"Ed I ain't got the time to explain . . . Gary Raven has . . ." Chrissy stopped her, an alarmed expression spreading across his face.

"*The package.*" He said finally making the connection. "That bastard's planted something and now we're gonna get a police raid!" Eddie looked on as if the pair of them had lost their marbles.

"What the fuck are you two talking about?" Chrissy turned to Eddie.

"Right Ed . . . listen up, that group of Pakistanis I was telling you about," Eddie nodded, "they're in the club and they are mixed up in all this somehow, we saw them talking to Gary Raven and giving him some sort of package, it looked well dodgy"

Hazel interjected.

"They're on the top floor, in the Bernard Manning show." Eddie shook his head,

"So what, we always get a few Pakistanis and Indians showing up for Bernard's shows and that package could've been *anything*. You two are worrying about nothing as usual!" She could see Eddie was in denial about the situation and turned back to Chrissy,

"There's no point in explaining it to him Chrissy we ain't got time, bab. Bomber and Tony are upstairs keeping an eye on those Pakistanis, the most important thing is that we find that package before the old bill show up." Finally the penny dropped and Eddie was beginning to realise there *was* a reason why he had been offered the pop star for free.

"Drugs," he said suddenly, his voice loosing his normal charm and becoming deadly serious, "that little cunt Raven has planted drugs on the premises. Fletcher's always been desperate to nick me and now he's making his move." Hazel and Chrissy looked at each other. "He knows we've got a zero drugs tolerance policy and what better way to discredit me than to plant some drugs in one of my clubs."

"Well fuck me Sherlock . . . you've managed to work that out pretty fast our kid." Chrissie said sarcastically, Eddie smiled, ignoring the dig.

"It'll be a cold day in hell before that toe rag pulls the wool over my eyes, I can tell ya that!" Eddie turned to Nobby who had been standing within earshot, taking in the whole story. "Nobby, Chrissy, get upstairs and throw them Pakistani blokes out on their arses. I don't know who they are, but fuck em off out the door sharpish. Me and Hazel will go and search the . . ." At that moment the sound of police sirens filled John Bright street, as several marked police cars and the undercover, brown Rover pulled into the street from different directions.

"Fucking hell!" Eddie turned to Hazel, "Go, go, go ..." he said, gesturing that she should get inside and find the package. Nobby followed her and they began climbing the stairs as the road outside filled with police cars, their blue, flashing lights illuminating the narrow road, the sound of the deafening sirens bounced around between the red brick buildings creating a feeling of chaos and panic.

Hazel raced upstairs towards the office followed by the huge door man. As they reached the top floor Hazel broke away down the narrow corridor that led to the office. Nobby carried straight on into the cabaret room.

Hazel stepped inside the cramped office and switched on the long, florescent light that stretched the whole length of the ceiling. The light flickered a few times before bursting into a bright glow that illuminated everything in the small room. She shut the door behind her. The desk sat in front of the green filing cabinet that Raven had mentioned to Fletcher on the phone, its four drawers were shut. She ran through the conversation she had overheard.

"Back of the middle drawer." Gary Raven's words played through her mind. She looked at the cabinet and counted aloud. "One, two, three, four, there's four drawers ... there is no middle one." She crossed the room and knelt down in front of the old, green filing cabinet and drew out the drawer that sat above the bottom one. The metal shelf slid out silently on its rollers. The brown paper files stacked tightly full of receipts, bills, newspaper clippings and music artist photos packed the drawer. She pulled the brown files towards her, they slid along their rails with a screech of metal until there was a gap at the back of the cabinet. She reached inside, blindly sliding her hand this way and that, desperately searching for the package. She felt nothing at first, then her hands found something small like a folded envelope. Hazel pulled her hand back excitedly. She held the envelope up in front of her face, *Durex* . "Ugh," She flicked the packet away from her as if it were a poisonous spider. The little packet landed on the floor, feet away. She stared at it for a second, then uncontrollably she reached across for it, grabbing it in her hand. Her curiosity taking control of her senses, she flipped the envelope open, empty. "The bastard!" She threw the condom packet at the wall and continued searching and cursing under her breath.

Eddie and Chrissy were blocking the entrance to the club. The street had filled with a mixture of coppers and passers by, who, attracted by the huge commotion, had started to gather all along the road, blocking many of the police from getting to the venue. Not only that but the army of police vehicles had started to cause a long tailback that had begun to spread out on to the busy Bristol road. The cars, taxis and buses all beeping their horns adding to the cacophony of sirens. Fletcher stood eye to eye with Eddie, several policemen standing behind him, long black truncheons in hand.

"What's this all about then Fletcher?" Eddie asked, trying to buy time for Hazel.

"You'll see Fewtrell ... you'll see." At that moment Chrissy saw some faces he recognised amongst the growing crowd. One of the men shouted across the top of one the police cars. An ugly man with a spiders web tattooed across his face and empty spaces where his teeth used to be.

"Fucking hell ... can this night get any worse?" Chrissy said under his breath, Eddie turned to him and followed his stare.

"Alright Fewtrell ... having trouble with Old Bill are we?" Eddie turned to Fletcher.

"This your idea is it?" Fletcher just gave a sarcastic laugh and stepped back, assured by the fact that Haroom and his men were about to kick off upstairs, thus keeping whatever doormen Eddie had to help him otherwise occupied, leaving the two Fewtrell brothers to fight the Meat Market Mob on their own.

"Alright lads ... give em space!" The policemen stepped back behind their cars.

"Stone me Fletcher ... the fucking Meat Market Mob?" He laughed. "You must be fucking desperate." Chrissy and Eddie were staring at the seven or eight men emerging from the crowd. They came forwards between the police cars, rough and scruffy scrappers from the back streets of *Highgate* and the red light district of *Balsall Heath*.

"I thought we'd seen the last of you cunts the last time we gave you a good battering . . . back for more?" Eddie turned to Chrissy and gave him an apprehensive smile, Chrissy took over the insults.

"Well it's taken you long enough, you shower of toe rags!" The insults began to fly back and forth as they always do when men are about to fight. The vulgar names hurled are a way to boil the blood and harden the men about to battle and hopefully soften the enemy. A ritual that has always remained the same since the days of David and Goliath and tonight was no exception. The blinding, blue, flashing police lights spun around in their little plastic domes atop of the white and day glow orange panda cars that blocked the small road. The lights gave the place a strange futuristic atmosphere, causing the shadows of the men to jump around the tall, brick walls. The cursing and catcalling stopped, the fight was about to start. Chrissy peered through the blinding light waiting for the first strike. It came in the form of a beer glass thrown from the back of the group. Chrissy caught a glimpse of the glass as it sailed through the air, the blue light glinting from its surface. He moved his head to the side without too much effort and the glass passed over his shoulder to smash harmlessly on the wall behind him.

"Come on you fucking ponces!" Eddie took his suit jacket off and threw it into the road. He stood back to back with his brother, fists in the air and ready for anything.

Fletcher had taken the opportunity to creep behind the two brothers and make his way into the club. He stopped and looked at the stairs.

"Top floor." Fletcher repeated Gary Raven's instructions to himself. He began to climb the stairs as if he had all the time in the world.

* * *

Nobby joined Bomber and Tony and greeted them with a smile and a nod.

"Where are these Pakistanis Chrissie's been on about then?" Bomber gestured towards the group of men who were talking loudly in Urdu over the top of Bernard Manning's jokes, much to the annoyance of the other members of the audience. The group were sat around a table facing one another and seemed to have no interest in anything else in the room. Nobby rolled his eyes resigning himself to the trouble he knew was imminent. "Here we go!" He began to walk towards the group then stopped and turned back to Bomber and Tony. "Watch me back will ya lads?" The two men placed their glasses on the bar and followed Nobby across the room.

"This white bloke walked in to a Pub. He said to the Paki bar man."

Bernard Manning was settling into his show. He had no problem dealing with hecklers, he was used to it, his come back material was so strong he encouraged any drunken loudmouths to have a pop at him, so that he could humiliate them in front of their friends and the rest of the audience, but tonight, he was struggling. Apart from Haroom, the group of asians spoke little or no english and even though he was ridiculing them with his racist jokes, it wasn't having the desired effect.

"Give us a pint Paki. The Paki bar man looked shocked. You don't order a pint like that you ignorant bastard . . ."

Nobby closed in on the group. He noticed there were no drinks on the table in front of them, smiling he bent down and put his hands on two of the Pakistani men's shoulders.

"The Paki bloke says, let's swap places and I'll show you how to order a pint. The Paki bloke walked around the front of the bar and the white bloke stepped behind the bar . . ."

"Alright lads . . . can I see you tickets please?" The asian men turned to look at Nobby, puzzled looks on their faces.

"The Paki bloke says, can I have a pint of beer please barman. The white bloke says . . ."

Nobby's smile dropped, he held his right hand out flat. "TICKETS!"

"Sorry sir we don't serve Paki's in here."

The audience burst into laughter, drowning out Nobby's request. The group of Pakistani men rose from the chairs as one, Haroom at their centre. Nobby watched as the giant man stood to his full height in front of him. Nobby was a good six foot six but the Pakistani was at least three inches taller, Haroom's long beard gave him the appearance of an ancient warrior. Nobby felt that familiar feeling of dread creating a void in his stomach. Most of the audience had turned their attention away from the comedian and were now watching the scene at the back of the room. Without warning Nobby slapped one of the smaller men at the front of the group with the palm of his hand. The slap had such power it knocked the man off his feet, sending him sideways in a comical spin that left him sprawling across the table. Haroom stepped forward through the group. He could see the doorman was on his own and was happy to take advantage of the situation. Nobby backed away. He knew his job well, the sight of the big man had been a shock at first but now he was taking control of the situation. The slap to the smaller Pakistani had been a ruse, as was his retreat. The asian group began to follow the doorman who was backing towards the exit door to the room. The group of asians became cautious so Nobby stepped forward and slapped another, this time he looked straight into Haroom's eyes and laughed, knowing that it would antagonise the big man. Still he backed his way through the venue to the doors, the Pakistanis following him. Nobby reached the exit door and backed through it, gesturing to the big man with his fist. The door man continued to retreat on to the small, top floor foyer and one by one, the asian men followed him. Tony and Bomber, who had followed the whole group from a distance, brought up the rear. Bomber and Tony knew exactly what Nobby was doing. The door man was clearing them out of the room, the Pakistanis saw Nobby backing away and assumed he was afraid of them, in reality this was a technique Nobby had used hundreds of times over the years. Unlike the Pakistani men, who were without doubt a vicious bunch, Nobby was a boxing trainer, he trained himself, many of the other doormen and professional boxers every single day. The Pakistani men found courage in their huge warrior Haroom. Nobby, on the other hand, put his courage in years of practising fighting techniques. He was not only a hard man but a intelligent fighter too. As Nobby stopped backing up he raised his hands in a fighting stance and planted his feet into the lush red carpet. The group of Asians spread out across the foyer, Haroom in the middle, the smaller men either side. The man who had received the first slap was bleeding from his nose and top lip and Nobby could see from the man's eyes, he had already lost the will to fight. Bomber and Tony stepped through the doors behind the asians, silently and unnoticed.

* * *

Hazel pulled the third drawer of the filling cabinet open. The green metal slid out hitting her in the knees, so she stepped to one side and let the drawer slide out until it reached the end of its metal runner with a small screech. The brown files inside were mostly empty and at the back of the drawer was a half empty bottle of Irish whisky and two cut glasses. She peered inside the drawer. The brown paper package lay beside the bottle, greaseproof paper wrapped in brown parcel tape. Hazel grabbed the package greedily, breathing a sigh of relief. The paper felt soft and malleable, turning to the desk she found Eddie's paper knife sticking from a metal tube that acted as a container for a collection of pens. Grabbing it she poked the point of the blade into the package then pulled it free. There was a small speck of white powder with brown speckles in it, collected at the tip of the blade. She put it to the tip of her tongue and winced, the taste was bitter and acidic. She didn't have a clue what it was but she knew she had to get rid of it. She had to get to the toilets on the first floor and empty the wrapper. Suddenly a crashing noise caught her attention, she heard shouting coming from the foyer at the end of the corridor. Hazel crossed the room, package in hand. She inched the door open and poked her head out into the corridor. The commotion at the end of the corridor sent a shiver down her spine. She stepped out of the office and gingerly walked towards the foyer. The scene that met her eyes was surreal, Nobby and Haroom were trading blows with such ferocity that it made the other fighters, who it must be said were in the midst of a brutal battle themselves, look like comical, cartoon characters. She stood in the entrance to the corridor, detached from the violence as if she were watching a Shakespearian life and death play on a distant stage. Haroom was desperately trying to grab Nobby's throat, he fought in a way Nobby wasn't used to, grappling and trapping the boxer's arms and wrists in body locks, trying to put him in to an inescapable position. Nobby on the other hand fought with everything he had, fists, feet and teeth, all brought into play against the big Pakistani. Just when Haroom thought he had him, Nobby would bring his head around and bite his ear or thumb the asian's eyes, all techniques used to create space between the two men, so Nobby could bring about his massive right hook that would no doubt flatten the Pakistani, but, every time he made that space, Haroom would close it again in an attack of power, weight and speed. She looked towards the doorway of the cabaret room. Bomber and Tony were standing with their backs against the closed doors, surrounded by the asian men. The usual sound of fists against skin mixed with groans of pain were broken intermittently by the sound of loud bursts of laughter coming from Bernard Manning's audience. Hazel watched with a macabre fascination. Tony standing in a boxer stance, head down arms high, protecting his head from the constant blows rained upon him from the group, their punches didn't seem to register with Tony, who seemed to take the brutal attack in his stride and *still* find a target for his devastating punches. Bomber on the other hand, had more of a street fighting style, kicking, punching and head butts were his way of dealing with the onslaught. He constantly moved from side to side thereby preventing his opponents from finding a target. Hazel saw Tony grab a man's shoulder and bring his head back, before driving it at lightning speed into the other man's nose. The man's face exploded, showering everyone in blood. He dropped to the red carpet clutching his face, screaming Urdu curses in a gurgle of blood and words.

The Pakistani man who had been slapped by Nobby earlier had lost all taste for the fight. He had been there just to make up the numbers and now he could see Haroom, their champion, had met his match in the door man, and these two white men, that fought like wild dogs were not going to back down in the face of overwhelming odds, he was ready to make his exit. That was until he saw Hazel, she was watching from the corridor and seemed hypnotised by the events. He crossed to her, suddenly finding his courage in the face of the slight young woman. He raised his hand, clenching his fist as he did, he brought it down on Hazel with an angry war cry. Hazel turned at the sound, her reactions were lighting fast, she turned her jaw away from the punch, it crashed harmlessly into her shoulder leaving the man in front of her unbalanced and unprotected. Hazel's instant reaction was to bring her own hand up and poked the asian with her stiff index finger right into his left eye. She drove the finger deep, feeling the eyeball squash in its socket. The man staggered back, screaming. Hazel drew back her leg and brought her foot up with a hard kick into the man's balls. He dropped his hands from his face, grabbing his groin, sinking to his knees with a high pitched squeal.

"*Hazel!*" Nobby shouted her name and she lifted her head towards the bouncer. Hazel saw that the big Pakistani had rolled onto his back after Nobby had managed to create enough space between him and his opponent to bring his fists into play and finally floor the huge asian man. He shouted again before following his punch with a shower of kicks to Haroom who was desperately trying to get up off the floor. "Hazel . . . Fletcher!" he said gesturing towards the stairwell, she turned to see Ronnie Fletcher climbing the stairs. Their eyes met and Fletcher saw the brown, paper package. He stepped over the last step to the top floor foyer, pointing at Hazel.

"You're fucking nicked now girl!" Hazel looked at the package and again at Fletcher who had already started to cross the floor towards her. Nobby saw the situation and without turning brought his arm up to throw a punch but instead brought his elbow straight into the policemen's nose. Fletcher staggered back and fell down the first few steps of the stairwell. Nobby turned back to Hazel.

"*Run!*" He shouted before Haroom was on him again, this time grabbing his waist and lifting the twenty stone man clear off the floor in a rib crushing bear hug. Hazel turned and ran back down the corridor. There was no way out, except for the office the narrow corridor was a dead end. She heard Ronnie Fletcher scream from the foyer as he regained his feet.

"I'm gonna throw the fucking book at you *bitch!*" She stepped back into the office and looked around herself, nowhere to go and Fletcher was coming.

* * *

Outside Eddie and Chrissy were in a similar situation. The fight had started with beer glasses being thrown by the men from the Birmingham Meat Market. None of the glasses found their mark but were used by the men as a distraction for the real attack, started by the man with the spider's web tattoo who rushed Eddie with a short butcher's knife in hand. Eddie saw the attack coming and easily stepped aside, catching the man's right arm in his left, then bringing his right fist up into the man's jaw in one swift movement. The man's open mouth was pushed out of shape by the punch, snapping his teeth together with a loud crack that caused the tattooed man to almost bite off his own tongue. He screamed in a gurgle of deep red blood that was so thick it ran, almost black, down his chin and onto his neck. The other men saw this and charged Eddie and Chrissy with a combined attack that almost drove the two men back into the club's entrance. The men were hard and ruthless with nothing to lose. The bad blood that existed between the Fewtrells and the Meat Market Mob had lasted years and now it was exploding on the frosty streets of Birmingham once more. A battle under blue, flashing lights, blind roundhouse punches struck the brothers again and again. The meat workers were hard but undisciplined, good scrappers but untrained, unlike the Fewtrell brothers who were *all* fighters; for almost the whole of their teenage years and early twenties they had trained as boxers. Not only could they give a punch but they could take one too. Chrissy's granite jaw taking blow after blow without him losing his aggression or energy. However the seven men from the Meat Market that remained in the fight were slowly gaining the upper hand against the two brothers. The gang were pushing the Fewtrells back against the doorway, thus making it virtually impossible to swing a punch properly in the cramped space. A silver knife blade flashed in the blue light and Chrissy cried out, the blade had slashed his forearm and the cut was deep, weakening his right arm. Another knife slashed at the brothers but luckily this time it missed. Eddie, realising they were getting cornered by the gang threw a powerful, round, bolo punch at a man who was trying to get in under his guard, he brought his fist up under the man's chin and slammed his fist into the gang member's jawbone, shattering it and lifting the unfortunate victim off his feet. He fell backwards into the other men, a look of shock on his twisted face. Eddie took advantage of the short pause in the fighting to push Chrissy into the doorway of the club behind them. Once inside he turned and slammed one of the doors shut and threw the bolt at the top of the door into its latch. Now there was only one door they could come through, there was only space for one fighter, maybe two at a time and so now their numbers would count for nothing. There was a hesitation from the Meat Market men, no one wanted to be the first through the door. Chrissy was holding his arm, which had started to bleed badly.

"We can't carry on like this for much longer Ed . . . there's too many of em." Eddie, who was standing on the other side of the open door, raised his eyebrows.

"Well this ain't gonna make it any easier for em is it." He moved away from the wall and stood in front of the open doorway so the gang member could see him. "Come on then you shower of toe rags what ya waiting for?" Eddie was concentrating on the men outside, jibing them, trying to get them to attack through the door. Chrissy stood with his back to the closed door holding his bleeding forearm. He was expecting a rush from behind him and readied himself for the attack. Eddie ducked back behind the gap, as two beer glasses smashed against the wooden door frame. They heard curses and jeers from the men outside.

"They're getting themselves ready for a charge . . . brace yourself Chrissy!" The two brothers looked at each other across the gap of the open door, each preparing themselves for what might be a fight for their very survival. Suddenly one of the Meat Market thugs came running through the doorway, screaming bloody murder. Simultaneously both brothers brought their fists up, smashing them into the man's face and knocking him out cold. He instantly fell unconscious in a crumpled mess in the doorway. His body twitched as small electric currents ran through his muscles. Then from the back of the police cars came a familiar voice.

"What the fuck are you lot staring at, you lazy shower of bastards?" Eddie smiled at the sound of the voice. "Nick em!" The voice continued. "Nick em all!" Eddie peered around the doorframe. The police, who moments before had been given the command by Ronnie Fletcher to stand down and let the Meat Market mob do their worst to the Fewtrell brothers, were now charging out from behind the Panda cars and clubbing anyone who looked like they might be a member of the gang. The Meat Market men began to run in every direction but the police were on them and uniformed arms rose and fell, the heavy black wood truncheons cracking skulls and faces without mercy. Eddie couldn't see the man who had given the order. The blue flashing lights blinded him as he tried to see over the top of the police cars. He searched for Fletcher but he was nowhere to be seen, confused he turned to Chrissy.

"Come on this ain't over yet!" They both walked to the stairs and began to climb.

* * *

Haroom had wrestled Nobby to the floor, his huge arm around Nobby's neck in an unstoppable stranglehold that threatened to choke the doorman completely. Nobby's legs thrashed around uselessly trying to find purchase in the deep red carpet of the foyer. In such a position it was impossible for Nobby to throw a punch or even regain his stance. The Pakistani had him good and it was just a matter of time before he blacked out, he knew it and so did

Haroom. The two gargantuan fighters had been battling viciously for nearly five minutes and now exhaustion was beginning to become a factor in the struggle. Nobby desperately tried to twist his neck towards Tony and Bomber who were making ground against the unskilled asians who, although blooded and weakening, kept on coming at them. Tony had his head down, flaying his tired arms around him at anyone that came near. Bomber was kicking and punching without any real style, just an aggression and determination stemming from his Fewtrell genes keeping him going. A man came at him with a pathetically tired punch, there was no power behind it and it glanced off Bomber's head without causing too much pain. Bomber just stepped forward and gave the man an almighty push in the chest with both hands, the man, who was unbalanced anyway, began to stumble backwards towards Haroom and Nobby. He fell across the huge Pakistani's shoulders, breaking Haroom's grip on the doorman and releasing Nobby. The doorman rolled away, gasping for breath. He climbed to his feet and before Haroom could push the fallen man off him, Nobby leapt in the air and landed all twenty stone of his muscle and bone on the Pakistani's chest. The huge man let out a strange groaning sound as the air was forced out of his crushed lungs by his weight. Haroom's eyes bulged in his head as he tried to draw breath but found his solar plexus was paralysed by the weight. Nobby stepped off him but before Haroom could move, he brought his size 15 Doctor Martin boot straight into the his with a kick that wouldn't have been out of place on a Saturday afternoon, premier season, football match. *Wham!* Haroom fell back, unconscious. Nobby stepped over the prostrate man and grabbed the smaller man that had fallen over his huge friend. He pulled the man off the floor and grabbing the man's jacket with one hand and his groin with the other, he flung the helpless Pakistani man over the hand rail of the stairwell, where he fell fifteen feet or so on to the steps below, nearly landing on Eddie and Chrissy who were ascending the stairs. Both men stopped and looked over the man who lay twisted on the stairs groaning. Nobby, grabbed another man and threw him the same way. The asian flew over the hand rail into the deep recess, eyes wide, a fearful whimper emerging from his open mouth as he fell head first on to the metal lined stairs. When the group of asians saw their champion Haroom had fallen and the fate of their other comrades, the fight went out of them. They grabbed their fallen, all except for Haroom, who in truth, would have needed a bulldozer to move him from the place where he lay and they scarpered down the stairs of the club past the two brothers.

Eddie and Chrissy watched as the panicked Pakistanis fled the building, stopping only long enough to drag the broken men who had been thrown over the stairwell down the stairs to the exit.

"*Fucking hell* . . . what's been going on up here?" Chrissy shouted. Eddie looked at the bleeding Pakistanis as they raced past him.

"Bernard Manning must've been giving them some shit tonight." Both men burst into laughter as they continued to climb the stairs to the top floor foyer. The three victors stood at the other end of the foyer, bleeding and panting for breath as they were joined by Eddie and Chrissy. The audience were still laughing hysterically at Bernard Manning's jokes behind the thick venue doors. All five men looked at each other and without anyone saying a word, began laughing uncontrollably, more from relief than from the jokes coming from the stage.

* * *

Fletcher had crossed the foyer as the fight between the Pakistanis and the two doormen and Bomber was gaining momentum. He stalked the corridor looking for Hazel and more importantly, the brown paper package. He came to the locked office door. Hazel in the meantime had taken the package and stuffed it down her knickers. Then, standing on the green filing cabernet she had opened the small louvre windows and slid the long glass panes out of their metal holders. Fletcher could just make out the figure of a woman through the frosted glass of the office door.

"It's no use darling I can see ya!" He rapped his fist on the glass, "Come on bitch open up, there's nowhere to go!" Hazel swung her leg through the opening in the window and pulled her slim body into the pitch black night. She swung from the metal rim of the window for a second until her feet found the concrete window ledge. The ledge was only six inches wide and she stood there frozen for a second. *Bam!* Fletcher had started to kick the door of the office, it was only a matter of time before he would be in. Hazel looked down, beneath her feet lay only pitch black emptiness. She considered jumping blindly before remembering the labyrinth of old, red brick alleyways two stories below. She ruled out jumping, it would certainly end in injury or even death. *Bam!* She looked left and right trying to find a foothold or something to climb down on to but she couldn't see anything in the darkness. *Bam!*

"Sooner or later that door's gonna give and all of this will be irrelevant anyway." She thought. She must jump and hope for the best. Hazel looked down into the blackness, "One, two . . ." she braced herself, "thrrreee . . ." Just at that moment a light on the lower floor came on inside one of the toilets. The light brought a whole new perspective of the ground below. She looked at the ground directly beneath her. "Thank God!" she said under her breath, for right beneath her were a set of rusty, old spiked railings that protected the windows to the basement of the building. If she had jumped she would've landed on them and God knows what the consequences would have been. *Bam!* The noise of Ronnie Fletcher breaking down the office door brought her back to her senses. The light from the toilet below illuminated an old piece of rusted, victorian fire escape sticking out of the wall about two feet below her. The fire escape had long since gone and this piece of thick metal was the only clue that it had ever been there. Directly below the metal bar was one of the high walls that made up the alleyways behind the club. *Bam!* The sound of a breaking lock was accompanied by the sound of glass dropping from the office door. Fletcher was in. She could see him through the glass of the window as he looked around the room. The sight of him gave her courage and panic in the same measure. She stepped down on to the protruding metal bar without hesitation. Then, swinging her legs underneath her she sat on the bar and twisted with both hands gripping the metal, she let herself drop until her weight was caught by her arms. She did the whole manoeuvre in one graceful movement as if she'd spent her life on a trapeze. She heard a commotion above as Fletcher climbed on top of the filing cabinet in order to peer out the window into the darkness below. Hazel knew the wall was beneath her and she let go of the bar and dropped the three feet on to the top of the wall. She landed silently, swaying left and right as she found her balance. As she landed the light in the toilet went off and she stood there in pitch black silence. Fletcher, unable to see her, reached into his long, brown raincoat and produced a thin, grey walkie-talkie. He pulled out the telescopic aerial, and pressed the large button on the side.

"Fletcher here, Fletcher here, over . . ." The radio gave a little, fuzzy noise before a thin, crackly voice answered.

"Yes sir." Fletcher pressed again.

"Get some men around the back of the building, we have a female trying to escape!" Hazel sat on the top of the wall, turned, grabbed the top of the bricks with her hands and dropped three feet onto the old cobbles that ran along the narrow alleyway. She could see nothing in the darkness. The smell of rat piss was over-whelming as she began to stumble blindly along the passageway to nowhere in particular. Suddenly there were torches at either end of the entrance to the alleyways about fifty feet from her, they were slowly drawing nearer, slim threads of light slashing the darkness like laser beams. Carefully she picked her way through the discarded shopping trolleys, beer crates and ankle high rubbish to the junction that sat in the middle of the alleyway. The junction crossed the passage that ran towards the club. It was as far away from the club as she could physically get without climbing more walls. Fletcher was bellowing from the office window.

"She's down there somewhere, the bitch is carrying, search her . . . search her straight away!" Hazel reached inside her knickers and pulled out the package, ripping the thick, brown paper open as fast as she could, she began walking up and down the alleyway emptying the contents in as wide an area as she could. As the white powder fell from the bag she could hear shuffling noises around her feet. At first she thought she'd stumbled on a sleeping tramp.

Just then one of the black shapes scurried over her feet. Hazel froze. Then as her eyes became adjusted to the darkness she could see little black things moving all around her, scurrying here and there. She stifled a terrified scream. Hazel shared Eddie's fear of rats and here she was, surrounded by them. Unable to move, she just watched the growing number of the rats gathering around her, the brown, paper package dropped from her hand. She flinched, terrified, as the rats clawed around her feet. Another beam of light from one end of the passageway broke the moment of horror. A man's voice said something inaudible in the blackness, then the sound of someone stumbling and falling into a pile of rubbish and broken glass with a groan of pain. The voice began cursing and the beam of the torch vanished. Hazel daren't move an inch but she had to find the package else they would arrest her and with this much heroin on her, she would certainly be facing a long prison stretch. Fletcher bellowed at the policemen below him.

"She's down there, keep going!" The man who had fallen, regained his feet. He was cursing louder now to someone behind him.

"It's fucking broken!" He was slapping something in his hand. The man behind him said something and they continued to come forward without the torchlight.

Hazel crouched down in the stinking rubbish. She put her hand down onto the cold cobbled floor and began searching for the package. Rats darted this way and that across her outstretched hand. She gagged at the smell and at the thought of their black furry bodies and long tails. Then she heard another crash from where the policemen were approaching, more glass being broken and the sound of a man falling again.

"Fuck this . . . I can't see nothing down here . . . she ain't here." The falling man had had enough. "She ain't here!" he shouted towards the window, Fletcher exploded in an outburst.

"Stop fucking around and fucking find her or you're on report sonny!" The policeman in the alleyway stood up again, aided by his friend.

"Fuck off Fletcher!" He muttered under his breath. "If you want to find her, fucking do it yourself." He stumbled back past the other man. They were only ten feet away from Hazel who sat fumbling around the floor in the filthy blackness. The lone policeman came on. At last her hand found the brown paper package, it was covered in rats who seemed to be going mad for the contents of the package. Suddenly a torch illuminated the passageway once more. The rats scurried away in all directions. She looked down. Hazel decided to grab the brown package and throw it over the wall behind her. They would still nick her for it but at least it wouldn't be found on her person. She searched the ground as the policeman was almost upon her. Then in the torchlight she saw a large, black shape scurrying away down the alleyway in the opposite direction to the policeman. One of the rats had the brown package in its mouth and it was being followed by five or ten of its greedy friends towards what must have been its nest. She watched the little, black shape disappear into the blackness and out of sight. The torch was shining directly on her now.

"Hazel?" A soft voice came from the man holding the torch. "Are you ok?" Hazel was still crouching, watching the other end of the passageway. "It's me Dixie." She stood uneasily and reached out to him, as their hands closed she burst into tears.

"Oh thank God, Dixie, get me out of here, *please!*" Dixie put his arm around her shoulders tenderly.

"Shhh . . . keep it down, don't worry I'll get you out of here, but you must be quiet."

Fletcher was shouting again. "Have you got her?" Dixie called back.

"No boss . . . there's no one down here . . . it's empty she must have got away boss."

"What the fuck are you men doing down there . . . how the fuck did she get away?"

Dixie didn't answer. Fletcher became angrier as he tried to peer into the blackness of the alleyway. "What's your name sonny?" Dixie didn't answer, he turned and guided Hazel back the way he'd come. "I asked what your fucking name is, constable!"

Dixie stopped in the shadows and looked up at the man's silhouette, his head squeezing through the tiny, louvre window which Hazel had climbed through five minutes before.

"Me sir." Dixie shouted anonymously. "I'm DCI Micky-fucking-Mouse you arrogant old wanker!" The two fugitives burst into stifled giggles.

"What . . . who . . . who is that down there? I'll have your fucking badge." Fletcher brought the walkie-talkie up to his ear again. "Fletcher here . . . I need men in the back alleyway *now*." He let go of the button, the little, grey radio buzzed again before a voice answered.

"Hello DCI Micky-fucking-Mouse here, receiving you loud and clear, you old twat." Dixie kept his finger on the button of the walkie-talkie which kept the radio channel open. Fletcher could hear a man and woman laughing. Dixie released the button and the channel went dead. He ushered Hazel through the alleyway and straight to his car, which was parked at the opposite end of Navigation street, outside the Navigation fish bar. He opened the back door of the Ford Cortina and lay her down on the back seat. "Keep down Hazel . . . we don't want anyone to see you, I'll take you home then come back for Eddie." Climbing into the front of the car, he turned the wheel and pulled away with a screech of tyres into the night and away from the flashing blue lights.

* * *

After the laughter calmed down, Nobby suddenly remembered how Fletcher had chased Hazel into the office. He quickly tried to explain to Eddie who became serious in an instant. All the men raced to the small office at the end of the corridor just in time to hear Dixie's voice crackling on the walkie-talkie.

"*DCI Micky-fucking-Mouse, here, receiving you loud and clear you old twat!*"

Fletcher began stomping on top of the filing cabinet and screaming obscenities from the window of the office at the two shadows in the alleyway. Chrissy couldn't help himself.

"Hey Fletcher . . . you'll upset our neighbours if you're not careful." Fletcher turned with a spiteful grimace, Chrissy continued, "They'll call the police." Fletcher became purple with rage.

"We *are* the fucking police!" Eddie butted in.

"Nah . . . he means the police . . . the proper police . . . not a Micky Mouse outfit like you lot." Nobby, Bomber and Tony were giggling at the detective's discomfort like naughty school boys. Fletcher answered Eddie.

"We *are* the police." He repeated unable to think of anything else to say.

"Nah you're a Micky-fucking-Mouse outfit . . . I just heard him on the radio, did you lads hear him?" He turned to his friends who were all nodding. "Anyhow Fletcher . . . I hope you've got a search warrant pal, cos if you ain't I'm gonna be getting my lawyers onto this . . . I think it's called harassment. They got laws against police harassment you know *Ronnie* old boy." The detective climbed off the cabinet. Eddie and his brothers crowded around him. Fletcher became flushed by the closeness of the other men.

"I don't need a warrant, I have reason to believe . . ." Chrissy finished off his sentence.

"That Gary Raven planted drugs in our office on behalf of that big Pakistani bastard lying out there in the foyer, unconscious." Ronnie looked confused. Surely they didn't mean Haroom. He became flustered. Eddie grabbed the grubby collar of his rain coat and pulled the man in close to face him.

"I know your game Fletcher, always wanted to nick me ain't ya? You cost my old man three years and a few others I know of too." He pressed his face into the detectives so their eyes were only inches apart. "If I were you Ronnie, I'd be very careful, cos there's some real nasty bastards in this town who might get to hear about what you tried to pull tonight and take it to heart." Fletcher tried to dislodge Eddie's hand's but the grip was too much for him.

"Are you threatening me Fewtrell?" Eddie's eyes opened wide in a look of pure madness.

"Oh it ain't a threat, it's a fucking promise sunshine . . . now *fuck off*!"

The man backed out of the door, a growing scowl his face, when he reached the corridor he stopped and stared at Eddie.

"One day I'm gonna . . ."

"Yeah, course you are." Nobby said, slamming the door into the detective's face as he said it. Fletcher stood for a second staring at the broken glass of the office door, before storming off down the corridor to the foyer, a growing feeling of humiliation only made worse by the sound of the men laughing behind him.

Distant Thunder

Chapter 18

By the time Dixie returned to the club, Haroom had regained consciousness and vanished into the night. The police had made a hasty retreat too, leaving only the customers, who milled around the club exploring the floors and enjoying the disco that had replaced Gary Raven's show and the Northern soul night on the second floor, totally unaware of the dramas that had unfolded in and around the club that night.

Bernard Manning had been given two standing ovations, after which, he had retired to the dressing room, changed clothes, been paid and was already in his Rolls Royce and en route to the *Embassy* club in Manchester to perform another show. The club was quietening down. Eddie, Chrissy, Hazel and Dixie arranged to meet on Monday morning to go over the events and try and put a plan together to outfox Ronnie Fletcher should he try it again. Chrissy had already left for the hospital to have some stitches to his arm but had left a message with Eddie about a possible lead on the missing girls that he wanted to pass on to Dixie.

* * *

Belfast Jimmy had dumped the white van on the old Stratford road outside of the Vale-Onslow motorcycle shop. He took the remaining plastic bags with the bombs inside and took a leisurely walk back to his digs as if he were carrying nothing more deadly than his week's groceries. He didn't lose any sleep over the death of McDade, as a matter of fact he spent the hour it took him to walk the distance, to run over the plan of action for his next attack. By the time he got home, McDade's face was all over the black and white TV screen in his room. The *News at Ten* anchorman, repeating McDade's name again and again as he went through the events. Jimmy thought it was strange how the ITV news already knew so much about a man who had been blown to smithereens only two hours before. Maybe Ray McLaughlin was already singing the names of all involved. He knew if indeed he had, then he didn't have long to complete his mission before the old Bill would be knocking down his door. He knew he couldn't expect any help from Fletcher since becoming a lone wolf operator. One thing was for sure, the trick with the *Timex* watch had worked and it was something he intended to do again.

* * *

Dixie, Eddie, Hazel and Chrissy sat in *Rebecca's Brasserie* drinking coffee. The meeting had been postponed for various reasons and instead of Monday as arranged, it was actually Thursday early evening before all of them were free to meet. They talked about Saturday's events and Dixie filled everyone in on the shit storm it had created down the station. Chrissy's arm was already on the mend and Hazel had finally got the of the smell of rat piss out of her nose after taking constant showers all week and some Valium. Eddie wondered what Fletcher had had in mind with the stitch up. Chrissy was relaying the events in the car park behind the Navigation Fish bar. He was explaining that he'd seen a posh asian man giving orders and also how the other man, the huge Pakistani had treated the naked girl, throwing her into the back of the van. Just then a voice came through the door, Chrissy was needed to sort out a delivery around the back of the bar. He left the room. Hazel said she had made a mental note of the number plate of the van in question. Dixie tried tracing the number of the blue van by ringing the station but the officer on the other end of the police line said that the registration number was that of a *white* van from an address in Lancashire, meaning the blue van must've been ringed. Just at that moment fate stepped in to the room, in the form of Mo, the young Pakistani salesman with dodgy goods.

"Alright Ed?" He said with a big, cheeky grin, Eddie was pleased to see his old friend. The meeting was getting depressing anyway. Mo always had a few bottles of this and that for sale and today was no exception. Only, Mo didn't want to talk to Eddie, he had overheard the conversation and he now wanted to talk to Dixie, mainly about this blue van. He explained how he bought counterfeit clothing from a guy in *Moseley*.

"You know Levi's, Wrangler jeans, anything that'll sell quick. This guy called Khan always had stuff in and was always knocking it out cheap. I was told he had a brothel downstairs too, full of young birds. He tried to get me to go down there but it all seemed a bit weird so I made my excuses and left." Dixie shook his head,

"And how does this relate to . . . ?" Mo cut him short.

"*They've* got a blue transit van , it's always parked across the driveway like some sort of a rolling gate with a bloke sat in it, looking dodgy as fuck." Eddie laughed.

"Well if *you* say he's dodgy he must be fucking bad!" Mo gave Eddie a dirty look.

"I'm only trying to help and this bastard's taking the piss," he replied breaking into a laugh, "he's got some sort of bodyguard, a massive guy called Harum or Haroom or something like that. It's him who collects the cash once you've got the goods. I've heard some bad things about that bastard too, he's been around a lot of my friends shops on the Stratford road, pressing them for money. If they don't pay up they get their shops wrecked or a beating, some of em can't even go to the old Bill cos they're here illegally. That's how he gets the women making the clothes to work for him, he tracks down those without visas and threatens to report them if they don't work for him. He pays them next to *nothing*." Dixie could've kissed the little Pakistani, but resisted the urge. He crossed back to the phone behind the bar and called the station. The receptionist transferred him to Ronnie Fletcher's extension.

"Well?" Fletcher said angrily, not knowing or caring who was on the other end.

"D.C.I Dixon, sir." Fletcher remained arrogantly silent. Dixie told him about this new crime lead. He omitted Mo's own involvement, but went on to explain about the blue van saying he thought it was owned by a man called Khan. He told him that he thought he might be press ganging women and children into working in his clothing factory, through a protection racket amongst the Pakistani, Indian and Sikh communities of Birmingham. Fletcher suddenly perked up, he wanted to know *everything* Dixie knew.

Dixie explained about the connection with the missing girls, he said he wanted to check out when this Mr Khan had arrived in the UK, to see if it tied in with the first abductions of girls. Fletcher told him to continue. Dixie said that this *Mr Khan,* had a huge bodyguard who, he thought, had been involved in an attack at *Rebecca's* club last Saturday. Fletcher said he was't interested in the big man just Khan, he pressed him for more information to see if the detective knew about *his* involvement. Dixie saved the best till last. He explained that he had a reliable source who had informed him that this *Khan* had a basement full of prostitutes. Dixie thought some these girls *could possibly* be the girls that had gone missing over the past three years. Even if they weren't, it was still going to be a good nick and he wanted to raid the house. Fletcher remained silent for a minute, finally saying.

"You'll need search warrants, do *not* go near that house in Moseley without those warrants. Leave it with me." Fletcher hung up the phone leaving Dixie listening to the buzzing sound on the crackly line. He turned back to the group, who had all be listening.

"He said I needed a warrant." Eddie laughed.

"Well he made that mistake on Saturday night didn't he? I doubt that he wants to do it again." Dixie seemed puzzled. He returned to his seat and sipped his coffee. Hazel was sat next to Eddie her hand in his. Dixie hadn't seen them show so much affection towards each other for a long time, she was watching Dixie with a quizzical look on her face. After a minute she finally asked.

"Come on Dixie, spill the beans what's up?" Dixie shook his head.

"Well it's weird."

"What's weird bab?" Hazel continued smiling.

"Well it's something Ronnie Fletcher said." He ran over the conversation in his mind, Then continued. "Fletcher said '*the house in Moseley*?" Hazel shook her head puzzled, Dixie carried on talking. "I didn't mention anything about a house in *Moseley*, did I?" Mo, who had paid attention to the phone call, just to make sure he wasn't mentioned or implicated in anything, agreed, and assured Dixie that he *hadn't* said anything about *Moseley* at all. As the group mulled over the conversation, Chrissy returned to the room and seeing the puzzled looks on everyone's faces asked,

"Jesus, who's died?" Eddie turned to him and explained about the phone call to Fletcher. Chrissy's face went white as he worked out the situation. The image of Ronnie Fletcher with the asian man in the dark car park at the back of the fish bar ran through his mind. He turned to Dixie.

"You silly bastard Dix, Ronnie Fletcher is one of *them*!" Dixie looked at Chrissy as if he were mad.

"One of who?" Chrissy became animated.

"One of *them* . . . the Pakistani gang, I saw Ronnie Fletcher with them on Saturday night. He was with an asian man and the big Pakistani in the car park. That's when I saw the naked girl and all the other blokes piling out of the blue transit van, Fletcher knows all about it for fuck's sake . . . and you've just *warned* him!" Dixie just stood dumbfounded, Eddie interrupted.

"Mo, can you show us where that house is?" Mo nodded.

"Yeah it's easy to find, it's on the Wake Green road." Eddie rose from the table.

"Come on then let's go pay em a visit." Hazel jumped from her chair.

"Oh no Ed, you ain't going anywhere, you've got kids at home and we've got enough on our plate we don't need all this shit, we're gonna have a romantic night in, babe."

Chrissy looked at Hazel. She looked as if the weight of the world had been lifted off her shoulders. Saturday night's rat infested horror didn't seem to have affected her at all, demonstrating the woman's resilience. She turned to Chrissy, their eyes crossed for a second. He gave her a slim smile, she returned it with a look that said she had finally found her place within the family. Like all people, Hazel needed love, but she also thrived on the drama that went with the lifestyle she had chosen and after her close shave with the law on Saturday she was back to herself, her self-esteem returned to her by the bucketful.

Chrissy said he would go with Dixie and Mo to check out the house in *Moseley* and after various delays that mounted up to around two hours, they set off in Dixie's bronze Ford Cortina. Chrissy was impressed by the car and explained how the Pakistani gang had wrecked his Alfa Romeo and how the smaller gang member had pulled the machine gun on him. Dixie was amazed he hadn't been told any of this before. He pulled his leather jacket open to reveal a snub nose revolver in a black leather holster under his arm, thus assuring Chrissy and Mo that he was well capable of dealing with anything that came their way. The Cortina sped through the cold streets towards the big house that seemed to hold all the answers to so many puzzles. Little did they know the biggest puzzle of all was just about to begin.

* * *

James McDade was more trouble to the British establishment dead than he had ever been alive. His funeral procession had been organised by the Dublin IRA. The funeral cars were set to wind their way from Coventry, where the remains of his body were held in a police morgue, to Elmdon airport on the outskirts of Birmingham where an Aer Lingus flight had been arranged to take what was left of him back to Ireland. The road was lined with both IRA sympathisers on one side and British National front supporters on the other. They chanted and cursed at each other from either side of the Coventry road, held back by the thin blue line of policemen and women from the West Midlands police force. The tension between the two groups was palpable.

Belfast Jimmy sat in the second funeral car. Unlike almost everyone around him, the family mourners, the police and pro-testers *he* had a smile on his face, to him James McDade's death was a gift that just kept giving. He watched from inside the luxury of the limousine, as he passed the freezing cold, screaming men and women outside the window. McDade's death had done all this. So much trouble and such a good diversion to the real events that were about to take place that very night. If ever he needed an alibi in the future, then he couldn't think of a better one than this. He looked down at the *Timex* watch on his wrist. One hour to go, perfect.

* * *

As the Ford Cortina pulled up outside the big house on the Wake Green road, Mo noticed that the blue van, which normally blocked the entrance to the house was gone. The Cortina pulled on to the gravel drive with a long skid. Chrissy and Dixie leapt from the car, Mo shrunk into the rear footwell of the car and remained there, terrified. The two men slunk around the side of the building, Dixie gun in hand, led the way. The dark opening to the stairs of the basement on their left as they crept along the shadows of the house. Dixie took one stair at a time, pointing the gun ahead of him as he went. The basement door swung open to reveal a dark corridor. The little brick domed topped rooms that branched off of the corridor were dark and empty. Ruffled beds which looked as if they had just been vacated, lay in various states of dishevelment. Dixie continued down the corridor, Chrissy walked into one of the small rooms and pulled back the thin, rough woollen blanket that lay on top of a filthy mattress. As he pulled back the blanket a silver chain rattled onto the floor, its padlocked end connected to the metal frame of the bed.

"Chrissy!" Dixie voice came from down the corridor. "You need to see this!" Chrissy crept through the dark corridor and

David J. Keogh

into a large room. Dixie was stood at a table holding disk shaped metal container.

"What you got there Dix?" Dixie shook his head and waved one of the containers at Chrissy.

"Films Chrissy . . . films." Chrissy crossed to the table and picked up one of the containers. He examined it, placing it on the table, he levered the top of of the container. It fell to the floor with loud clang, Dixie turned to Chrissy and gave him a dark stare. "For fuck's sake Chrissy . . . quiet!" Chrissy took a roll of film from container, he turned it in his hand then noticed a name on the roll of film.

"Gary Raven?" He said rolling the film out and trying to look through the tiny 16mm frames. He could see nothing. Dixie in the meantime had done the same.

"This one's got Ernest Whirlington written on it . . . he's a fucking high court judge. Whoever was here left in a fucking hurry." Dixie said looking around the messy room. Chrissy looked over the films.

"There's about ten films here . . . whoever this Mr Kahn is, I think he's left these as a gift."

"Take em up to the car, I'll take a look around upstairs." He piled the canisters onto Chrissy's arms and led the way out onto the large gravel drive. Chrissy took the cans to the car as Dixie, gun still in hand went to the front door of the building. He stood outside of the big Victorian house and looked up at its gothic style turrets that sat either side of the huge frontage. As his eyes wandered over the architecture he noticed the wind that danced around the tree tops suddenly stopped. A stillness came over the place, no birds or cars, not a breath of wind. Dixie stepped inside the doorway of the huge porch. The stillness of the air and sudden silence of the night, gave the great entrance hall, with its black and white tiles and sweeping elm stair case a haunted atmosphere of long lost of ghosts. The building was empty, silent and abandoned. Dixie placed his gun back in it's holster and walked back out into the still night. He walked to the driveway and stood watching the tree tops against the yellow lights that lined the Wake Green road.

BOOOOM! What sounded like a soft distant rumble of thunder rolled across the sky from the direction of the city centre, Dixie took note of the time on his wrist watch. 8.26pm precisely. Then, *BOOOM,* again a few minutes later, another low rumble of thunder rolled out of the dark, November sky. He searched the tree tops for a flash of lightning, but nothing came. Then suddenly the wind returned, only this time it blew the tree tops from the other direction.

"Well the wind has certainly turned for someone tonight." He thought to himself.

* * *

As the Are Lingus flight departed from Birmingham airport, Belfast Jimmy was concentrating on his watch . . . 8.26pm. He sat in his chair and raised the glass of complimentary whisky to his lips. His job was done, now it was all out of his hands, the British media and general public would do the rest.

* * *

Dixie returned to the office around 10pm that night, he had the canisters of film in an old cardboard box and a story to tell. The office was almost empty except for the telephone operators who seemed busier than usual for that time of night and the Chief superintendent who sat behind his desk, head in his hands. Dixie marched past Fletcher's office. He gave a short look in his direction. The man was sitting at his desk behind a glass wall, talking earnestly to someone and didn't even notice Dixie pass by his big window. He walked into the Super's office with a little knock on the glass paned door.

"Sir." The superintendent looked up. He looked older, more haggard than Dixie remembered.

"Yes Dixon, what you got?" Dixie was surprised by the sudden interest in what he had to say.

"Sir I'm onto something big sir." The chief looked relieved.

"Thank God we've got a lead ... come on then!" Dixie was confused but continued regardless.

"Sir I think I may have solved the missing girls case, I've come across a house in Moseley with what looks to me like a brothel of sorts in the basement. I've found chains and ..." The chief stood up, a scowl growing on his face.

"What?" Dixie gave a thin smile trying to hide his growing feeling of foolishness.

"It's a brothel sir run by a Pakistani gang sir ... and it's a bit sensitive but I think DCI Fletcher may also be involved sir." The super's face began to grow red, his interest in the subject turning into a scowl.

"Just what fucking planet have you been on tonight DCI Dixon?" He screamed. The men and women on the phones in the main office turned at the sound. Dixie suddenly felt stupid. "I don't know if you've fucking noticed but the IRA have just blown up most of the fucking city ... people are dead Dixon ... fucking dead, and you're coming in here talking to me about DCI Fletcher being mixed up with some Paki bloke who's got himself a few whores." The chief stood behind his desk and checked his voice.

"We are at *war* Dixon ... at fucking war son, we need every-man on deck, there could be more bombs out there!" The chief's attention was drawn to the box under Dixie's arm. "What's that?" Dixie shuffled his feet nervously.

"Well sir ... there's this is box of films too sir, I found them in the cellar used as a brothel in the building, they've got names on sir, some of the names are quite sensitive sir, I think it might be pornography." The superintendent looked over the box a growing look of concern on his face, suddenly interested again.

"Names you say, who's names?" Dixie spoke again.

"I haven't looked at all of them sir but there's at least two names I recognise." The chief sat down again.

"Ok Dixon that'll be all!" He gestured with his hand for Dixon to leave.

"Sir, I really think DCI Fletcher's involved in this ..." The chief interrupted him again.

"I said that'll be all Dixon, if there's any connection between DCI Fletcher and Mr Khan we will get to the bottom of it in time, but for now, get your arse out there and catch those IRA bastards!" Dixie turned to leave. "*Leave* the box Dixon!" the chief ordered. Dixie placed the box on the chief's filing cabinet. As he left the room, the chief rose from his chair and came around the desk to examine the contents of the box.

"Yes sir." Dixie answered with a growing feeling of dread in his stomach. There was something wrong but he couldn't tell what it was. He shut the door behind him and stepped into the main office. As he walked past the window of Fletcher's glass box office, he could see the detective rocking back and forth on the back of his chair. As he passed he gave Dixie a cold smile. The look on Fletcher face gave Dixie shiver that ran up his spine as he realised what was wrong. He had never mentioned the Pakistani by name so how had the chief known of the name Khan? He stopped, wondering if he should return to the chief's office and ask how he knew the name when from behind him the chief's voice bellowed from his office doorway.

"DCI Fletcher . . . in my office *now!*"

Epilogue

As Davey Keogh sat in the back room of the Irish centre in *Digbeth* on November the twenty first, 1974, learning to play his guitar, he saw first hand how well Belfast Jimmy had done his job. The British general public reacted to the brutal murder of 21 of Birmingham residents with understandable rage on that awful night. As the windows to the Irish centre came through, showered by bricks and petrol bombs, the children inside cowered behind their parents as they were herded away for protection. Although twenty one innocent people were killed by the two bombs in the *Tavern in the town* and the *Mulberry Bush* pubs, in reality there were many more victims than just those poor unfortunate souls who were murdered on that cold night, whose only crime was to be in the wrong place at the wrong time.

British and Irish relations sank to an all time low and the Irish community in Birmingham was pushed back twenty years by the actions of the three murderers that attacked the city. Public reaction drove the police to find someone responsible and six innocent men who were also in the wrong place at the wrong time would spend sixteen years in prison, blamed for a crime that didn't commit. Of course the IRA denied all knowledge of the bombs.

But it must be said that the murderers actions were assisted by a naive belief shared by many in Irish communities all over the world, that somehow, the Irish rebellion was in some way, a romantic rebellion, with its feet still set firmly in the far off days of the 1916 uprising in Dublin. But after the pub bombings, nothing would ever be the same again. For the friends and relatives of those poor victims, it seems as if the British justice system has failed them again and again, many years have passed and still they suffer the loss of their loved ones, without any answers as to who committed this atrocity or any justice for their loved ones.

The real murderers still walk free to this day.

Zulu Warrior

Nearly two thousand Tottenham Hotspur football fans had rolled into Birmingham New Street station. The chanting could be heard from the station's main entrance by the Saturday shoppers that were commuting home after a day milling around the Bull Ring shopping centre. The Tottenham Hotspur football hooligans were being led by a hardcore calling themselves, *The Yids*. A mismatch of young and middle aged men which included everything from villains, builders, business men and even a lawyer. It didn't matter what their job was in London, today's business at hand was chaos, destruction and violence. Football was only the excuse for the group to be here, the real reason were the Zulu Warriors. The few policemen who were on duty at the station didn't stand a chance as the two groups met on the streets of Birmingham. The battle that ensued can only be compared to something from the pages of a medieval history book, as the *Yids* took the fight to the Zulu warrior stronghold. Eddie Fewtrell had seen many such battles over the years, but tonight he would have to, literally, stand alone amongst the carnage brought on by the waring tribes. Across the other side of the city, the Chinese were spreading their wings. Birmingham's own little Chinatown could not contain their ambition any longer. This 1980s deadly phenomena namely *The Triads*, were spilling out of their motherland, threatening to wash away the families and businesses that had become so loved by many in the second city. Between the Zulu

Warriors, the Triads and another recession, it seemed to Eddie Fewtrell that things couldn't get any worse ... and then, the girl from his nightclub went missing.

Lightning Source UK Ltd.
Milton Keynes UK
UKOW02f1559160516

274358UK00001B/20/P